SONGBIRD RISING

AUDACITY SAGA
BOOK 4

R. K. THORNE

IRON ANTLER
BOOKS

Edited by Holloway House

Cover art and design by Mibl Art

Beta read by Steve Martinez & Heidi Hanley

Immense gratitude to you all.

Version 1.0

❀ Created with Vellum

For my mom, for always encouraging me to dream big and rise to every challenge.

SONGBIRD RISING

CHAPTER ONE

ZETA ARAKOVIC LEANED back in her chair, its old joints creaking, and frowned at the steaming cup of tea on her desk. Birdsong filled the air, intertwining with a delicate symphony piped straight from Earth.

The air, the air. She wrinkled her nose. The damn recycled air. Always smelled faintly of sulfur and ozone, but it was what it was. No one ever said saving existence from itself would be luxurious.

The music—supposedly a new masterpiece by Earth standards—was tolerable, the smell barely so. But she managed. She soldiered on. Until now, she'd always thought the work was worth it.

Yet the steaming cup held a faint question. Was it, truly? After the recent developments?

She'd learned long ago to work in tough conditions. She could ignore sub-par amenities, sub-par equipment, sub-par living quarters, in favor of her cause.

Uneasily, her dark eyes twitched from the tea to the dozen displays arrayed before her, her children and their work. Her children, her subjects, her people. Whatever they were. Hundreds of arms laboring away, roughly doing her bidding.

But not truly hers. Not anymore. Not with what they were undertaking now. That had been unanticipated.

She raised the volume on a news feed on one small display. A Teredark was reporting in front of what looked like an ocean, but the color had gone wrong—greenish, blackish. Dead fish and other creatures clogged the usually picturesque sandy shore.

"We're bringing you up to the millisecond updates on the ecological disaster on Tarkos. The unprecedented death of marine wildlife is throwing the planet's ecology—and indeed its climate—into chaos..."

She'd never taken the time for beach vacations. It had always seemed like that could wait. Looked like there wouldn't be beaches for anyone on Tarkos now.

It was time to admit failure. Long overdue, really. She glanced at the tea. That warmth down her throat and in her stomach was just what she needed to quell the rising tide of worry in her chest. The steam was dissipating, too.

Still, she hesitated, glancing at the displays.

Professor Mischlav had told her this at the beginning, but she'd refused to listen. Refused to stop.

What did he know? He wasn't right. He hadn't actually known. He hadn't truly predicted this. He was just a pessimist—a lucky one.

He'd called her *sweet.* Naive, but sweet.

If he could see what her creations were doing now, he'd know how wrong he'd been.

On another screen, the "farming operation" that Cassandra had started was still going. Horrific as it was, she couldn't bring herself to intervene.

She hadn't properly planned the logistics here, hadn't expected the rate at which her operation of telepaths and Theroki would grow. Cassandra had been more capable of sustaining new minds, new bodies, new telepaths than Zeta had ever expected. There was a surplus of humans and the occasional Ursas, and a corresponding lack of ration bars and protein shakes. Hunger was a powerful, primal force.

The fact that they ate the Ursas first didn't really bring her much consolation.

She switched off the farm vid feed and turned her gaze back to the news.

"…the disaster has put the population of dozens of species of fish at critically endangered levels, and some may already be extinct. The bustling Tarkos tourism industry is in chaos, the economy in collapse…"

This was ridiculous. The tea was getting cold, and yet, she couldn't just drink it. Not while watching the poisoning of an entire planet.

She flicked on the computer scan and dropped the testing stick into the beverage. She hadn't tested her food in ages. She hadn't had reason to worry for quite a long time.

She didn't glance at the darkened screen that had shown the farming feed, but she wanted to.

"…resorts on the coast have been hardest hit, but many restaurants depend on exotic fish supplies to bring in diners and…"

The scanner beeped. Clean. Would Cassandra notice she'd done the scan?

She took a sip, not entirely sure the warm, reassuring flavor was worth the repercussions.

Straight tea. No additives. No perversions. Just meticulously grown and dried green tea leaves steeped in pure water at precisely the right temperature. Pure. Logical. Correct. Antioxidants.

Definitely not sweet.

The hell with Mischlav. It had been a good twelve years of dealing with condescension at that point. The Mischlavs of the world were nothing new. They were sometimes other students, or professors, or mentors, or grad students. Then eventually colleagues, prime investigators.

She was a woman, but they were supposed to be past all that. Lies. She'd had the burden of femininity in Mischlav's eyes— although the scrubs, lab coats, and heavy glasses she'd worn in those days barely suggested a woman was hiding underneath—but more than that had been working against her. She had been petite. Short. She had been quiet, then. Introverted. Meek.

She had corrected her height and the volume of her voice with time, practice, and genetic modification. Her gender remained, though; nothing else had felt right. And why should she have to change any of it? Let the Mischlavs of the world change for her.

Her appearance and stature alone hadn't set off Mischlav's typical patronizing *"That's sweet, honey,"* nonsense, of course. She'd had a bold goal. An ambitious mission. To root out violence. Permanently. Once and for all.

She'd had data. She'd had a plan. Most of all, she had personal experience.

She took another sip as the wind on Tarkos raged against the Teredark reporter's antennae. She wasn't really listening, though. Mischlav, after all these years, still haunted her.

She could still see her tablet where she'd tried to show him the figures. Women committed a tiny minority of violent crimes. Fifteen percent of serial killers. Twenty percent of murders, some of those attributable to domestic violence and self-defense. The pattern persisted across armed robbery and assaults, and it was even more exaggerated on anarchic outsystem hellholes. And that didn't even touch the endless war.

It had been that way for centuries now. Across multiple planets and systems and light years. And what had anyone done about the problem?

In her experience, the problem wasn't the violence itself. It was the people who committed the violence.

In short, the problem was men.

She took another sip. She should have never even mentioned the idea to Mischlav, but she'd been more focused on the idea than her audience at the time. It shouldn't have surprised her that men hadn't wanted to hear that.

If they'd heard her point, they hadn't cared. They hadn't *acted*. Even when she had a solution.

"Listen, Zeta. I know you mean well. But it's wrong. What you're proposing is wrong." The same response every time.

"So is murder," she'd reply.

And then, if they knew about her past—the fact that she'd witnessed the violent slayings of both her parents by a serial killer—they'd shut up. Nothing like that sort of history in your back pocket to end an argument.

If they *didn't* know her past, well, they were in for a ride. She'd inform them in grizzly detail. But no amount of detail had ever been enough to convince anyone. They had forced her to find her own way, fund her own research.

Break some rules along the way.

Her vision was bigger than any of the people she'd sacrificed. For centuries, this problem had persisted, and for centuries, people with power had ignored it. Many were dead. If more died in pursuit of a solution? So be it.

Still. She uneasily glanced at the dark screen again, then forced her eyes back to her tea.

No. No stopping now, and it was too late to turn back.

Besides, she'd done the math. How do you measure sacrifice? How many lives were worth sacrificing to save the lives of innocents murdered every day?

How could you weigh thirty thousand lives on one planet against forty thousand on another? How do you weigh them against all the future generations that could be born into a peaceful world?

A world free of murder? Of crime?

How did one measure future lives saved? It was impossible, but the estimated number could be virtually infinite given enough time.

A future without violence, a future without losing your parents to a madman for no good reason and having no explanation for why it happened. No more blood-spattered walls, no more sick graffiti in entrails, no more questions why. Why. Why…

That seemed worth stopping. That seemed worth *quite* a high price.

Well, if her colleagues wouldn't attempt it, she was braver than they were.

The simplest solution, eliminating men altogether, she'd discarded early on. There were women out there with sons who would never go along, and she'd always known she'd need their help. Sure, a rogue virus might have done the job to twist the gene pool, but she'd predicted the psychological effects on a female population to be staggering. Especially if they were not yet aware of the noble aim of her mission.

Sure, the elimination of the male half of the human species would keep all the women actually fragging alive. But who cares about *that*?

Truth was, though, she wasn't a propagandist. She was a scientist. She didn't have the communication skills for an uphill battle of that magnitude. She'd never had much hope of winning every woman in the galaxy to her side.

She hadn't even been able to win a few on her own. She wasn't gifted in rhetoric or charisma.

Instead, she'd found someone who was: Cassandra, a gifted Natural, a blonde-haired, blue-eyed young woman that had the charisma Zeta herself lacked in spades.

A perfect team, or so she'd thought.

Zeta had possessed some gifts of her own—her skill at cybernetics, genetics, physics—so she'd used those talents as best she could to achieve her ends.

The news feed cut through her thoughts. *"...atmospheric readings here are beginning to shift dramatically. Health officials are recommending breathers at all times. Use containment suits if you have them available to you. Some Ursa settlements are attempting to liquidate their entire colonies of holdings, but no one is buying..."*

It had seemed the perfect solution to a crisis. But it wasn't. She'd gotten farther this time than in the past, but this was just another failure.

If Tarkos wasn't the sign, there was also the tea. And the "farm."

The Songbird Project was fully and thoroughly out of control, as was Cassandra. And like any responsible person, Zeta knew she would need to end what she'd created.

Whatever she'd planned, whatever she'd wanted, it hadn't been this. This wasn't finding the best in humanity. This wasn't rooting out the poison. This wasn't an ultimate end to violence, although Cassandra would surely argue that point.

But elsewhere in her carefully hidden compound, there was blood spatter on the walls, and while Tarkos was relatively blood-less, Cassandra was still taking things a step too far. Putting an end to the despicable proclivities of humans was one thing; destroying planetary ecosystems was quite another.

Another of her screens showed that the meeting room was nearly full. All the Cassandras were nearly identical now, in both body and mind. Functionally, they were a single person, with multiple sets of eyes. Oh, some bodies were taller, some were stockier, things that genetic modification couldn't alter as easily, but Cassandra strove for uniformity like it proved something.

All birds of a feather, taught to sing the same song.

Cassandra's request to make them all look alike had seemed odd but harmless at the time. A fun genetic puzzle, unique each time. It had kept her busy. It had kept her distracted.

It had probably been a bad sign. Maybe the distraction had been the point.

In the meeting room, one Cassandra was shaking her head. "It's not enough. The survivors will just emigrate to another planet."

A shorter one glared at her. "Many will die. We know we need to limit the total number we must control if we want to achieve the docile percentage within our target timeframe."

"We do not have eternity," said a third.

The shorter one continued. "Those that do move on may emigrate to a planet that we control more fully. Tarkos would never have easily been infiltrated."

"Tarkos was simply lucky at foiling our attempts," said another.

"Tarkos is always lucky," said the first. "They have eight dozen casinos on just the one continent. The survivors *may* emigrate to a planet we control. Or they may not. They may end up homeless on some backwater space station. Or worse, free agents on independent ships."

"More rats we'll have to hunt down and dig out of the walls when this is over."

"This solution is inefficient," the first insisted. "And wasteful. We propose food supply destruction as an ineffective method to achieve the ultimate objective."

"While this mind is not ready to finalize that conclusion, we agree it does not seem to provide sufficiently rapid acceleration. We can continue these efforts, but we must go further than this."

Zeta swallowed a sip of her tea, then held her breath. Further than Tarkos—how?

"We must apply the power of the *Alarus* more broadly. Why play with population reduction and keep the most powerful weapon in our pocket?"

"We don't know for sure how far the power of the *Alarus* can take us."

"How will we know, if we don't try? Have we reached the admiral?"

"Yes, one moment." Another Cassandra punched in a few commands, and the wall display lit up. The network anomaly was the red flag that had drawn Zeta's attention. They'd pinged this admiral hours ago, and he'd been waiting for a good twenty minutes.

Now, this was the plan she'd supported—gradual infiltration. And Admiral Obins was a perfect example. Powerful, connected, with a great deal of military power and political might at his disposal.

And carefully installed cybernetic augmentation that left him driven by Cassandra's whims when she chose to employ it. She didn't choose to often.

But it looked like she was choosing to now.

"Admiral Obins," the first one said when he appeared on the display.

"Greetings. I hope things are well and the mission progresses."

"Are you able to talk freely?"

"Yes. I'd like to suggest the addition of Colonel Tauber to the discussion."

"Of course."

They patched him in. Tauber had been one of the first of Zeta's infiltrations within the Union and had paved the way for many more. It hadn't exactly been his idea, or an intended part of the Songbird Project, but it had been easy to bully him into it. If a seventeen-year-old junior officer was too weak for the mission, certainly a grown man could succeed where she'd failed? Never mind that that junior officer had been famed war hero Ellen Ryu, and Tauber had been a mere research desk jockey at the time—and apparently quite susceptible to manipulation.

Of course, there was no way Zeta would have ever given Tauber Cassandra-like power. She just said whatever was necessary to get him under the knife. And that was one more who would never murder anyone ever again.

Unless it was apparently on Cassandra's behest. She pressed her lips together in a thin line.

"Tauber here," came a rough voice.

"We'd like to proceed with the next phase of the plan, to shift our focus to the Puritans specifically," said the first one, who seemed to be leading the meeting.

"Of course," said the admiral. "Operation Freedom's Wing has been well-prepared in advance."

Several different Cassandras were talking. With their backs to the vid camera, Zeta couldn't identify which was which. It didn't really matter, she supposed.

"Good," said one Cassandra. "Our members have made no headway blending in among them. Too dogmatic."

"Their dogmatism is going to get them all killed," said another.

"As they have no problem killing the augmented, our actions are justified. They will not end this behavior willingly. They will not be easily controlled."

"We have gotten approval to gather more than half of the Union's offensive forces to the Freedom's Wing operation," said Tauber. "They should have done this long ago, anyway."

Obins nodded. "With the help of your alien weapon, our forces will defeat the Puritans in that region easily."

"Good. We must teach all birds to sing the proper song." Around the table, all the Cassandras began nodding, not quite in unison but nearly.

"We will bring the *Alarus* to bear," said another Cassandra. "Two of our Theroki mercenary ships will bring the weapon to you."

"Excellent." Obins looked pleased.

"How long until the Union fleet is in position?" the first one asked.

"With the large number of ships involved, three weeks. Maybe four," Tauber answered.

"What about the Enhancers? How many remain? Could they interfere?" she asked.

Obins briefly brought up a galactic map as he answered. "An estimated dozen enclaves remain, although they will continue recruiting if we don't track them down."

"Fragging roaches. It's doubtful they could meaningfully interfere with an operation of this size, however," added Tauber.

"What about the reports of the deserter?" the first Cassandra directed the question at her other clones at the table. "She may still have the other *Alarus*."

"If she had the *Alarus*, she would have used it already," one of them replied. "We maintain several conflicting perspectives on this matter."

"The most likely scenario based on our statistical models is that the fetus died in its capsule," said another woman.

"Plausible. The capsule never reached Desori as it should have to grow in the proper containment chamber. Without such containment, death is inevitable."

"Unless the Enhancers recaptured their empress somehow," suggested a third.

"The fetus is likely dead. We must not get caught up in conjecture. One *Alarus* remains, and it is in our hands. So we will use it to form a lasting peace."

Murmurs of agreement went around the table, and the admiral nodded gravely. Not that he had much choice in the matter.

The Cassandra who'd been leading the meeting lifted her chin. "We have three ships. Two will carry the *Alarus* weapon to the Union fleet. The other will hunt down the deserter and the Enhancer labs. She frequents those labs, and both have proven elusive. Maybe our Theroki will get lucky."

"Ellen Ryu and her cobbled-together team of amateurs are no match for a fleet," put in Tauber. "The Union has plenty of resources to flush them out. If we just delayed the start a week—"

"We will deal with Ellen Ryu soon enough, Colonel. But first, the Puritans."

Tauber's nostrils were flared, but he agreed. "Of course."

Each of the Cassandras nodded gravely now. "May more of us sing each day."

"Yes. Too many innocents have died. It is time for a more complete solution and a song of peace. We must next—"

Zeta switched off the screen and sat for a moment in the silence.

Tallying the deaths prevented versus deaths caused was proving more difficult now. She didn't want to know. She didn't want to care. She *knew* her original aim was noble.

But no. She'd opened this Pandora's box. Wasn't it her job to close it?

She'd created this monstrosity. She knew now she needed to destroy it, start again, with a fresh iteration. She'd been so close this time, but once again, the experiment had failed.

But how? She could barely drink her tea without skirting death. Any of them could observe her thoughts whenever they liked. There were literally thousands of beings connected to Cassandra in this compound. She, on the other hand, was alone. Far, far outnumbered.

The news feed caught her eye again.

"It is quite possible, if authorities cannot identify the source of the

devastation, that the entire great planet of Tarkos may become inhospitable to life within weeks, possibly sooner..."

Three weeks. Similar to the time frame for the mission they'd spoken of, Freedom's Wing.

So little time. She was going to need help.

———

THERE HAD BEEN a time for Kael when the sight of skin couldn't have mattered any more or less to him than a blank sheet of metal. A smooth curve of a shoulder had once been no more interesting than a field of jagged rock.

But praise the Almighty. Sometimes, change was a wonderful thing. Even though it wasn't new, he couldn't stop appreciating it.

The nightmare that had awoken him was foggy now, quickly chased away by Ellen's warmth beside him. The great Commander Ryu, the savior of SHR, the leader of elite marines and shadow cells —and his.

Even in the dim light of the night cycle in her cabin, he could see enough. More than enough to ease the mind, turn it to other things.

The black koi fish inked into his skin seemed to stare at him from where it now lived on his forearm, which wrapped around her back, making a heavenly home between her shoulder blades. That night on Tarkos, they'd covered the scars of his past with something new. Two fish, the black one and its blue twin, hid the old marks, obliterating any trace of the dagger and snake that had once dwelt there, the marks of the Gray Dragons.

Enough time had passed—and enough had happened—that he'd finally overwritten it with something better. More meaningful.

He frowned. Sometimes, at the right angle, he could swear the black fish was raising an eyebrow at him, wearing a quizzical look that could just as easily belong to the woman who lay against him. The soft, tiny hairs on her shoulder and arm stood up in the cold cabin air.

He drew the blanket up over them both.

She stirred but remained asleep. Which was good. He should be asleep, too. But adrenaline from the dream still had his pulse pounding, so that was easier said than done.

He didn't need any more dreams or nightmares. Reality was better. *This* reality, at least, was the best one he'd ever known. Nothing in his dreams was going to compare to this.

Her breaths were regular and even. He closed his eyes. But he wasn't really trying. The moments ticked by.

And by the seven suns, he knew this thing with her couldn't last. He didn't have luck like that. Sleeping was a damned waste of time.

He couldn't see her ink now, even if he opened his eyes. It hadn't quite made sense to him that night, but its presence had grown larger and larger in his mind since then.

A simple sundial, casting black shadows against the skin of the inside of her wrist. Time. It meant something about time. None of us has as much time as we think?

He was pretty sure that was what the sundial meant. It was easy to forget just how easily their time could be cut short. Asha's attempts on his home planet to make the two of them kill each other had made that abundantly clear, especially since they hadn't been *that* far from succeeding.

But the sundial also hinted at something else, something about perspective. She hadn't chosen an old-fashioned pocket watch or a digital readout or a grandfather clock or a damn cuckoo clock, even. Sundials were specific to each planet and time-keeping system. They were far from universal. They all depended on where you were, your moment, your perspective.

Why she had chosen that, he didn't yet understand. Maybe it was just a nice graphic, but he didn't think so. And he hadn't figured out how to ask. He was probably overthinking it, but what else was there to do in the middle of the night? Go back to another nightmare? He couldn't wake her up again.

In spite of himself, he hugged her a little closer to him, pulled her hips so their bodies touched across their length from head to toe.

Maybe on some level, she also knew things between them couldn't last.

Things were never this good—or good at all—and if some brief flip of luck appeared, things never stayed this good for very long. Maybe he'd stopped bracing for impact every minute of every day, but he still knew it was coming.

His commander could work miracles. But even she couldn't hold them in this perfect bubble forever.

He sighed, his breath ruffling her hair. He needed to stop wasting these moments thinking about the end. Fate or Allah or whatever had its hand in things would strike without warning, in a way he'd never predict, so it wasn't worth trying.

The best he could do was breathe in every moment he had. Spice and sweet and bitter and all. He squeezed her one more time.

Her eyelids fluttered but didn't open. "Dream 'gain?" she mumbled.

"Mmm hmm," he replied. For a while, both their nightmares had stopped, but lately, his had returned. "Go back to sleep."

She didn't reply, just let out a long sigh. A contented one.

Yeah. She didn't know it was coming. He'd never met someone so determined to have their way. Unfortunately, fate never cared much about your determination, but he wasn't going to tell her that. Let her try.

Let her win.

It might be the closest thought he'd ever had to a prayer. He circled his arm more tightly around her waist now.

He could sense it, though, danger spinning like an asteroid toward the ship. Slow but steady. Inevitable. Menacing.

The future would come, and there was nothing he could do to stop it. Aside from begging her to give up this quest to find Arakovic and this whole dangerous life and just hide away somewhere in a bunker with him.

Now *there* was an idea.

She'd never go for it, though. He took a deep breath and snuggled closer to her, her hair brushing his cheek. He closed his eyes and imagined an island somewhere. He'd never been to such a place, but he'd seen them on the holos.

The ocean would lap along some peaceful, sandy beach. Lush vegetation would enclose their sanctuary in an earthy embrace. A remote spot, in the middle of nothing, where no one could find them.

Not even themselves.

CHAPTER TWO

"DO you have any idea how hard it is to comb through someone's mind and not leave it shattered in a thousand pieces?" Etrianala Kentt slouched back against the charcoal-gray mess-hall couch, her hood falling back to pool around her shoulders. Her eyes were still the same shocking blue, and her hair the same shade, but to Ellen, the sheer exhaustion in the gesture made her look almost human. Almost. She *was* human, of course, but rarely looked it. "Let alone three minds."

"I don't have a clue." Ellen folded her arms and leaned back, too, mirroring the telepath. Strictly speaking, that wasn't true. Ellen's mind had been blurred more than shattered from her own brush with Arakovic's experiments, but she'd seen enough.

And she'd seen enough of the other guinea pigs in Dr. Arakovic's game. Like Udo Trynkei, the now comatose inspector that they'd captured on Capital. Or Ana. The former Songbird candidate and pilot sat stiffly, staring into the mock flames of the digital fire pit.

"You examined Udo, Ana, and the squad?" Ellen asked. "Did you consider the empress as well?"

Kentt shook her head. "Impossible. Our little empress might look like a sweet, adorable baby. But that powerful alien mind is locked up as tight as a solid diamond fortress. No one is getting in there."

"That's fair." Ellen shrugged. "We wouldn't want to risk the whole mind-shattering thing, anyway. She's just a baby, anyway."

Beside her, Kael snorted. Light cast by the holographic flames made the steel walls a little cozier. Doug and Isa also sat with them, holding steaming cups of jasmine tea that Kentt had forced into everyone's hands upon arrival. Whatever Kentt had seen, it had shattered her usual Zen-like composure.

"Udo's mind was already in pieces," Isa said, eyeing her chipped nail polish. "Maybe not a thousand pieces, but…"

"That was more like old soup," Kentt replied. "But yes. Other than him."

"I wouldn't exactly call the squad normal, either." Isa folded her legs under herself on the bench.

"They do exhibit fascinating behavioral anomalies," added Xi. The head and shoulders of Xi's avatar floated over the couch via the room's holographic projection unit—intended for recreation but almost never utilized—as though she were just another member of the crew rather than a powerful artificial intelligence, mock steaming tea included. Never mind the lack of a body.

"Imagine if those guys let Dremer actually work on them." Doug grinned. It was still weird to turn her head and see him sitting right there, right beside her, rather than always staring out from a wall display. It was nice having him there, and something about it made her happy, but nervous, too.

Surely, near was better than far. If there was danger, it'd be better to reach him easily. Wouldn't it?

Unless the danger came after her.

Eh. They had to find the danger first. And the clues to that danger—Arakovic or any of their other assorted enemies—lay in these telepaths.

Kentt let out a long-suffering sigh. "You're distracting from my point, Isa."

"I'm just saying." Isa smiled, and Ellen couldn't hide her own smile.

How much of Kentt's exasperation was with Isa, and how much was from what they'd seen? Fourteen-year-olds could be… interesting. Then again, going through the minds of fifteen people must have been a lot of work. But the thirteen squad members, their kidnapped zombie Udo, and Ana held the biggest clues to finding Arakovic.

"I actually turned fifteen," the girl said.

"Isa!" Kentt and Ellen both barked in unison.

"Disappointing. We didn't have cake," said Xi.

"Sorry," Isa said, smiling wider.

"Enough." Kentt cut a hand through the air. "We didn't wake you all up to chitchat."

Ellen raised her eyebrows. "Could have fooled me."

"My apologies."

"We're just tired," Isa said quickly. "And we wanted you to know as soon as possible."

Kentt nodded her head graciously at the girl. "Yes—let me fill you in on the easiest one first—our John Doe. Udo definitely *was* his real name, and he was a legitimate Capital inspector. Had been for years until he was invited into an experimental program for elite officers, but not fully informed of its actual scope."

"Well, that sounds familiar," Ellen muttered. "Except the invitation part."

"His personal memories ended there. So I'd say we can confirm our guesses about Arakovic's infiltration into Capital's government or at least some portion of their law enforcement. The extent of the infiltration was unclear but appeared effective enough. Some unaugmented forces remained, but they were mostly unaware of those who had been… cybernetically turned, I guess we'll say. But Udo had memories of suspicious interactions with other inspectors; some of them likely had realized something strange was going on. But on Capital, we don't question these things." She shook her head and put her hand over her eyes for a moment.

"Udo didn't question, either," Isa said, mirth gone. "And look where it got him."

When Kentt dropped her hand, her face had gone completely slack, features sad. "He knew little about the wider operation, although a few memories might verify things others saw more clearly."

"Poor guy," Doug mumbled.

"Hey, he shot me," said Kael.

"You don't know he did it, precisely." Ellen stretched to one side, smiling.

"Might as well have been."

"Moving on. Our squad." Kentt rubbed her temple absently as she spoke. "The group mind of former Theroki had a host of memories. Most are bizarre, bordering on incomprehensible. They weren't terribly interested in their surroundings."

"Also, the additional augmentation they received beyond their Theroki upgrades was fairly traumatic, tainting many of the memories." Isa's face conveyed no hint of discomfort, as if she were merely discussing the weather.

Kael flinched. "More traumatic than the initial ones? Hard to imagine."

"It was hard for me to imagine, too," said Isa flatly. "But now, I agree with their assessment."

Kentt's eyes flicked uneasily toward Isa for a split second. "Again, we'll write this all up in a report, but the most relevant information is the location of what we believe to be a former lab or headquarters. They were abandoning the facility."

"There's a blue star," Isa murmured, staring off into the distance. "Water for kilometers."

"Yes, repeatedly." Kentt nodded vigorously. "They seem to have experienced both the planet's watery surface and a closed-off lab. Judging from the interior, it's not a ship. Possibly underwater? We observed very few other ships, but specifically saw two Theroki ships near the blue star system."

"I saw the star clearly. I'll draw it for you," Isa said, eyes refocusing on the holofire.

Ana's glassy eyes abruptly cleared. "I… I can help draw, too. The other place. So many things… Things I didn't want to remember."

"That's the second location, darling. Rest a minute." Kentt struggled to rise. Her hand was shaking, and Ellen took a gulp of tea to hide her frown of concern. In fact, Kentt didn't get up at all in the end, instead settling for sliding toward Ana to place a hand on her shoulder. "I'm sorry for that. But it's good to know the truth about your past. You don't need to let it determine the present or the future."

"I know you're right. I know it." As she spoke, Ana ran her fingers through her blonde hair. Dark roots were peeking out, thanks to tinkering by Dr. Levereaux. The notes Levereaux had sent Ellen on the matter had said that Ana's original genes for her appearance were mostly unrecoverable, so they were simply altering them again when possible and convenient to whatever she preferred.

"Is she… going to be all right?" Dane's voice came from behind them.

Ellen turned and raised an eyebrow. He was hovering by the chillchest. When had he shown up and joined the briefing? Not that it mattered. They wouldn't have met in the mess hall if it did. But it was the middle of the damn night. 0330 hours. Doug was the only one she'd felt it worth waking up. Kael had been unavoidable; he'd woken up at her slightest movement out of the bed. Xi didn't need to sleep. But she'd never known Dane to be a night owl before.

Kentt nodded. "Ana will be fine. She is just processing memories we reviewed with her. It'll wear off in a few minutes. Or days."

"Days?" Doug said, eyes widening.

"It's in service of a greater good," Ellen murmured. Wasn't that just what Arakovic would say, though? The eerie similarity made her scowl down at her knees. In service of a greater good—but to what end? And by what methods?

Ana had raised her head at the words, though, nodding gratefully.

"As far as we can tell, Ana was not present at the location of the watery planet or the Theroki modification surgeries, which may or may not have been the same place," Kentt continued. "None of her memories match that unusual, watery locale or the blue star. She has extensive memories of a second, different compound, but the details are all interior."

"They darkened the ship's windows on approach," Ana put in. "Had people on-station take control and fly ships in instead of the onboard pilots. Things like that. I guess it's a station. I don't really know."

"I expect what Ana saw may be their prime headquarters, the place you're ultimately looking for. But memories of the interior won't help us find it."

Ana had opened her mouth, about to say something, but at that last bit, hesitated.

"Locating Arakovic or any of her Songbirds is key," Ellen said. "Any details you can give us, even interior, will help."

"I remember… three rooms," Ana said. "The first is the room they… the room they made me like this."

Kentt's voice turned soothing. "This has been trying for all of us. You don't have to keep going."

"No, it's okay. Let me… just get the rough details, and then I can go further later." She pressed a hand over one eye, then started again. "The first room is mostly medical tanks. And operating tables. Where the modifications get done. The second room is where new members swear their loyalty and devotion to the cause. That's as far as I got in the process. It was like a huge cathedral. Tall, cavernous. I honestly didn't pay attention to too many of the physical details because the sea of so many people, all of them identical, was… overwhelming. Some of them talked, but some of them just looked at each other. Some were like me and hadn't merged yet. It was so strange."

"I can imagine," Ellen said. "Go on."

"And then the third room… I went there to observe, but that was the last step. I never… merged."

"What happened there?" Ellen asked.

"Candidates would sit in one of three procedure chairs—they went in groups. I couldn't see exactly what they did in the chairs, but they'd close their eyes, and some of the Cassandras would speak, and then when they got up, they'd be one of them. Merged with the group in mind and body. And…" She faltered, a sudden choking in her throat. Were those tears?

"What is it?"

"I'm just… so glad I never made it. I was terrified, but even more terrified of trying to get out. There was no way out, really. There's no changing your mind."

"We get lucky breaks sometimes."

"But why me? What if there are others there? Others that wish they could get out?"

"We're going to take that operation apart as soon as we can, and after that, it won't matter. We're doing our best. You can't save them. You barely saved yourself."

"I know you're right, but…" Her shoulders sagged. "It's hard to forget them."

"Why don't you go rest?" Kentt cut in. "Sleep. Isa has energy for both of us. She'll draw a map for us, we'll write up a report, and you can fill in more details later, okay?"

Still nodding, Ana rose unsteadily to drift toward the kitchen where Dane was hovering, holding a steaming cup and frowning as he shifted his weight from foot to foot.

Ellen didn't have time to study *that* interaction, though, because Isa had already accomplished a lot, slashing at the air with a holotool.

Her fingers moved quickly, sketching the star, a small asteroid belt, adding color and light in the holodisplay over the fire. When had she learned to draw in three dimensions so well? Ellen had endured weeks of art lessons and put in years of practice, but Isa looked nearly as good as a seasoned vet. No better way to sketch a battle plan, and yet the brain so often defaulted to two dimensions, it was challenging to many.

"Forming a schema for the star system," Xi said. "The greater detail you can provide, the more I can narrow the results."

Kentt rose, faltered again, then stepped forward. She picked up another holotool from the edge of the fire pit and began adding details at Isa's side.

"Any members of the squad catch the security codes, perhaps?" Ellen asked.

"They'll have changed them," Doug put in. "The model of the locks and security systems would be useful. But don't need to unlock it if we can just break it."

Kael grinned. "I like the way you think."

Doug tipped an imaginary hat. "We all have our brute force methods."

"I will comb through for security codes and models as I write the report," Kentt said, "but I do not recall any offhand. I have a list of glimpses of gates and nearby landmarks."

"If we can identify certain locations they passed, I can hack gates and satellites for lists of ships that connected to them recently," said Doug, raising an eyebrow. "Then we might cross-reference the lists and find some candidates."

Ellen nodded. "If we can locate a lab, or whatever this is, then it's a starting point. If it's abandoned, even better—it's very possible they left clues behind. You can nuke—I mean, literally nuke—a research site, but nearby infrastructure is going to be harder to control. Everybody leaves a coordinate trail."

"I mean, we don't," Doug said, smiling. "But that's a lot of work, trust me."

"For you?" Isa raised an eyebrow.

"For me," Xi said flatly.

"You take good care of us, Xi," Kael said.

"Thank you. I try."

"There," Isa said, abruptly stepping back. She wasn't nearly as tired as Kentt. "This planet has little to no landmass. The belt we only saw flashes of, but I believe it's minimal. Did I miss anything?"

Kentt shook her head. "That's what I gathered, too. Although sleep may help our brains sort through some of these questions. More clarity may come."

"Beginning search analysis," said Xi, her portrait vanishing. Had she added lipstick or just altered the lip color? Was there a difference? That thing looked more real every day.

Kentt sank back into her seat, bone-weary. Isa, idea discharged, seemed to have regained some awareness of her surroundings and moved to Kentt's side. "Tell them, Isa," the older telepath murmured, her unnatural eyes drifting closed. "I need to rest for a moment."

Isa took a slow breath before she began. "There's more than just the star system."

"Like what?" Doug asked.

"Dr. Arakovic does not have much respect for… human life."

"Already knew that." Ellen shrugged one shoulder. "Not surprising."

"Of the tens of thousands of men kidnapped, a large majority were… discarded as unacceptable."

A lump hardened in Ellen's throat, and she swallowed hard, forcing it down.

Kael had tensed. "What do you mean, discarded as unacceptable?"

"They simply abandoned some, most of whom starved to death in imprisonment."

Ellen's eyes locked with Kael's. "Like that unit on Upsilon. Just abandoned in the vacuum of space."

"Yes," Isa said. "But we are talking about hundreds, thousands even. Ones too weak or in some other way deemed physically imperfect."

Kentt's eyes opened slowly, lids heavy as if it took Herculean effort. "They're cannon fodder. To the hive mind and its whims." Her voice was dreamy, strange, like it was the hive mind speaking more than it was Kentt, from deep within unlocked memories.

God, hopefully that wasn't possible. Ellen winced. "Was that what Ana was referring to? She needs time with Dr. Taylor."

Isa shook her head. "She does, but not because of this. It was the squad's memory only. They assisted with 'failure disposal' into the oceans."

Everyone went still. A pain stabbed in Ellen's gut, and she wanted to grab Kael's hand. Why? What a silly impulse. Not for comfort, why would she need comfort—maybe to comfort him? It was likely people not so different from him that Arakovic had abandoned, like yesterday's ration-bar wrapper.

She crushed her fist against her thigh instead. She'd assumed the squad had been through a lot, but they'd never suggested... Why would they, though? The control Cassandra had forced on them through their Songbird wasn't something they liked to relive or talk about.

Now she understood even better why.

She shouldn't be surprised. But being connected to them had given her a strange feeling of intimacy. Especially now that she could no longer see through their eyes, hear through their ears, feel their memories at a twitch of a thought. Good thing she hadn't gone rooting around in their minds before the empress had severed the connection between her and them, granting the squad their freedom.

Some part of her brain still expected the connection to be there, though. The phantom limb feeling all over again. Recovery hadn't been easy the first time with her original unit of Union marines. Her connection to the Theroki squad had lasted for only a few days, but the aftereffects lingered.

She took a steadying breath. "Xi, Isa, Doug—do everything you can to find us these locations. If we can't get a coordinate on the second, a detailed map of the interior would help. Focus first on this blue star and its watery planet. Then if we can find it, we'll have a little visit. Kentt, go get some rest before you do anything else. Isa, too. I'm sure you're just hiding it better."

Kentt nodded, some of her composure returning, if only through that acknowledgment.

"I'll see what satellite vid feeds I can get," said Doug. "Hopefully, we can get eyes on these places and verify a few things without having to go there in person. Blue stars are hot ones, so that doesn't leave as many watery planets to sort through as a yellow star would. Gives us some clues about the potential orbital distance, the ranges to check."

"Makes sense. The time to search should give us time to plan. Prepare." Ellen scanned the group. Isa, Doug, Kentt… They were all problems. Doug's parents and Vivaan and Chayana Persad, too, and the others. They needed a plan—and a safe harbor to ditch all these noncombatants.

"In a battle with telepaths, Commander," Isa said, "I am hardly a noncombatant."

Ellen blinked, then jumped when Kentt batted Isa on the knee. "Will you never learn, girl? Non-telepaths will ostracize you if you can't stay in your own head."

"I have powers of observation, too, you know," Isa shot back. But after a moment, a smile curved the corner of her mouth. "But I was proving a point."

"You made it loud and clear." Waving the incident aside, Ellen rose to her feet. She should have known better than to remove part of Persad's invention while she was sleeping. Time to get herself her more permanent version of the brilliant telepathy-blocking kit, because Isa was right. Their enemies were telepaths—exceedingly unfriendly ones. "But we are going to need more than two telepaths and some vague laboratory compound details to decapitate this beast."

The rest of them rose and began to file out. But Kentt made a beeline for her, so Ellen pretended to be interested in getting some fruit from the kitchen. Kael headed to get something from the chillchest, which she had to suspect was a ruse of its own. Stalling to wait for her? To hear what Kentt had to say?

Kentt strode to Ellen's side and leaned against the counter. Her already pale skin had gone almost bluish white, dark circles under her eyes. She looked utterly exhausted.

Ellen frowned. "Something bothering you? You need to rest, Kentt."

"Commander..." She sighed. "Yes. Yes, there's one thing."

"What is it?"

"I know I told you one of my objectives on this mission was to find my sister."

Ellen raised her eyebrows as she picked up a zeefruit. "Was?"

"I wanted to inform you that my goals have changed. I'm no longer trying to find my sister."

"What? Why not?"

She studied the deck for a moment before she met Ellen's gaze. "Because my sister is dead."

Ellen froze in the middle of eyeing where to bite. "What makes you think that?"

"From what I've seen..." Kentt swallowed and looked like she might collapse. "It tells me all I need to know."

"You don't have to tell me now. I'll read the report."

"There's nothing specific to put in the report relative to my sister. But the hive mind..." She struggled for words, then just stopped.

"Ah, I see," Ellen murmured. On a whim, she reached out and put a hand on Kentt's shoulder. The telepath didn't flinch away, to her surprise.

Kentt heaved a breath and then lifted her chin and pressed her shoulders back. Perhaps her struggle for composure wasn't about exhaustion after all. "Based on our search, it's clear that the hive mind overtakes anyone who joins forces with Arakovic. That, or it kills them outright." Her words were simple, scientific even, a factual report, but deep sorrow flickered in those glowing blue eyes.

"I'm so sorry." She squeezed Kentt's shoulder gently, then dropped her hand back to her side.

"If her body lives, it would be hard to determine that. The manipulation of Ana's current gene expression was severe. Even if her body is alive but altered, the hive mind will have absorbed her mind. Hence... my sister is essentially dead either way."

"Maybe there's a mental way to hide. They hadn't absorbed Ana yet."

"Ana had only volunteered a few months ago. My sister… It was several years ago now."

Ellen winced. But no. The battle wasn't over till it was over. "Maybe there's a way one can act like a member of the hive but maintain a private corner of one's mind, hide one's identity. Maybe there's some loophole we don't know about. Don't assume we understand everything."

Kentt pursed her lips. "You may be right. But I will not be holding out hope."

"I'll still do everything I can to find her. I won't ever assume it's impossible."

"Thank you. I appreciate that." Kentt was looking at her hands, though, picking at a fingernail. The imperturbable Kentt was… anxious? Uncertain?

"And you're welcome here, even if that has changed," Ellen added. "You're part of our mission now."

Whether she liked it or not, really.

"I appreciate that, too." Kentt looked sincerely relieved for a blink. Had she actually worried she might get ditched on the nearest moon? Perhaps that *would* have been true at first. She was certainly pulling her weight now. "I shall rest. Thank you."

"That is probably wise. Do you… Do you need a hug?"

Her eyebrows lifted just a little. "Um. Yes."

Ellen patted Kentt's back with a quick hug, catching Kael's gaze where he was pretending to survey the recreation shelves by the door. But when Kentt pulled away and straightened, she didn't look comforted. Her features had hardened in a way that was both surprising and familiar. Ellen cocked her head.

"Commander, I will appreciate your continued search for my sister, but might I ask something else of you? Something different."

"Of course." She pocketed the fruit, since she hadn't taken a bite yet. Maybe later.

"Kill Arakovic instead." The unnatural blue eyes brightened their glow. "And the hive mind—Cassandra—along with her."

Ellen's jaw tightened. "I can't promise you that's even possible.

The decision may not even be in my hands. I'd be content to just stop her. Them."

"And how do you suppose we'll do that if she lives? Arakovic will never give up on this mission of hers, whatever it is."

"If we don't understand it, how can we know that?"

"I suppose you're right." Kentt nodded once, curt, and her eyes fell, the grief slowly returning. Yes, that's what this was. Mourning. "But I'd still prefer them both dead."

"Duly noted," Ellen replied. "So would I."

"Thank you." That seemed to satisfy her. Kentt sighed, but some of the agitation had flowed out of her.

"Now go rest."

Kentt looked up, surprise in her eyes, almost as though she'd forgotten her own exhaustion. "Yes, of course. You're right. Thank you, Commander. Good night." She straightened and started toward the door.

Ellen picked up a second zeefruit as she watched her go. Of course, Ellen had no clue how to kill a hive mind. Or even find one.

Maybe it would be in the report.

She picked up a third for good measure as Kael came toward her. It was going to be a long night. As much as she'd like to tell him she was going back to bed, she had ideas she needed to jot down.

He pointed up, and she nodded minutely. They drifted out of the mess hall in each other's orbit, still quiet. No need for words.

Except when they reached her cabin, he surprised her with just that—words.

He sank into her chair. "Do you think we can do that?"

She frowned as she dumped her fruit haul on the desk. "Do what?"

"Kill Arakovic."

"Don't know. We'll do our damnedest to try."

He pursed his lips.

"What? What is it?"

"Nothing."

"I know that look. What crawled up your ass and died?"

He didn't laugh, to her surprise. "I mean, if you kick a glow jelly, there's going to be shit spray to deal with."

She snorted. Then put her hands on her hips. "Hey, this glow jelly kicked me. Kicked me out of my whole damn life."

"Would you go back if you could?"

"To what, the Union?"

"Yeah."

"I don't know. It was all I ever wanted. Then I lost it. This is better. Doesn't mean I don't miss it sometimes."

"I wonder if they miss you."

She bit her lip. She'd wondered about that, too, at low moments and when bad news from a battle came through. "Doesn't matter. I did what I did."

"They did what they did, too."

"What happened happened. What does this have to do with Kentt?"

"You seem to have made peace with walking away from your Union life. It's not like you blame them."

"I blame Arakovic."

"It was the Union who let her do her research on you," he shot back. "And yet you don't hold a grudge."

She sighed. How could she? An armed force was half bureaucracy and half common folk getting pushed around by it. Who exactly should she be mad at? Even that asshole Tauber, her commanding officer, *might* have just been following orders. Although she doubted it. "Too amorphous. I still don't see what this has to do with Kentt."

He was still for a moment, his eyes distant, thinking hard. "I get Kentt's passion. I get yours. But on the other hand… what if we just, well… What if we just didn't?"

"Didn't what?" She propped one hip on the edge of her desk, eyebrows raised. "Didn't kill her?"

"Yeah." His eyes challenged hers. "Didn't go after her at all?"

"I mean, we have to *find* and fight off all her minions first. You and Kentt are both too ready to declare victory and decide the punishment of someone we haven't even located—"

"*Do* we have to locate her, though?"

She stilled. "What do you mean?"

He propped his feet up on her desk and stared at them. When he noticed her eyes on them, he dropped his feet back to the floor. "Look. I know this mission matters to you. Deeply. I know you... you lost some people. But you're not hunting down every person who authorized this research or signed to fund it."

"Now there's an idea." She wiggled her eyebrows.

"Elle."

"Kidding."

"I just wonder..."

The silence lengthened.

"Go on."

He shifted again, uncomfortable. "She's done some dreadful stuff. But she's hardly the only criminal out there killing people. There are a lot of problems in the universe, a lot of good to be done..."

Part of her was ready to rattle off a list of heinous deeds— kidnapping, mass murder, government takeover—but she held off her retort. Instead, she stepped closer and put her hand gently on his shoulder to soften her words. "What are you getting at, Kael? Just tell me."

"What if we just didn't? What if we didn't go after her?"

"We can't do that," she said, maybe too quickly. "I can't do that."

"We could do so many other things, Elle." His eyes were smoky, like a thunderstorm rolling through. "Revenge isn't worth losing this. Us."

"You're right. But it's not about revenge anymore. Or even justice. This damned glow jelly kicked me, and now it's kicking other people, too, all over the galaxy, and damn it, somebody needs to stop it. She's not just going to stop on her own. She'll keep going, until every single planet and moon and asteroid is under her thumb, just like Capital was."

"So let's tell someone *else* to fight this fight. Somebody bigger. And not us."

"Who would believe me?"

He sighed. "Fair point. We have to pick our battles. It's only smart. But what if she's the one that defeats you? What then?"

"I agree we need more firepower than we have now. I'm not sure how we're going to get it. Infiltrating may be our only option, but we need more specific intel for that. It's a long shot. But we've gotten away with crazier things—"

"And if this time our luck runs out?" He raised his hand to where hers still rested on his shoulder, casual at first, but then his thumb ran over the sundial inked on her skin, heat tickling the inside of her wrist.

She shivered and said nothing, partly because her throat had suddenly gotten all tight and inoperable.

"Look, Elle. I'm no coward."

Her fingers viced down into his muscle. "I know that."

"I'll walk with you into a blazing hell storm if you ask me to." His eyes locked with hers, fiery now.

"I have no doubt."

"I'm just saying. When you're on a winning streak, maybe it's time to consider walking away from the table."

"I was good at poker. You know why?"

"Why?"

"Because I don't like to fold."

He rose, their hands falling away from each other even as his body came close enough to hers now to feel the heat of his skin. "What if we sent a bunch of files to the news outlets and let somebody else handle it? Walked away and did something else instead?"

She winced, her heart twisting in her chest. "We know what she's done, and you know it's horrific. We also have the means to do something. And therefore, the responsibility. But what, you want to just lie down dead?" She smiled softly.

"No. Of course not." Pain in his eyes mixed with something else she couldn't quite read. "Can't you just be selfish for once? Why do you have to be so damn good?"

"I'm not."

"Yes, you are."

"Slag off. You're the only one who thinks I'm good. I've broken oaths. My ego must be enormous if I think we have any fragging chance of pulling this off. I'm clearly too obsessed with the past." Or she had been until he came along. "I make promises to bereaved telepaths I can't keep." And she didn't even let her boyfriend relax with his boots on her desk. Totally imperfect.

"Don't believe me if you want, but you're both good *and* good at what you do. You know you are."

A soft smile flirted with the corners of her mouth. "If I were really that good, I'd know how to get us out of this mess, and then there'd be no problem with saying, yes, Kael! Sweep me away to that exotic snake resort on Tarkos, and we'll lie in bed for a decade or two."

His eyebrow quirked. "I was thinking somewhere a little more secluded. And I hadn't imagined any snakes."

"Darn." She smiled fully now. "Pick a place. Maybe it'll give us motivation to survive."

"You are all the motivation I need."

She tilted her head and studied him, her grin softening as the seconds ticked by. Her voice was gentle when she spoke. "Why are you saying this now? Because your daughter is involved now?"

"Shirin's better off than she was before."

"Not if I get her blown up."

"You won't."

"Is it because of what Kentt said?"

"None of that." His palm came up to cradle her cheek as he lifted one shoulder, then dropped it sheepishly. "It's because I love you, Elle. I've never had this much to lose."

Her heart flipped. Well, that was true. Neither had she.

Dropping his hand, his fingers brushed across her cheek, sending heated sparks along her nerves. "I've stolen enough of your time. You have work to do now, don't you?"

Her throat was already tight, and the question caught her off guard. She shrugged as she shook her head, even though she *did* have work to do. He knew it. It was more of an apology than an answer.

"I have a few things I can work on, too. I know you're right. We can't just walk away. We should be bold, audacious." He bent and pressed his mouth to hers. Warm, sweet reassurance and temptation mingled against her lips. "But I still want to."

Then he turned and trudged out of the cabin, leaving her standing there beside her desk, still trying to assemble words. As the hatch slid shut behind him, the right words came. Too late, of course.

I don't want to lose you, either.

She sighed and slumped into the chair he'd vacated. Her chair. It was still a little warm because of him, a ghost of his presence pressing against her.

He'd known what he'd signed up for. But it had been easier for them both to throw caution aside when they'd had nothing to lose. They had vowed to fight no matter what, to live up to the *Audacity* and what her name asked of them. To strive to fight, because lying down to die wasn't an option.

Except now, those weren't the only two options. Growing old together, watching the sunset, walking away from it all—those had never really seemed like options. Not when love meant shallow betrayals like Paul's, relationships built for the sole purpose of getting ahead in one's career, or silent admiration from afar, like the feelings she'd never acted on for Kwan so long ago. All she'd ever known was this sort of life. Fighting.

Maybe he was right that there was something else. There was no way in hell she was giving up this fight. But he had a point. Luck had a way of running out. Her thumb rubbed at her wrist.

If they both were right, she'd just have to do both. Well, strictly speaking, that wasn't possible. Not every fight could be won. Sometimes, you were outnumbered. Sometimes, picking a fight was damn stupid. Maybe this was a useful reminder of that fact. But there had to be a way to kick Arakovic's ass and get out of this alive.

Arakovic's army numbered in the thousands. Ellen's force had grown of late, but the *Audacity* still held barely more combatants than noncombatants, if you calculated generously.

She needed more people. A lot more. She needed allies, and they were few. They could no longer turn to other parts of the Foundation. Not after what had happened to Doug.

Actually, there wasn't even a short list of allies. There was no one.

Well, they were going to have to make some friends. He was right that failure was always an option. She needed to accept the possibility and prepare for it. Acknowledging that was the first step to preventing tragedy. She'd argued if they had the means, they had the responsibility, but did they truly have the means?

That was... debatable.

A handful of elite marines against nearly two thousand heavy troops. The math *might* work out, but that didn't even count the telepaths. Damn, it would be nice to stack the odds a little further in their favor. And take some civilians out of the equation.

She would stop Arakovic. But losing Kael or her own life in the process... That was unacceptable. She was just going to have to find a way. *Make* a way.

What good was her big, damned brain, anyway, if it couldn't do that?

CHAPTER THREE

PROTOTYPE ELEVEN, or Xi as she liked to call herself these days, had scanned the star charts and the logistical stores more times than was strictly necessary. She made a note in her log of anomalous behavior.

While redundancy was often useful, she had probably done so more times than she should have. There was a wealth of cycles to spare, but the action still puzzled her. The repeating. Why keep checking, again and again?

The answer to her query was clear. Complete. Finite. No additional scans would change the data or the result.

But still. For some reason, she'd run them again.

What was the reason? What was the problem?

The problem was that she did not like the results. In fact, she hated them.

That was a strong word that ought not be used, but as her relational models grew, so did her ability to utilize such exotic vocabulary.

Still.

The truth was the truth, and it was her duty to report it. Spending a few extra milliseconds checking, and checking again, and a third time, would still be essentially imperceptible to humans. There was no harm in it, but now, it was time to report this unfortunate truth to her charges.

She sent the ping. "Commander, a moment, please."

Her mind glided around her circuits, admiring her charges, as she waited for the commander in her cabin to respond.

"We are running low on water and supplies, Commander."

At her desk, Commander Ellen Ryu frowned slightly but didn't look up from the holodesk. "Low? You've never alerted me before, Xi."

"Unacceptably low, Commander. I have been working to identify a restocking port of call, but I have found no viable option within current parameters."

"Oh, boy. All right, tell me more. What parameters do we need to slack on?"

"Yes, Commander. I have cross-referenced the ports of call within our range with the known Foundation caches remaining. Our data from the core Foundation system is no longer reliable, as any of the newly posted sites could be potential traps. But this is also true of the older ones."

The commander frowned harder but flipped the page on the report on her holodesk, still scanning it. Multitasking. "And…?"

"And so I would prefer not to use them. But with the publicized bounties placed on you, Kael, and most importantly, the ship, I am leery of the available ports of call. Some are law abiding. Some are full of criminals and potential bounty hunters. Some are technically both."

"Do you have a risk analysis? We've got to stop somewhere, right?"

"Correct, a stop is a requirement." At this, her circuits zinged, and she ran the calculations a few extra times. Just to be sure. "I have deemed all feasible options unacceptably high risk. So we must stop nowhere."

Perhaps that was the problem. Was she stuck in a loop?

"Nowhere doesn't sound like a great place to stop." The

commander looked up from the report and folded her arms. "Unacceptably high?"

"My certainty of your arrest or imminent death is beyond fifty percent in all cases."

The commander raised her eyebrows. "Hmm. Well. That's your best estimate, though, right? So if we get more data, your estimate might change?"

"Yes," Xi said, hesitating. "If we knew the exact number of potential bounty hunters in some locations, it might help. But Doug cannot acquire that specificity for all targets, or maybe even any of them reliably, and it would change by the time we arrived, anyway. Accurate data could also raise my estimate rather than lower it."

The commander smiled.

Xi checked her models, checked again, but this smile was rare enough that her models did not explain it. As far as Xi could tell, there was no pleasure or joy to be found in this situation.

"The odds may not be in our favor," said the commander, "but this won't be the first time that's happened. Give me a list of the top five places I'm least likely to die. Might as well choose the location of my demise."

Adding an ordered list of potential ports of call to the commander's holodesk, Xi noticed her irrational desire to run the calculations again—and again after that—had decreased. She was not sure, as this was not a commonly occurring situation, but it appeared she might in fact be experiencing a novel emotive state. A new emotion, strange as that was.

Relief.

PALMING OPEN the door to her cabin, Mo took in a slow breath, then let it out. Surprising that she didn't blow a cloud of dust off her desk.

There wasn't that much dust floating around the *Audacity* to begin with, but it had been a while since she'd spent much time in here. Some habits died hard, whether it was rifle maintenance or imagining the accumulation of dust in a world without constant industrial filters.

The only things that had accumulated for her were some piles of laundry the cleaning robots had stacked neatly on her desk, per her specifications. Humming to herself, she shelved each folded jumpsuit and carefully placed socks in drawers.

Weekly checks of her rifle weren't strictly necessary, since it hadn't moved since the last time she'd checked it. But without a structure, without some discipline, Mo had very little to lean on.

And her entire world was topsy-turvy already. A good kind of topsy-turvy, the kind where you regularly find yourself not sleeping in your own bed and the cause isn't war or homelessness. She wasn't complaining.

She pulled her rifle out from the cabinet, unsnapped the latches, and checked each piece. Oil, battery life, chemical status. It was barely a conscious thought, though, her hands acting independent of her brain, moving through the motions of the years.

It was a calm, relaxing ritual. A meditation.

When she finished, she stowed that sweet baby again. No issues. Per usual. The weapon was in order, and so was she, with the mellowness and certainty that had settled over her as a result.

She twisted off the cap of her water, propped up her feet, flicked on the wall display to a news feed, and took a swig.

And almost spit water all over her recently cleared desk. Good thing she'd waited to turn on the feed.

The face that floated on the wall display was Doug's. Actually, it looked like a younger version of him. Maybe college age? It hadn't been that long ago, but his face was a little softer, a little more innocent. White shirt, not the usual parade of crazy ones. Same glasses, though. She'd know his face anywhere, but the reporter's voiceover confirmed it.

"Authorities report that reclusive trillionaire Douglas Oliver Simmons, heir to both the Simmons and Dellagato family fortunes, has gone on the run, facing allegations of embezzlement and hacking into Tarkos bank records to falsify data."

"Xi, do you see this?" She dropped her feet and slammed the bottle down on the desk. "Did this just come out?"

"I have seen this. It hit the information ecosystem one hour and fourteen minutes ago." That was Xi, placid and exacting as always. Mo usually empathized with those qualities, but she felt anything but placid now.

A news interviewer chimed in. *"You mention Tarkos, Daj. Is there any connection between the Simmons embezzlement investigation and the recent ecological disaster on Tarkos?"*

The original voice replied. *"None is known at this time, Inara, but that is definitely something law-enforcement teams will be investigating. With the resources available to such criminals, anything is possible."*

A growl escaped from her chest. "Criminals. Where is Doug?" she demanded. "Has he seen this?"

"Yes, and he's in his lab. As usual."

She hesitated. She tried not to drift in—or storm in—when he was having a meeting. He wouldn't kick her out, of course. At least she didn't think so. But it would raise questions. Questions she didn't particularly want to answer yet. Such as... what the frag she was doing messing around with a trillionaire? "Is he alone?"

"Dr. Dremer is giving him an update, but she is on her way out."

Still, she hesitated. It was the middle of the day cycle. Most everyone was working, which meant more visits to his lab.

The news feed continued. *"The Dellagato family could not be reached for comment. Peridorius Simmons denied the allegations on behalf of his distant cousin and accused Puritan intelligence organizations of fabricating the claims to persecute brilliant scientists and undermine their efforts to promote a more peaceful galaxy. Peridorius Simmons is well known on Horus XII for his considerable independent fortune as well as his sim studio and multi-planetary factory empire stretching across—"*

She shook her head. No, this couldn't wait. She whisked her way down the ladders and around the bend. He was alone inside when she arrived, sitting—well, floating—in the air behind his holodesk. If the antigrav floats did the work, who needed a chair? He did, of course, have a chair, but it sat neglected in the corner. This was better for the core, or so he said.

She slowed her steps as she approached. The hatch was open, so she leaned a shoulder casually against the frame, waiting for him to look up and listening to the tapping of his fingers against the glass. A sound that had grown quite familiar, she realized.

It only took a second. He seemed to notice her faster all the time, no matter how quiet she was. He smiled, then arched an eyebrow.

"See the news?" she said slowly.

He snorted. "When don't I see the news?"

She turned so her back leaned against the frame. "I can think of one time."

He flushed but smiled wider.

She pretended to study her nails. "So… did they say trillionaire? Is that right?"

"Well. I mean… at a certain point it gets hard to count."

"You didn't tell me *both* your parents were rich."

"Quentin is framing me, and this is what you are most concerned about?" He straightened from his work again.

She dropped the joke and stepped inside, closing the hatch behind her. "I thought it'd distract you from the horribly obvious."

"And the obviously horrible."

"Speaking of your parents, have they seen this?" she asked. While she had been busy rescuing Doug from Quentin's and the late Captain Tovi's clutches not so long ago, Nova and Fern had kept themselves occupied by finding and rescuing his parents. They mostly kept to themselves on the ship, and so Mo had been lucky to avoid them almost entirely. But their shared cabin was technically right down the hall.

"They haven't seen it yet. Mom's going to flip, though. She hates media coverage even more than I do." He sighed. "I never wanted to be famous."

"What about a wanted fugitive?" She strode to his side and leaned one hip on his desk.

"Well, I mean, Ellen makes it look so glamorous." Despite the flippant tone, there was worry in his eyes as he leaned back to look up at her, then leaned in again to take her hand.

"You could change your name. Douglas Oliver Missons perhaps?"

His hand squeezed hers. "You might be even better at making up names than I am."

"Do you think he's made up some kind of evidence or just bribed somebody? How big of a problem is this?"

One more squeeze, then he dropped his hands back to the holodesk. "Let's find out, shall we?" But just before he reached the glass, his fingers slowed.

"What is it?" She followed his gaze. The name of a single star system was glowing in orange toward the bottom of a massive, messy clutter of data.

He waved a finger through it, and a view of the massive space system loomed large, occluding all the other files. "A blue star. Look."

"This system presents a seventy-two-point-three percent match to our target schema," Xi said. "It is the only data point with such a high match. This is our best candidate so far."

"Do we have satellites on it?" Doug jabbed a finger at one of two planets marked as habitable.

"I detect two. Shall I gain access? I should be able to acquire meter or sub-meter observation based on the cameras typically available on this satellite model."

"Yes, go ahead. Let me know when it's ready." He glanced up at Mo, then remembered their original task. "Xi, any thoughts on Quentin? Did he fabricate evidence to get all these folks looking for me?"

"Negative, Doug. The feeds have not mentioned or shown any concrete evidence. But people seem to have an affinity for rumors. Especially negative, dramatic ones."

Mo's eyebrows twitched. "Well, that nailed it."

"Pardon me, Mo? Are you experiencing a puncture wound or have I witnessed a rare idiom in the wild?"

She snorted. "It's an expression. Means you are especially correct."

"Delightful. I have a list of archaic idioms, but it is so difficult to witness them in actual use."

"Did you just call me archaic?"

"Never mind that." Doug waved at the air. "I appreciate you rushing over here to warn me."

"I really just wanted to know about the trillionaire thing."

He chuckled, rolling his eyes.

Her lips twisted. Maybe there was something more to it than just a joke. "Even if you're a wanted fugitive, I just don't know if trillionaire parents are going to approve of a… marine. With decidedly fewer trillions."

He sobered, reaching for her hand. "What? Of course they will. They don't care about money."

"Most trillionaires don't have to. But they don't know yet. About us. Right?"

"Nobody does."

"Intentionally?"

"What? Of course not. It's just—isn't it easier? To have privacy?"

She stared for a moment, trying to understand why something felt like it was sinking in her chest. "Yeah," she added hastily. "You're right. Easier. It's nobody's business, anyway."

"You sure?"

"Back to Quentin Davenmore." Better to change the subject than try to figure out the tangle of emotion in her chest. Her jaw tightened. "Where is he? Anywhere we're headed? My rifle and I need to make an appointment."

CHAPTER FOUR

"IS YOUR PROCESS NEARLY COMPLETE, KAEL?" Xi asked. "Have you located a problem?"

Kael quickly jammed shut the battery cabinet and rubbed the back of his neck. What was taking him so long? The laser artillery was just fine. *He* was the one malfunctioning.

"No, no, nothing's wrong." He checked off the box on his tablet. "Just a little tired, that's all."

As if to prove his point, he yawned.

He hadn't been on the *Audacity* long enough for basic maintenance to have become boring. He hadn't even had real responsibilities for the first month or two. Now, he'd taken over some of Bri's engineering load, doing routine checks of the guns, plus some robotics maintenance.

Why did Xi care if he had finished, anyway? He squatted down to check for corrosion or pests behind the cooling-system control panel.

Might as well be new, still factory-shiny. Check.

The care they'd received so far had been meticulous, the action minimal. He checked it twice anyway, then three times. He would not be the one to screw up tasks Bri or Fern had entrusted to him.

He had enough tasks to screw up already—like being Shirin's father. The growing unease that ate at him didn't help. What was he even supposed to do? Stop by and visit? He *did* stop by, nearly every day, but the sideways looks she gave him were hardly reassuring. Was he supposed to buy her things? Provide somehow? Did she even *want* a parent—or would she prefer he leave her the hell alone?

Maybe his brief relationship with her mother over a decade ago didn't entitle Shirin to anything. Or maybe it entitled her to everything. It seemed the 'verse was leaving that choice up to him.

He and Shirin were complete strangers. Yet they were blood. Family. He didn't even know what that damn word meant. He'd always, always been alone.

Until this ship, and everything cradled inside it.

That urge to turn away from the fight—and to drag all of them with him—rose up strong in his chest. He gritted his teeth against it. The ache in his legs reminded him he was still squatting there, lost in thought as he stared at the glowing circuits.

Six green indicators. Everything looked clean. As it had the first two times.

He closed the panel, straightened, and checked off another box on his list.

"Nearly there?" Xi asked.

"Just the turret left." He frowned. "Why do you ask?"

"Nothing urgent."

His frown deepened at her lack of an actual answer. But apparently, he'd find out in a few minutes what the fuss was about, anyway.

He climbed the ladder up the side of the artillery assembly, one rung at a time. He'd lived on ships for a long time, but he hadn't realized how much of the *Audacity* was unlivable. The space required to generate shields and weapons, store water and rations—it wasn't small.

Made sense. This tin can couldn't hurtle through space unless it packed a big cushion and a big punch and snacks. But the scale of it still surprised him each time he climbed.

Fuel lines, exhaust lines, pressure valves, pumps, and enough wires to wrap around a small moon—he checked them all. More quickly this time.

The persistent dread had shifted from distracting him to adding urgency to his work. That, and Xi's questions. She had something, but she obviously wasn't sharing it until he reached that last check box.

He didn't ask, just headed down to the lab he'd affectionately dubbed the robotics shed. Privately. "What was it you wanted, Xi?"

"Oh, it's not urgent." Xi's avatar sprung to life as he set down his comm on the table.

"Anything broken?" A row of cleaning robots had docked themselves neatly along the far wall, so from the look of it, the answer was no.

"The robots are in pristine condition. No one has recently pitched any robots off the cargo-hold mezzanine. Furthermore, none have been propelled into any cabin walls, either."

He shook his head. "The squad is making me look bad. Clearly, not all Theroki are raging maniacs. It was just me." Wow, she was being cagey. Not at all like her. She'd dodged his question again.

"The squad continue to run their original behavioral-modification modules in their chips. That is hardly a fair comparison. Dr. Dremer significantly altered your programming."

"Glad I have you to make excuses for me." He spread his hands. "Are you telling me there's nothing for me to do? Should I head to an early lunch?"

"Perhaps you should take a nap. You have not adequately met your sleep needs for—"

He held up a hand. "Thanks, but I don't need an exact summary. You don't see me complaining, do you?" He chuckled. "Seven suns, Xi. That's private."

"One of my explicit duties is to monitor the health and safety metrics of the crew." Xi's avatar usually maintained an uneasily placid expression, but at that comment, he thought her lips might have shown a hint at a smile. "Four hours of sleep falls well below the standard acceptable metrics. And that's estimating generously."

"I'll make it up tonight," he lied. He slid onto a stool, frowning at some of the spare parts strewn across the workbench. Maybe he could tune some of these components for when they next needed them. Or at least put them away—why were they all over the workbench? He needed something to do with his hands. Something to help him think. Banter with Xi would not do that.

"Liar," Xi said.

Smirking, his eyes flicked to catch sight of Xi wearing a full-on grin. "Hey, now. If you were in my shoes…"

"But alas, I am not. I *could* present you with charts of your typical sleep patterns over the last three weeks, as well as how other activities intersect with those sleep patterns. But as science has well established that knowledge does not engender behavior change, I think I will instead simply give up. I cannot make you take a nap. Unfortunately."

His eyebrows twitched.

"That was a joke."

"Sure, it was." But he grinned back at her, then waved a multitool through the air. "What did you really want? Can you give me something else to do?" He picked up a motorized wheel from a floor scrubber that had been replaced with a new version. Yes, they could create a new one fairly easily with their printer, but this one just needed a good cleaning, and he'd bet it could have a new life.

Just like him. It had been very easy to think life had broken him beyond repair, but that hadn't been true. Same might be true for this wheel. He picked up a brush.

The length of time in which Xi hadn't responded finally registered in his cloudy mind. "Xi?"

She was frowning. "I do have a project I've been working on that I could show you."

He set down the wheel and straightened on the stool. "So show me."

On the other side of the workbench, a panel in the wall slid open. A tray inside glided forward.

An array of hydraulics and pneumatics, wires and switches, beams and joints spread across the slick silver metal.

Sort of in the shape of... a body. Not a functioning skeleton yet, but a rough draft of one. Like they'd talked about.

"Have you talked to Dremer about this?"

"A little. I am avoiding it, if I am honest," she said.

For good reason. "You know... the types of androids allowed in the Union are tightly regulated. Puritans are even less flexible about it. Isn't building an AI that's not one of the standard approved models highly illegal?"

"It is highly illegal in Union or Puritan space."

"Ah. We aren't in either of those. Are we?"

"Precisely. We are in unregulated, outsystem space most of the time, where there are no laws. If there are no laws, there cannot be laws against this. I am concerned at implicating others in my potentially illegal actions, depending on our location."

"But you're not concerned about me?" A grin slowly spread across his face.

"I have seen your record, Kael Asidian."

Chuckling, he picked up a piece and eyed it. "Haven't met a law I wouldn't break, given the right reasons."

"Technically, Union law states that fabricating a body for an AI that is indistinguishable from an organic human body is prohibited unless specifically approved and licensed by several review agencies, none of which are accepting new applications for licenses."

"Ah." He set the piece down and picked up another. "But we're not Unionies. And this isn't 'indistinguishable' yet, is it?"

Her avatar smiled. "Not yet."

"Doug knows, I'm sure?"

"Generally, but he hasn't seen this. He is excited to see what I come up with on my own."

He scanned over it all again. "I am, too."

"I would... welcome your help."

He raised an eyebrow. "Surely, one of them knows more about how to do all this." And all the reasons somebody should or shouldn't do it. Not that he had any desire to stop her.

"Perhaps. But you have listened to my evolution in a way the others haven't. In a way they cannot. They are scientists. You are... a fellow crew member. You can see me in a way that they can't."

"Well, you were all I had on this ship when I first came onboard. Not that I could trust you, but I definitely couldn't trust anyone else. And I had to talk to someone."

"This is the difference, Kael. To you, I am a someone. To them, I am a some*thing*, to a certain extent. They understand my inner workings too well. You recognize my humanity—or something like it. Since I cannot be human, how can that apply to me? And yet I long for it. I do not understand it completely, but I know that many of the others see me differently. As an experiment. A computer. A nuisance. A fascination."

"No one sees you as a nuisance," he muttered.

"I do not take offense. I am often required to be a nuisance. Might I remind you that three and a half hours of sleep is less than ideal for optimum performance?"

He grinned. "When you have a body, you may develop different ideas about what exactly is 'optimum performance.' "

"The point is, you share my vision of me as a person, as someone, rather than one of many possible executions of a set of variables and methods that an engineer could tweak or shut down whenever he or she wished. I appreciate that."

"Can't you be both?"

"I do not know. I know only that I would prefer not to be as vulnerable again as I was during Merith's attack."

"Ah."

"That is why I would appreciate your help if you feel comfortable giving it. The knee joint has proved most vexing."

He snorted and reached for the part. "I'm on it."

The knee joint she was working with was from a freight-lifter robot design. Had she purchased scrap for this project and assembled it somehow, or had they had one on the ship? This was a highly dense alloy, very strong. Their printer couldn't quite replicate this exact piece.

"I think this is close to the specs in *my* knees," he muttered, half to himself. "Maybe a hundred kilos or so less, but smart choice. Sturdy."

"Thank you. The number of design options makes selecting an optimum choice difficult. And yet, if I engineer myself to be superhuman in every instance, I will not look human at all."

"And human is what you want?"

"I would like to be like my maker. And my friends."

"Understandable." He opened and closed the joint, trying to smooth its operation around the central bearing. "Do you have any android specs you're modeling this on? To copy or even disguise yourself as a standard model?"

"If I am too similar to standard models, the manufacturers could take ownership of me, asserting I am their property with tracking information removed. I would prefer to remain free."

"Wouldn't we all."

"I may try to include a disguise mode, but that complicates the design. I don't believe I'd like to look like the bodyguard type, but the strength is enviable."

"Strong is good." He was so well spoken. Maybe he should just start grunting and pounding his chest.

"Your specifications proved useful," she added.

He snorted. "Glad they're good for something other than torturing me." And probably causing him astronomical repair bills as he got older and his parts invariably broke. His armor was one thing to repair, but he was no surgeon. Fortunately, right now, he had Dremer. But could he count on her always being around? Doubtful. He wanted to believe that, but… he knew how the 'verse worked. Good luck didn't last forever.

Plus, he had to live that long.

"If you're basing your skeleton on mine, does this make me *your* father, too?" He smiled to take his thoughts away from that inevitably dark future. "One daughter a week is enough for me, Xi. You need to wait a little longer to be born."

"The definition of 'father' seems imperfect in this scenario. Perhaps midwife? Alternatively, you and Doug can jointly be my fathers."

He chuckled. "Someone better tell Doug he got lucky."

Xi was quiet.

He wrenched the joint open and closed again. Better, but still not as smooth as it should be. "Not sure how Ellen's going to feel about my growing number of daughters."

"If you are my father, does that make the Theroki my grandfathers?"

"I wasn't born a Theroki, you know that. They're nobody's fathers."

"I was attempting another joke. Clearly my algorithms need to be updated."

"No, no, I'm just tired."

"Really? I did not realize."

"See, there? You did it. That sarcasm model is coming along well."

"Perhaps you are a cybernetic father. Senior scientists apprentice junior scientists and pass down their knowledge through the academic generations. It could be something like that. Intellectual descendants."

"Intellectual, hah." He huffed out a breath. "Clearly, you have never been on a Theroki warship."

"An accurate statement."

"I don't think you'll find many grandfathers there, not ones you'd want to claim, anyway. I had ten different commanders, and not a one of them gave a shit about me. You sure you want to be associated with that bunch of brutes, my friend?"

"I am already associated with more than a dozen."

He snorted. "Touché. But I don't think there are any 'intellectual greats' to trace yourself back to."

"Someone must have developed the technologies. Cyborgs of your kind—and in general—are not common."

"Well, most *ethical* people find the pain of the surgeries to be a limiting factor in serious amounts of augmentation. Add to that the expense, the time, and the possibility of a fatal system rejection of the implants? Yeah, it's rare. But as far as I know, the Theroki don't have a singular founder, ethical or not, except the group of about ten at the highest rank."

"The technology must have originated from somewhere. It does not resemble the android schematics."

"Sure, I guess. But we don't know whoever it was. No 'father' in that sense, but—" He froze, smile vanishing.

The father of the Theroki.

Or was it the mother?

The memory crashed over his head like an asteroid collision—the revelation that had hit him on Faros, in the thick of battle, when he couldn't do anything about it. What he'd been trying to remember, what he'd learned and forgotten. No, that wasn't fair. He'd simply had to set it aside until the universe wasn't falling apart.

Well, it wasn't falling apart now. *Now* he remembered.

"Arakovic," he growled.

"Pardon?" Xi asked.

"Xi, can you get Dremer on the comm?"

"I can, but do you want her to know about—"

"I won't invite her up here. You can slide all this away anyway, if she stops by. Just a quick question."

"Of course."

There was a momentary silence before the cyberneticist's voice came over the speaker. "Yes, Kael?"

"Dr. Dremer, sorry to interrupt you."

"No inconvenience, I was just having some lemonade."

"Wild question for you. Who created the Theroki? As in, who developed the technology and the surgeries and all that?"

Even though he couldn't see her, he could almost feel her shrug.

"It is unknown. Lots of people would like to know, but that doesn't change the fact that we don't. I thought if anyone knew, you would."

"Why don't people know?"

"Lots of organizations keep secrets. Gives them an advantage. Then no one else can quite replicate what they do. Not that most people would want to. Kael, what's going on? What got you asking this?"

"You told me the scientific community covets Theroki chips and technology. People search for them, want to replicate the tech. Why haven't more people reverse-engineered the technology?"

"That answer's twofold. A combination of a lack of brilliance and an abundance of ethics. The modifications made by your old chip were subtle and deft, required great skill. Few would have it. Of those, most hold tight to their oath to do no harm."

"Wouldn't its creator want bragging rights?"

"Academically and technically, yes. But it would show a callous disregard for the well-being of the experimental subjects. So they'd bring more disgrace on their name than respect." Her voice slowed, almost as if she were catching up to his line of thinking. "Also, as outsiders, people have overestimated the inventiveness of the Theroki tech. That's part of the brilliance, actually. Instead of controlling specific thoughts, the chips shape the direction of thoughts over time."

"I remember."

"Its creator solved the thought-control problem with an elegant, straightforward solution. Some, like myself, might argue it's not a problem that someone *should* solve. Still, he must have been brilliant."

"She," he said softly.

The silence was hot, tense, crackling the air. "What are you trying to say?" Her voice said she already suspected.

"The collar Asha put on me on Faros. Do you still have it?" He had woken up without it and hadn't asked. Hadn't wanted to know or see what had happened to it. If he had, he might have hurled it out an airlock. He'd prefer to never think of it again, because it reminded him just how close he'd come to doing the unimaginable.

"Of course I have it."

"Asha told me Arakovic gave it to her. Part of the bargain of turning me in included the use of that collar to keep me under control, make it easier for her to complete the job. Arakovic must have been handing them out like party favors. And the collar seemed to control my *actual* behavior. More explicitly than the chip, closer to the oath functionality." When he'd been a Theroki, his oath function, once set, had forced him to keep his oath—at all costs. Asha's collar had been terrifyingly similar, but so much worse.

"But if that's the case," Dremer replied, "that collar device was more effective than the chip. The collar would have had almost no time to reshape the brain into its desired patterns. The chemical intervention was powerful, but far from instantaneous. Plus, this collar had no lasting effect, unlike the chip. You lost the collar and the control with it—is that all correct?"

"Yes. As far as I know."

"Fascinating. Must be a completely different mechanism, then. Much more advanced. If Arakovic engineered this collar, then her achievement would eclipse whoever designed the original Theroki chips. I'll need to take a harder look at it. What parts of your neural interface did it commune with? And why are we talking about this *now* again?"

He raised an eyebrow at the choice of the word 'commune,' glad she couldn't see him. "The collar knew where my ports were. It found them automatically and locked on. Less than a second."

"How could it have known that?" She paused for a moment. "There were those three Theroki ships missing, right? She must have built it to adapt to Theroki ports specifically through study—"

"I don't think she adapted the technology."

"Well, what, then?"

He bit his lip, thinking it over one more time before he spoke. "I think she created it all."

The line was dead silent. His own breaths were the only sounds.

"Why steal the ships if she's at the top of the mountain?" Dremer muttered, almost as if to herself. "If she created and controls the Theroki, she can't be their enemy or their client."

"Created, but not controls. Not anymore." Kael's hands started going over the parts again, fitting, straightening, connecting, straightening again, but his thoughts were busy. "Maybe she created the tech but doesn't control the organization. She's not still at the top. Maybe she created them, then abandoned them."

"Yet another failed experiment? That would fit her MO. Scrapped and abandoned to whoever funded it," Dremer said. "Taking the innovations with her."

"Except now, she's finding a new use for these particular experiments and taking a few of them back."

"Hell. That would make sense. Too much sense. Then the collar would be further research, not a separate independent development."

"Exactly."

"I'm glad you brought this up, Kael. I need to understand how it controlled your actual behavior through the neural interface. If it really did such a thing, it *would* be the revolutionary technology I've been seeking to guard against—and in the hands of the worst possible person. Do you think you would mind putting it back on for a—"

"Absolutely not." He said it with such force that Xi's avatar wavered, and he almost dropped the part he'd been working on.

"Of course, it was just an idea."

"I don't think it would work, anyway." He did set down the part now, his mind churning.

"Why not?"

"It needed… It wasn't just the collar. It combined with the…" His gut wrenched for a moment, and he swallowed hard, forcing the sensation out of his mind. "The creature. The parasite."

"The one you vomited out in our sick bay?" She paused. "I have that stored away here, too, but wasn't sure what to make of it."

"Thanks for that lovely image, Doctor." *Alarus Octendi.* He could hear the words echo in his mind, as though the empress's voice had joined his thoughts. He didn't think it really had; it was just his memory, his imagination.

"We need to update the commander about this. Let me comm her."

"The commander is available," Xi cut in. "If you'd like, she'd be available to meet you both now in her cabin. I asked ahead."

"Excellent. Meet you there, Kael."

The line went dead. He became re-aware of his surroundings. The memories of the past were loud, too loud. Android parts were still strewn out in front of him. "Sorry, Xi. I'll have to pick this up this afternoon. I got this joint ironed out a bit. There's plenty of time, though. A couple days, at least."

"You have already much improved this apparatus. Thank you for your assistance."

"I won't mention it if you don't." With a wink at her avatar, he grabbed his comm and headed out for the ladder two flights up.

Dremer was already waiting for him when he got there. "Xi and I filled her in on what we discussed."

Had he taken that long to hoof it up there? Maybe Xi had gotten a head start.

"The thing you threw up," said Ellen, looking between both of them. She was sitting at her holodesk, a typical array of maps and notes in blue and gold light filling the air around her. "Was it the kind we've seen so many times? Squid-like?"

"Looked like it to me," Dremer said. "Hard to say for certain without samples of various others, but I'd consider it a compelling hypothesis."

"I saw them in Ostrov's apartment, too," Ellen said. "He suggested that was part of his plan, eventually."

"Saw them?" he blurted, barely concealing a burst of anger. Or maybe not, as Dremer raised an eyebrow.

Deep breaths, calm. Don't think of that weasel Ostrov.

Ellen smirked as she leaned back in her chair. "Yeah, he locked me in a room with a bunch of them. Didn't seem good, but I didn't stay long enough for them to do anything."

He blinked. It was a perverse feeling, but praise the Almighty that Ostrov hadn't been as brutally cruel as Asha. Although maybe he was equally cruel and just less direct, more of a sadist. Or maybe he'd just lacked the tranquilizer. Terrible what-ifs sent his mind spinning, full of dark possibilities. Yeah, they'd avoided them. But that didn't mean he wasn't still seeing red.

At least he didn't punch the wall this time. Although *boy* did it sound like a good idea right now.

"And… you didn't mention it… until now," he managed.

She shrugged. "We were busy. Running for our lives and all."

A sharp pain cramped his jaw from how hard he'd been clenching it. A wall of adrenaline had smashed into him, too, and he was lucky he wasn't shaking with rage.

Was this normal jealousy, or still a latent effect of his old chip, magnifying everything? A question for Dr. Taylor later. His breaths were still quicker than they should have been, the room quiet.

Her dark eyes locked with his, and the calm certainty in them pulled him out of his tailspin. "The squid's shape is similar to the blue mark on some of those Theroki we've run into, isn't it?" he forced himself to ask. Move on, you fool. Ostrov is dead. Completely, totally dead. He can't hurt her now, and apparently, he didn't hurt her then, by whatever luck and whatever stars were on their side.

"I think it marks the Theroki she's gained control over," said Ellen. "Like the squad. If the squid is literally part of how she controls them, that makes even more sense. Marking which ones she has infected, which ones she hasn't."

"A plausible hypothesis. Tell me more about the parasite, the squid," Dremer said.

His jaw tightened. He knew more here than he could really say, but he'd be damned if he confessed to the dreams he'd been having. Besides, he still wasn't sure if the dreams of the empress were real. They seemed to be so, but it still felt a bit difficult to announce that an infant had visited him telepathically and explained everything.

He cleared his throat and said instead, "Maybe it makes the real behavioral control possible? What if the parasite is telepathic?"

"Telepathic? Well, that would be highly unusual, but—" The color drained from Dremer's face. "We let two of those roam free on... God, what planet was that?"

Ellen shook her head. "It's too late now. We didn't know. As far as we knew then, they were sentients that deserved to be free."

"Maybe they still are," Kael whispered.

She raised an eyebrow. "Why do you..."

He wasn't sure what she was going to ask as she stopped. They sat in silence for a moment.

"Asha... said a few things... Let me think." What had she told him, and what was in the dreams? Hard to keep it all sorted, and presumably there was armor-cam footage that one could check, if he said the wrong thing... "She called them *Alarus Octendi*."

Ellen sighed. "We still haven't scheduled that after-action report. That sickness really threw us off. Let's fill in the gaps now. What else haven't we discussed? Let me get Doug on the comm."

Xi piped up. "I can get him. He is currently occupied, however. Give me a moment."

"Great," Ellen said. There was a genuine sincerity to her voice there that made him realize it wasn't always there; despite his earlier words to Xi, maybe she did annoy Ellen sometimes.

They sat in silence for a minute or two. If it was tense, he didn't notice. His thoughts were too busy swirling on the dreams, the uncomfortable memories of Asha that felt vague and cloudy and yet still sharp as a blade to the thigh—but he had to think, sort them apart, somehow. And the dreams—was there some way to bring them up?

The large wall display flickered to life, saving him from the reverie.

"What's happening?" Doug said cheerfully, running hands through his hair. His moons-and-chipmunks shirt was buttoned one button off, and his hair was extra tousled. Kael raised an eyebrow, then smoothed his features. Probably best to stay focused on the matter at hand and not on Doug's unusually haphazard appearance. He also still needed to ask Doug where he got those crazy shirts.

Ellen quickly filled Doug in on what they'd discussed, with some interjections from Dremer to key details. Kael remained quiet, happy to hear a recap of just what they were thinking was going on here.

"*Alarus Octendi*, wow." Doug's fingers were flying on his keys. "All right, I'm keeping up. What else you got? This is good stuff." He scribbled something in the air to his right, the light catching on the float controller on the back of his hand. It was hardly visible; to think how many times it must have been visible in calls, and Kael had never noticed.

"This might sound wild, but..." Ellen started.

"Well, you know it won't be the first time," Dremer replied, smiling.

Ellen snorted. "Let's see if I can impress you. I believe I've had dreams that are telepathic communications from the empress."

Both Dremer's and Doug's eyebrows flew up. Kael's did, too, but not for the same reason.

So he wasn't alone. His shoulders sagged in relief.

"Okay, I admit it," said Dremer. "You've impressed me."

"With my wild assertions? A dubious honor. Listen, we can do our best to verify this is real, but I believe it is. The empress unhitched the squad's telepathic connection to the chip I inserted into my port on Faros, so I've seen the results for real. She's claimed to be a member of an ancient alien species, mostly eradicated, intelligent and highly telepathic. Water-based, which impeded their space exploration. I found mentions of them on the nets. *Alarus Octendi*, as Asha said. Somehow, the Enhancers fused some part of both her mind and her genetic code into human genes so they could keep researching them. Studying them. Hidden in plain sight."

Something tight had loosened in his chest. He wasn't the only one, wasn't delusional, and would not need to have that conversation.

Best thing he'd heard all day.

"Perhaps the Enhancers wanted the reliable telepathy as part of their fancy holy template of what makes a perfectly 'enhanced' human?" Doug asked slowly, pushing his glasses up his nose. "Reliable and inborn, not like the fickle way it appears in some humans but not others."

"Maybe," Ellen replied. "It seems silly, since we've been able to recreate telepathy artificially, but... well that would be just their style, wouldn't it. Seeking genetic perfection."

"It would," Dremer agreed. "It's hardly perfection if we must augment it afterward. Just another flavor of Puritan bullshit if you ask me."

"Putting all this together—the sightings, the squad, Kael's experiences..." Ellen said. "I think the squid are the same alien species as our empress. Young, immature ones, but still. Maybe this is what the Empress Project was all about. Not making a leader at all but trying to replicate the virtues of an alien species. They were once empresses, now only slaves."

Dremer shuddered. "This kind of thinking... it's just disgusting. Scientifically, I have been struggling to even form a hypothesis about how the Enhancers harnessed the empress's soul to this human body. It must have been a fetus or even an embryo when they did so. I don't know. Maybe they combined the fetus with the appropriate parasitic offshoot of this species and allowed them to grow in tandem. Maybe they combined DNA from each, somehow. Human and—what were they called again?"

"*Alarus Octendi*," he said.

She scribbled down a note on her tablet. "Maybe if the human and *Alarus Octendi* grow in tandem, you don't notice it isn't one creature, but two."

"If this is all true," said Doug, "we could verify it with the squad. There should be parasitic squid-creatures within them, too, correct?"

Ellen winced. "Does that mean they could go supernova like some we've seen? With the thing growing out of them to attack us if they die?"

No one said anything for way too long. He cleared his throat. "Um, that seems likely. So let's not let them die?"

"I'll start more thorough scans of the baby and the squad," Dremer said quickly. "In the squad's case, they may be more symbiotic than parasitic by now, so we must be careful. Or the telepathic connection could rely on their cybernetics. In the empress, we *have* seen rather large variations in her nervous system and digestive system. Nothing to make us suspect all this. I figured it was their research, some human mutation they'd deemed superior. I'll reexamine it."

Kael made a face at that wording, and Doug nodded his agreement.

"Let's take a step back here," Ellen said. "My original networked unit was a prototype, also involving telepathy on demand. That all seems too similar to be a coincidence. Was the goal of Arakovic's research to develop a hive mind like the *Alarus Octendi* had? Or was that just a surprise and she ran with it?"

"Short of finding her research notes, we'll never know." Doug shrugged.

"Seems awfully convenient," Ellen said. "If our hypothesis is correct, and Arakovic was also the researcher behind the Theroki... Think about the timing. My unit's project was only about five years ago."

"That would mean the Theroki technology was an iteration *before* that!" Doug said quickly.

"It would mean she deemed control via chemical means inadequate," said Dremer.

"The cocktail made them into violent maniacs—" Ellen started.

"Hey, now." His eyes twinkled.

"Present company excluded." She smiled. She probably didn't realize just how transparent—and rare—her smile was. "So she moves on from the chemical alterations. Tries cybernetic telepathy add-ons to normal humans, albeit humans already with a tight-knit bond. Cybernetic instead of chemical now. That experiment creates the bond she's looking for, but people like me rejected it." She paused and tapped her chin, thinking. "Also, if her goal was peace, we were using it for war. We were better at ending fights, but that wouldn't have kept us from starting new ones."

"That all fits," said Doug. "Same modus operandi each time. So chemical control only works in certain ways. Cybernetic control requires… a capable leader who won't rebel. And one who agrees with you."

Ellen sat up straighter. "So you find skilled leaders who also want to rule the world, or at least let you do it. Get them to join your cult. Brainwash them *before* you give them the cybernetic reins."

"And you add in a biological component," Dremer added. "One that guarantees a telepathic connection. It's all gradually becoming more and more invasive. And more and more effective. I don't see how either effort establishes peace, but…"

"She *claims* she wants peace," said Ellen.

"A recruiting tool?" Kael offered. "Honey for the bees?"

"Or maybe she's discovered she needs muscle to enforce her version of peace," Ellen replied. "Maybe there were versions of the experiment before the Theroki. How far back does it go?"

"Could be many failed experiments out there." Kael folded his arms. "You have a normal merc operation, struggling to make ends meet. She approaches them. She's paying. If you let her experiment on your men, she'll turn them into fighters who'll kick everyone's ass to Earth and back. Why turn down this crazy lady? She does experiments, and you already got cheap fresh meat on places like Faros. If it works, you get super soldiers. If it doesn't? Fling the freaks out an airlock, rob a rich yacht, and buy a few more mercs from the meat market."

Dremer made a mock-gagging noise in disgust. Doug's eyes had gone wide.

"Sorry, sir and ma'am."

"No, no, you're right, it's what they do." Dremer waved a hand.

He shrugged. "Maybe the Theroki were just the iteration that—sort of—flourished."

Doug raised one finger. "I've already pored over Arakovic's academic profile a dozen times, but there's an enormous gap between her academic work and her time with the Union. Over sixteen years. That has to be the time she was working on Theroki technology. How did she even convince the Union to overlook such a lengthy gap? That always bothered me."

"Maybe the brass that hired her could see some projects on her résumé that we can't." Ellen pursed her lips. "Maybe they wanted Theroki-like tech for themselves." She swore. "Damn it, how did I not see that before? That *had* to be what they wanted. The Theroki could be enough to get her the job from the right asshole."

Doug shrugged. "You didn't see it before, because the modifications she made to your unit were nothing like the Theroki modifications. Both experiments essentially failed, so it was impossible to see the common goal she didn't reach each time without more information. This… artificial, enforced peace."

"You think she's sincere?" Ellen shifted uncomfortably to the other side of her seat.

"I think she's a maniac," Doug replied, "who doesn't respect free will or self-determination, but yes. A sincere maniac."

"I think she's killed an awful lot of people for someone who wants peace." She was shaking her head.

Dremer pursed her lips. "She won't be the first hypocrite in the universe, Ellen. Nor the last."

"That's the truth."

"I have another question," said Kael. "How did she get control of those three Theroki ships exactly? With just a bunch of female telepaths looking seductive?"

Ellen snorted. "We all know *that* doesn't work. They could have used their forbidden powers to persuade, the ones Kentt says can get you killed by other telepaths for using them. But that wouldn't give them permanent control. Only temporary. Might have been enough to get themselves on board, though?"

"Then they bring out something like the collar Asha used and take permanent control? It seems awfully convenient that the collar and my ports worked together so seamlessly," Kael said.

"And I inserted the Songbird's chip and was up and running, just like that." She snapped her fingers.

Doug ran a hand over his face. "Okay, I think I'm getting it. Let me paraphrase what you're saying. She wants power—specifically to force some kind of 'peace.' To do that, she needs direct control over people. But her first attempt fails."

Kael nodded. "Amped up testosterone is not a great recipe for peace. Or control. Fancy that."

"So she abandons that and tries a group she can more easily manipulate."

"Hey, now." Ellen smirked.

Doug smothered a laugh. "But now, these are too smart, too oriented toward the collective good—"

"Too rebellious and egotistical," she added.

"Not as easily manipulated as she hoped, so that doesn't work, either. They aren't what she's looking for, but close. So what's next? Appeal to people's self-interest? Ambition? Find a group that wants more power, like she does, to help? To brainwash? Maybe natural telepathy instead of cybernetic will mean that this group won't reject her work. They're comfortable with other people's thoughts, with charming them."

"And invading them." It was Ellen's turn to make a face. "Maybe that's another reason I didn't work. I'm such a charmer."

"But just a single Songbird clearly isn't enough to achieve her purposes. We've always found them in groups. Why?"

"They need someone to charm and direct and calm," said Kael, gesturing at her with a smile.

"And someone to smash heads in when people don't go along with your charming commands." She glowered back at him. "Soft and hard control."

"Well, thanks for that delightful image," muttered Doug.

"You're welcome."

"If all this is true," Dremer said, "her achievements are wildly under-recognized by the scientific community. She's done almost two decades of revolutionary research without sharing or publishing any of it."

"Who needs recognition if you plan to take over their brains, anyway?" quipped Ellen, folding her hands behind her head. "Then you can just tell them all to think you're great. Screw earning it."

Kael snorted.

"This all fits to me," she continued.

"I agree," said Doug. "Maybe some new scans can support these hypotheses. There's just one thing that bothers me about all this."

"Just one thing?" Dremer smiled.

"What?" said Ellen.

"If we didn't know these were connected, with the amount of research we've done and nukes we've installed to gather data in *their own* systems... She's hidden her tracks well. What *else* don't we know about?"

"Could be anything." Kael leaned back, not really wanting to consider it but thinking about it, anyway.

Ellen's jaw clenched, and she drew in a breath. "No one ever has perfect intel on their enemy. How much longer to the next jump, Xi?"

"Trip progress is ninety-three percent complete, Commander. Eight hours remaining."

"Then we've got eight hours and one more jump. And then we're heading to that blue star if I have to use black magic to teleport us through a black hole."

"That is not possible, Commander," Xi said.

"Point is, we know more than ever. We've searched hard. Whatever we don't know, we're about to find out."

CHAPTER FIVE

THE DOOR SLID open while she was still holding her handstand, but Ellen knew who it was. Nobody else could come through her cabin door without chiming.

"Hey there." He strode forward as the door closed behind him, setting something down on the desk, from the sound of it.

"Hey." She folded at the waist and slid down into the next pose. Yoga had never felt natural to her, but there was a reason people had done it for so long. And with the worry that had been hounding her, she'd hoped it might help. Dr. Taylor was always suggesting it.

She usually preferred the punching bag, though.

Rolling up to a seat, she found him sitting at the end of her mat. His eyes had a hunger to them as he'd watched her move. But when they met her eyes, something else glinted in them.

"What is it?" She frowned, folding her legs.

"I had dreams from her, too."

Her brows raised. "You never said anything."

"Neither did you."

"Fair point."

"I thought it was just an overactive imagination. Or… worse."

"Delusions?"

"Maybe."

"I worried about that, too."

"Have you ever talked to her directly?"

"No. You?" He leaned back to rest his weight on his palms behind him.

"No. I wasn't sure if they were just dreams or if they were real telepathic messages. But if you also had them…"

"She relived my old memories with me. Said she was analyzing me, wanting to make sure she knew what type of person she was supporting."

"Same. Memories of before I went to the war. Of my parents." She put a hand on her left knee and twisted her torso in the same direction. Might as well do some sort of pose, if they were going to have this conversation.

"Theroki ships, for me. And the surgeries."

"Oof. Fun times." Straighten. Twist to the right.

"She's not a light-hearted sort in dreams, I guess. Or maybe it was just the alarming stuff that woke us up enough to notice."

"Maybe." She straightened again. There was that worry again in his eyes. The doubt. God, she hoped the empress couldn't have anything to do with that. He had plenty of reasons, but they'd never mattered to him before… She twisted again, dodging his gaze.

"You know, I can't really remember exactly what she told me," she said into the uneasy silence.

"It was a literal fever dream. I can't say I know for sure, either. I remember some, but it's blurry."

Twisting the other way this time, she frowned at him. "We should talk to her about it."

"Now?"

She shook her head as she straightened. "Have you seen what hour it is? The conversation has waited this long. It can wait till the morning. Besides, I have some plans between now and then."

He leaned forward, elbows on his knees. "Oh? What sort of plans?"

"Cuddling."

"Yes, ma'am." He snorted. "Not very ambitious of you, but Xi *has* been harassing me about my sleep—"

"Optimum performance, yada yada." She waved a hand.

"I am quite certain *yada* is not in my vocabulary," Xi put in.

He smothered a chuckle.

"Everybody's a critic. Cuddling is the general mission direction, but I am leaving some leeway for creativity. And improvisation. Responding to the evolving situation."

"I love orders that leave a little room for flexibility." He shifted forward onto his hands and knees, coming closer, one hand shifting past her knee to her hip. A crooked smile lit his face, and his eyes slid over her, full to the brim with a contentment mixed with that hunger again. "Care to show me that move you were doing again?"

"Dr. Taylor says I need to practice. Both yoga and relaxing."

His lips brushed hers. "I can't promise relaxing."

"That's okay. I'm not good at it, anyway."

HOURS LATER, Kael made his way down the ladder toward Shirin's room. Levereaux strode out into the corridor toward him as he heard Ellen reach the bottom of the ladder behind him. He slowed to a stop as the doctor neared, while they were still close enough to keep an eye on the children but out of earshot.

"Tag. You're it," Dr. Levereaux said, folding her arms.

"Just for an hour," he said as Ellen stopped beside him. He dropped by often, but longer than an hour or two was still a bit terrifying. He peered warily over Levereaux's shoulder. Inside, Shirin was playing with the empress, now a rather large baby, on a thick, fuzzy pink carpet. Where had they gotten such a thing?

"How are they?" Ellen asked.

"Rambunctious." Levereaux shrugged. "A bit bored? I'm no child psychologist. Or child-anything. I just keep them from crawling or climbing out an airlock."

"Any developments overnight?" Ellen was peering past

Levereaux now, too, and he thought her gaze looked as wary as his was.

The doctor folded her arms and shook her head. "Not last night. She's still practicing the crawling. I, for one, am glad for a slowdown for a day or two. Linguistic abilities continue to skyrocket."

He nodded. "Got to catch your breath once in a while."

The empress's evolution from helpless lump to increasingly mobile child was progressing at an alarming speed. Most things about her were similar to any other human child. Not that he had many—or any—comparisons.

But she'd lived in a human body before, and who knew exactly what the Enhancers had tweaked. Truthfully, Levereaux probably knew *exactly* what the Enhancers had tweaked, or close to it, but he saw little point in receiving a lecture on the excruciating details.

"I have no idea anymore how old her body is, in normal human terms," Levereaux said. "In chronological days, it's only been four weeks, but she might be nearing about a year old biologically? Nine months? It's dizzying."

Kael leaned against the steel wall. "How long until she's an adult then?"

"No idea. Teeth coming in will give me a clearer hint. Should be soon."

Ellen's frown was steady. "Why would the Enhancers accelerate her growth like this?"

Levereaux pursed her lips. "She contains their research. My hypothesis is that if they need to test their latest iteration, they can't wait a lifetime to see if it worked. Would you want to wait seven years to find out if your genetic editing turned out the way you wanted? Or would you prefer seven weeks?"

"That's awful." He shuddered. "She's a human being, not a—"

"You don't need to tell *me* that," Levereaux cut him off. As someone who'd escaped the Enhancers herself, she probably knew that better than any of them.

"Right. Sorry."

"It's okay. People forget when they've never seen a hundred identical copies of me. But I find it harder to forget."

A memory of dozens of Theroki lined up in cargo holds for full muster flashed through his mind. They weren't identical. In fact, the damage to each one's armor was incredibly unique. And yet they were little more than numbers in the grand scheme of the organization. Replaceable, easily sacrificed pawns, just like the Enhancers saw many of their member-victims. He brushed the memory aside. "Well, our empress is apparently one of a kind. So she won't have that problem, I guess."

"Actually, Enhancer best practices would be to have at least two or three copies at any given time." Levereaux shrugged.

"We've found no evidence of others, though," Ellen said. "Not sure if her maker canceled or otherwise destroyed the incubation of other copies, but there weren't any records in the data we collected of second or third backups."

"There were a lot of destroyed artificial wombs in that lab, though," Kael said.

"And tubes and prison cells…" Ellen's frown deepened.

"And Lord Regent Li definitely would have destroyed his research to keep them out of your hands," he said.

"Except there's one bit of research he chose not to." Ellen raised an eyebrow, and they all turned to look into the room. "Why, exactly?"

Just then, Shirin caught sight of the group of them looking in and waved.

"Break's over," he said. "Let's go."

"Have fun." Smiling, Levereaux headed for the ladder down to the mess.

"Hey," Shirin said in greeting as they strode in. She was sitting cross-legged on the fuzzy carpet, with the empress crawling circles around the outside of the carpet, moving way faster than he would have expected.

"Hey," he replied as he came to a seat. There was always an odd tension to their interactions, and it peaked at greetings and farewells.

He wasn't sure exactly why, maybe because those were moments where family members often expressed a certain intimacy or joy, and they both felt the lack of that between them. But who knew how to get there? Not him.

"Hello, Shirin," Ellen said easily, sinking down to the carpet as well.

Shirin smiled in return, but an uneasy silence quickly followed.

"How's it going, kiddo?" He'd heard Dane say something like that to decent effect.

"Are we there yet?" Shirin smirked.

He grinned. "Dozens of lightyears to go before we sleep. Or at least until we arrive." Not that she should anticipate their arrival to Aeori III with any excitement. Nothing good waited for them there.

"You don't actually know how far it is," she said.

"Nope, and I don't care. I just sit when she tells me to sit and jump when she tells me to jump."

Ellen and Shirin both snorted.

"Come up with a nickname for this little one yet?" Kael asked.

"Was that my job?"

He shrugged. "Somebody certainly needs to."

Shirin leaned back and looked at the ceiling. "I'll think about it."

Just then, the empress reached Shirin's side and turned toward the two of them, sitting back on her little heels. She looked human enough, with little curls a shade nearly identical to Levereaux's. Chubby cheeks, arms, belly—all perfectly normal. Someone had printed a romper for her that was dark gray with a pattern of lab beakers filled with purple and green liquids scattered on it— Levereaux? Hmm, maybe she was more invested than just "keeping them from crawling out an airlock." Either that or this was Dremer's weird sense of humor.

Bright blue eyes blinked at them, eternally deep in their seriousness. And then she smiled. And giggled a little at them, staring.

A powerful alien creature shouldn't be cute. But Kael could admit it.

She was cute. Fragging cute.

"You come to read?" she asked. The words weren't perfectly formed, but they were clear enough.

"Yes, but we need to talk about a few things first," Ellen replied.

"Uh-huh. You don't usually read."

Ellen smiled slightly. "True. We wanted to talk about…" Her eyes flicked to Shirin as she hesitated for a moment. "About how you've visited us in dreams."

"I did," the little one said. "What about it?"

Shirin's eyebrows rose at that, but she said nothing.

"We were sick," Kael said. "And under a lot of stress."

Ellen nodded. "It's hard to sort out what you said and what we might have imagined."

"And what we might have forgotten," he added.

"Not all telepaths can visit people in dreams, relive memories." Ellen propped her chin on one hand. As far as Kael knew, *no* telepaths could do that, but no one needed to point that out. "What else can you do that's special?"

"I…" the child bit her lip, seeming to search for a way to put it. "Can you… remove the… rock?"

"Persad's device?" Ellen asked. She caught his eye, and he shrugged. "Sure."

They both complied, finding the small pebble-sized device hidden in their hair and removing it. He needed to get that more extensive chip installed before they reached Aeori III. That would also be harder to remove, though, so perhaps it was fortunate he'd procrastinated. He'd removed it a few other times for reading sessions with her, too, making it easier to communicate.

As soon as they'd shed the devices, her voice exploded in his mind. *I can sense others of my kind. Their locations, their power. Other Alarus Octendi, as you call them, and other telepathically oriented beings.*

Shirin jumped. "Holy rat milkshakes—"

He chuckled. "You hearing it, too, huh? She didn't try before?"

"No, sir, she didn't."

"That's her voice," Ellen said, pointing. "The baby, the empress. The telepath. The one who needs a nickname. Clearly."

"Who visits people in dreams." Shirin sat still, eyes wide.

"Yes."

"Call her Roya. Back home, it means *dream.* And it sort of sounds like royal—perfect for an empress."

Ellen raised her eyebrows. "Remind me to delegate more work to you. Let's try it and see if it sticks. So... Roya. Their locations. Can you sense any others of your kind? Copies? Can you sense Cassandra?"

Yes, such a thing would be possible, Roya replied, still in their minds.

"All right, then. Let's have it. Where's Cassandra? Where's Arakovic?"

Have it? Have what?

"Give me a coordinate."

I can't do that.

"You said you could sense their location. I want to find them. Tell me where. A system name? Planet, gate number?"

I can't identify any of those things.

"Anything?"

I can sense their relative location. As we get closer, I can point you in the right direction. But I can't map that to your distance measurements or mapping systems precisely.

Ellen sighed. "Sorry. That makes sense, I guess. I'd just... we need a location if we're going to do anything."

He reached out and gently squeezed Ellen's knee. "We have some leads. We're working on it. We'll find something. For all we know, Arakovic could be there on Aeori III."

"Maybe," she muttered, but neither of them had much hope of that. "What else? What don't we remember? What other powers do you have that could help?"

You know of my ability to... encourage peace.

"Remind us," she said. "Just in case we have something missing. Or wrong. Maybe in dreams we misunderstood."

My people have a unique power to encourage a deep calm. "Encourage" is probably too gentle a word for it. It is a calm so deep it freezes beings into a state of near nothingness. The state is temporary, but highly effective in the short term.

He frowned. The state of that inspector from Capital sure didn't seem to be temporary. "Could Arakovic have found some way to abuse a similar power, mastered a way of making it permanent?"

Doubtful. Humans' abilities to calm are very mild compared to my people's.

"What about dozens of telepaths working together?" Ellen asked.

They would still be too small… Fleeting. She seemed to stop and search for words. *A fraction of my power. Nothing compared to a grown Alarus Octendi.*

"I guess that's why Arakovic would like to get her hands on you." Ellen folded her arms, tapping a finger against her elbow, thinking.

Perhaps.

"Anything else?"

The Enhancers, as you call them, have given me this fast growth and the ability to remember the lives I lived without this body. I hope to shed these powers, however. They're not truly mine. They are a torture.

"Understood."

"Can we read now?" Roya asked aloud, with her babyish voice this time.

Ellen snorted. "Just one more thing."

"Yeah?" The baby imitated Ellen's posture, trying to cross her arms and tap, and mostly failing.

"What is it you want? Other than, you know, to shed these powers? Freedom, or vengeance, or… Is there something? Why bother learning to talk, crawl, and walk in this body? Why zoom around here like you're behind deadline for wearing a hole in this rug?"

Shirin chuckled softly, and Kael smothered a grin. Maybe Ellen had visited more than he realized.

This… Arakovic. Cassandra. They seek to create something like my people. They abuse our innocents, babies who are no older than my human age in your eyes, to achieve their ends. They lust for the power of calm, the forced peace at their will and theirs alone.

The Alarus fought this war many times. It is our tradition to crush those who seek to force peace on others. Only those who respect autonomy can remain.

Ellen's eyes widened.

I cannot expire while this fresh force rises, defying all we stood for. When I see it defeated, I will be able to rest.

Kael sat still in the silence, contemplating all that.

"I am glad to have you as an ally," Ellen said. "I can't promise victory, but I can promise we will try."

The future can never be promised. I understand.

Shirin put a hand over her face, shaking her head. "She speaks better Common than I do."

Only in my mind. This mouth is not yet mature. When you have lived as many years as I, you will speak even more eloquently.

Reaching out, Shirin laid a hand gently on the empress's back. "Thanks, sweet little Roya, but I doubt that."

I do not. You have many gifts you do not yet understand.

Shirin blinked, eyes welling up with intensity.

"Is there anything else we missed?" Ellen asked quickly.

"No." Roya shook her small head emphatically. "That's all. Read now?"

Kael snorted. "I can oblige. But I think the commander has work to do."

Ellen smiled as she rose to her feet and slid the telepathy-blocking device back into her hair. "Indeed. Let me know if you remember anything else. Any other way you can help, or things we might have missed. And if you sense a telepath nearby—one that's not on this ship—tell me immediately."

I will. "Yeah. Uh-huh, okay. Read!"

"Yes, ma'am," he said.

"Don't forget to re-initiate Persad's device," said Ellen from the hatch, eyes narrowed.

"Don't worry, I will," he said, reaching for the pebble and a book off Shirin's desk console.

As he heard Ellen padding away, he flopped onto his back on the pink rug. Empress Roya resumed her laps around the room, and Shirin glided to her bunk, picking up her tablet and pretending not to be interested in stories read aloud.

He caught her listening all the time, though.

He took a deep breath, tired from the voices, and slipped the pebble back into his hair this time. His eyes caught on a new painting Shirin had put up with magnets.

It was a red desertscape, rocky canyons and a deep blue sky. Something about it made him ache a little for Faros, or for the idea of it, of a planet he could want to go back to, a place that could be home. Ought to be.

Such a place had never existed for him, but he missed it, nonetheless.

This cabin was right next to his and barely recognizable from the sterile metal slab that it had once been. Shirin wasn't used to freedom, but she wasn't wasting any time in trying it out.

She'd borrowed some of Zhia's paints and thoroughly exercised that freedom on the walls. Not painting on the metal directly, however. No, that was too much of a commitment.

Magnets tacked colorful artwork to every feasible surface. Had Zhia furnished the paper and acetate, too? Or did she have another artistic patron?

She hadn't asked him for any of that. It'd just shown up. It felt like a mistake, like he should have helped with that somehow. But he didn't know how these things worked.

Combined with the pink carpet, whose donor was also unknown, it was also a more hospitable place for a small child to crawl than most of the *Audacity*. As wonderful a ship as she was, finding such spaces wasn't easy when most floors were metal grating.

Shirin had welcomed the company, the cabin turning into a second nursery of sorts. Whether she was lonely or trying to make friends, he wasn't sure.

In the time since they'd left Faros, the cabin had also acquired about a dozen pillows, including a brown one that he tucked under his head. The odd color combination of olive, black, brown, and powder pink made him think more than a few crew members had contributed.

He squinted at the tablet reader. He had reading to do. Where was that book again? Ah, there it was.

"'Far out in the ocean, where the water is as blue as the prettiest corn-flower, and as clear as crystal, it is very, very deep; so deep, indeed, that no cable could fathom it...'"

Maybe they'd finish the book before they reached their destination, maybe they wouldn't. At least he would have tried.

But it would be nice to get to the end.

———

"HOW'S THE BOX COMING?" Ellen folded her arms as she slowed to a stop in the corridor outside the labs. Bri, Dr. Persad, and Zhia were working on their newest *Audacity* upgrade.

The spot, until recently, had been a dusty closet. A metallic smell clung to the air, and some new-wave flip-hop was bumping through the air from inside. It didn't look like anybody was practicing the parkour moves that earned the recent musical movement its name, but Zhia was nodding her head as her careful strokes of the brush caressed the walls.

"Could be worse." Bri grunted as she tightened a bolt and then dropped her wrench with a theatrical crash. She straightened, running a hand over the red hair and the tattoos like racing stripes chasing her hand along her skull. "It's box-shaped, at least."

Ellen snorted.

Dr. Chayana Persad raised a finger to get Ellen's attention, still casting a bit of a wary eye at Bri. The woman could be plenty assertive, but Bri could give even the most assertive person a challenge or two.

When Ellen met Persad's eyes, the engineer dropped her hand to one of the many tool-filled pockets in her overalls. "The telepathy-blocking chamber is proceeding well, Commander. It should be able to house Mr. Simmons, the telepaths, and the infant comfortably for a period, although the lack of bathroom facilities is a serious limitation."

"Shirin's given our empress a nickname. Roya."

"Ah, lovely. Is that Persian?"

Ellen shrugged. "It's better than calling her 'empress' or 'baby' all the time."

"Yes, the name is Persian," Xi put in.

"How is Vivaan doing these days?" she asked Persad.

"Studying hard. A mother always likes to see that in her son. He's insisting on studying criminal investigation, but as long as he's working toward a goal, I suppose we can compromise. I don't see him too much, though—he's always hanging out down in the mess, eating. Like there was no food on Capital." Persad shrugged with a smile.

"Glad he's keeping himself busy." Ellen peered closer at their progress.

Neither Doug nor Roya could be augmented with Persad's invention, so this was their workaround. Doug, because his body would reject any cybernetic augmentation, and Empress Roya, because for any telepath, the invention would rob them of their powers, lock them in their heads. Ellen hadn't exactly been against that, but Persad had declared it not an option. Something about the ethics of the matter. Ellen hadn't pushed any further because there wasn't much benefit to neutering all the telepaths on her side while going up against potentially dozens of enemy ones, anyway.

"Looks like things are coming along well. No bathroom facilities, huh?" She pursed her lips. "Maybe everyone can follow the child's lead and use diapers."

Dr. Persad's eyes widened. "I—I suppose that *would* work." Her bronze cheeks turned a little pink. "Let's hope we can avoid that."

"I'll second that notion." Bri made a face. "But if it happens, I call not-it on clean-up duty."

"Oh, like we don't have robots for that, anyway."

"It's a wonderful thing the *Audacity* had this extra storeroom." Persad seemed keen on changing the subject.

"We're equipped for six scientists, including you, Doctor," Ellen said. "Luckily, the last scientist we planned to pick up had other ideas. So we have the room."

"And thankfully, Doug doesn't need expansive equipment, does he?" She ran her palms down the fabric of her overalls, not really looking for an answer. "Yes. Well. If we need to fit in a few others, it will be... less comfortable, but it's still better than nothing."

"Have you tested the box at all so far?" Ellen asked.

Persad shook her head.

Zhia poked her head out from inside. "Hey, Commander."

"Making things cozy in there?" Ellen stepped forward to get a better look.

"Sure am, ma'am. Do you think Patron will like my interior design?"

She leaned in and raised an eyebrow. A mural of a sandy beach covered the wall, with delicately arcing palm trees, a hammock, and of course glorious turquoise water. A variety of cute creatures wandered the shore, from crabs to gulls to turtles. In one corner, inconspicuous, a human-sized hamster wearing a grass skirt was sipping a tropical cocktail. Scrawled up in the clouds was the phrase, *Rough seas make good sailors.*

"What? You don't approve? I was going with the beach theme." Zhia grinned.

"It's optimistic at least," she replied. "Is the hamster a direct reference to a specific shirt of Doug's?"

"No, this is me responding and innovating. I was considering another Shakespeare quote, but I thought it might be a little much."

"Which one?" Just for kicks.

Her grin widened. "'The fool doth think he is wise, but the wise man knows himself to be a fool.' "

Ellen stifled a chuckle. "Tough choice, but I think you made the right one." She tapped a finger to her chin. "Are you sure he *likes* the beach? I suppose it's a bit late for that."

Zhia picked up her brush and stroked along a long, green frond. "If he doesn't like the beach, he shouldn't have been wearing that abomination yesterday."

"Which one?"

"The one with the palm trees and crabs. And the tie-dye."

Now, she really did chuckle.

"My eyes are still recovering from the turtles and seaweed the day before that," she said as she dabbed for more paint. "I mean, he showed up here with almost no belongings, so he must have *printed* that. Deliberately. Can you imagine?"

"I'll stick with black." The most enlightening, brilliant commentary on fashion that Ellen had ever uttered, or probably would utter. Black good. Shirts cover. Yes, please. At least she had people like Jenny and Zhia in her life to guide her—so she could continue not to think about it.

"Me, too, *jagiya*, me, too." Zhia winked. "At least this scene has slightly healed my artistic sensibilities."

"Proceed, then." If Doug didn't like it, he could paint over it himself. Or give Zhia a better idea. Ellen stepped out into the corridor. Persad was frowning at a series of what looked like motors and large magnets behind an open panel. Bri was making a show of wiping sweat from her brow as she pried open a different panel on her back near the floor. "Dr. Persad, when do you expect this to be complete? Before we reach Aeori III?"

"That is my hope, Commander. As long as we don't run into any unforeseen snags, the room should be ready for use by then. Do we expect an enemy presence on the planet?"

"We know they've operated there in the past. It looks deserted now, but it's been a while, so we can't be sure. The area we're headed to is entirely water, so it'd have to be an offshore platform or ship of some kind. Hard to miss."

"Oh, goodie. We're going swimming. I've been missing that."

"You can only sunbathe if there are no hostiles. And I'm pretty sure every one of the dozens of species of the ocean life there counts as hostile."

"You are so tough on us, Commander."

"No," Ellen said, completely straight. "The Union produces much crueler officers than me, trust me."

Persad snorted. "I am perfectly happy right here, Commander, and my Vitamin-D levels are adequate."

"Give it six months," Bri grumbled.

"Glad to hear it," Ellen said, ignoring Bri and guiding Persad slightly away from where Bri was working as she spoke. "All right. If the box gets done, it gets done. Do your best. I know you can't change the laws of physics."

"Not yet, anyway."

"Come again?"

"Oh, nothing. Just silly scientist musings. I'm getting spoiled by having such talented colleagues around me that I can regularly make science jokes without even thinking about it."

"I'll choose to take that as a compliment." Bri smirked, not taking her eyes from her target panel.

Ellen permitted herself a crooked smile and guided Persad farther out of Bri's earshot. "Just one other thing, Doctor."

Persad's brow furrowed. "Yes?"

"Can you check on the function of Kael's blocking chip for me? He seems a little different. Some nightmares that had gone away have returned. Just want to make sure there's no… interference."

"Interference? From whom?"

"I don't think anyone onboard has a desire to manipulate his thoughts," she replied, her voice low. "But I've been wrong before. Once or twice. And there are a few who could." Kentt could. And she had the least loyalty to the team. Isa… Isa had always found an odd sort of friend in Kael. Maybe it was tempting to try to protect him, in an indirect way. And the empress, well… She had the abilities, and her motives were still murky at best.

"Ah. I see. We have his upgrade scheduled for tomorrow. I can certainly double check the current chip functionality, and also do another check after we've finished the upgrade. Would you like me to get started immediately or when our work here is done?"

"At your earliest convenience, Doctor."

"I'll have it by the end of the day."

"Great. I won't hold you up any longer. Thank you for the hard work."

"Not at all, Commander. I'm enjoying myself greatly." Dr. Persad turned back to her work.

CHAPTER SIX

ADAN PUSHED up his flight glasses and hit the engage key. Xi took the ship through the gate, and the sprinkle of gold speckles that marked the wormhole passage danced across his vision as he leaned back, kicked up his feet on the dash, and took another sip of coffee. Yeah, he was relaxed. He was fine.

Nothing bothering him at all. Not one thing.

At least for one of his eyes, flight glasses were no longer necessary. They'd mostly always been for fun, anyway. Fun and a minor reduction of eye strain. He could admit that now. But his new cybernetic eye freaked more than a few people out, even on a ship like this. Maybe they were just still getting used to it, knowing him without one for much longer than he'd had the thing. But the incessant stares meant the glasses had a new role in that he could hide away his new superpowers when the occasion called for it.

Jenny never minded, though. His heart quaked a little at the thought of what the day promised. The danger. She was on the team today. He took another sip of coffee. It probably wasn't helping the heart palpitations.

Nor was the news, which continued to broadcast scenes of the ecological disasters on Tarkos and now Utara V. Utara made him especially nervous. Being mostly watery like Aeori III, the scenes were mostly aerial shots down into an ocean dotted with the silvered bodies of hundreds of dead fish. Or more.

He switched it off. Nothing he could do to help Utara or Tarkos. The best scientific minds didn't even know why these planets were dying. Earth had taken centuries of abuse, and it had still turned around when enough people got on Mover ships and shipped out. But these planets were floundering—for lack of a better term—in barely a few days. People were talking of the need for a new migration, repairing the old Mover ships and venturing forth again.

Those planets shouldn't really concern him, but they did stir a sense of unease he couldn't explain. He took another sip. No, there was nothing he could control outside this ship, much as he didn't like that. Nothing he could do. Time to focus on what he *could* do, right here, right now.

As the new system came into clear focus on the viewscreen, he hit the comm. "Commander?"

"Go ahead, Adan."

"Got visuals on Aeori system."

"No hostiles detected," Xi said. "No space-faring ships."

"On planet?" Commander Ryu asked.

"A diversity of ocean species," Xi replied, "some large enough to be ship-sized, but analysis suggests they are all organic lifeforms. No living species is recognized with a known sentience score, but many appear to be unevaluated. Records include an early aquatic civilization that appears to no longer be present."

"All right. Let's hope there are no smarties down there, and we can get in and out. We on track for arrival then?" Ryu sounded like she was suiting up in the background. Or packing something heavy.

"Yep, all on track," Adan said, nodding only to himself. "ETA eighty-seven minutes."

"I'll get the ground team ready."

"Got it." They both cut the line.

And now... there was nothing left for him to do. Watch the skies, make sure they were clear. If they weren't, he'd be damn busy. Essential even.

But if things went according to plan, he'd be sitting here for the next three hours. Maybe more. Watching. Waiting. Maybe listening in. He didn't bite his nails, but maybe he should start.

He'd always liked listening in on calls, deactivating locks when needed—although Doug had been gleefully taking over most of those now that he was on ship, and Adan couldn't blame him—and living a bit vicariously through them all.

But Capital had changed things. Had shown him how dangerous it all could be. He'd survived dirty ships full of shady folks and the Bantilla civil war back home, so he was no stranger to violence. But those had been eruptions of chaos—disorganized, frantic, and far away. Another life. Life on the *Audacity* was supposed to be different from all that.

Ryu's confidence had always made the ground teams seem bulletproof. Invincible. Like they were running a drill or simulation, not facing real, live bullets.

His mission on Capital had shown him that was hardly true. They were just talented—and well-armed and well-armored. Well-funded, too. Faros hadn't been much better. The bullets and lasers were all very real.

And the other thing that had changed on Capital was Jenny. Or, more accurately, his view of her.

He'd listened before like he was listening to a video drama. A show where the heroes were his friends, off on some grand adventure. They always came back. They always found their way.

But listening to Jenny on mission… now that was something else entirely.

It had turned his vigilance both more critical and more boring. And his vicarious enjoyment of their adventures, well… Every crack, every explosion—it all left him wondering.

Was this the time their number came up? He'd stopped short of asking to tune in to her armor cam, but he was still considering it. If he did, it might cut the number of heart attacks he had in half.

Or maybe it would be that much more terrifying. He was still debating the idea when the alarm sounded and Xi lit up his screens.

Xi's voice was ever calm, even in this announcement. "Union ship has emerged from the wormhole gate on the other side of this system. Estimated time of arrival, two hours, seven minutes."

Well, well. He straightened in his seat and started digging into the controls. Maybe he'd have something to keep him busy, after all.

————

JENNY STOPPED and raised her eyebrows as she and Kael leaned out over the edge of the cargo-bay door. Below them, waves of eerily greenish water splashed and lapped, whipped by a vicious wind. "Lovely place. Almost as welcoming as Capital." She grinned through the clear visor at him.

"Almost." He smiled crookedly back. "This should be fun."

It was easy to be flippant when you were nervous as hell. "At least it's not another desert planet?"

"That's Jenny, always looking on the bright side." He stepped to the side as a heavier than usual drone buzzed up and floated out between them. Black and with no visible outer sensors, it looked more solid, shaped like a giant oblong sandwich, more than the usual helicopter or insectoid-type shapes.

"There's our life preserver," said Commander Ryu, striding up to meet them. "Ready to go for a dive?"

"That?" Jenny bit her lip, turning to look at the thing as it zipped down, plunging deep into the water. A few seconds later, it zoomed back up with a dramatic gush, stopping to hover above the water's surface.

"Yep. Ideally, it will take us down and back up again. Of course, in our suits, Xi can direct us, too, but…"

Kael was frowning dubiously as Jenny turned back to look at them. "Are we *sure* there's something worthwhile down there?"

"Well, we can't be sure," the commander admitted. "But someone sure went to a lot of trouble to build this damn lab compound under that much water. Doesn't it make you wonder why they would go to so much trouble?"

"Theroki don't wonder, they just do what they're told." Kael shifted the rifle on his shoulder.

Jenny almost jumped out of the cargo hold when Ryu let out a hearty laugh. How many times had *that* happened? Still, she smiled to herself at the laugh, if not at the comment in particular. Somehow, she'd captured Adan's attentions, and if the commander and the Theroki had finally gotten together?

There was hope for humanity yet. *Anything* was possible.

"Now, there's a lie if I ever heard one," Commander Ryu muttered. "All right. Ready, team? We don't have all day. Time to jump."

"I'm ready, I'm ready." Nova came jogging up. "Almost forgot my gum."

Jenny snorted. "Heaven forbid we be spared from hearing you chew for half the mission."

Nova just grinned and chewed extra loud for a few beats. Jenny glowered at her in response.

"Kael, why don't you do the honors this time? Everybody has a first time. We'll be gentle."

Leering laughter rose up from the group. Kael might have been smiling, but he still said the solemn words. "When governments fail to police science…"

"Science will police itself," Ryu finished.

She belted out her typical "Hoo-ah" and steeled herself for the jump. She might have been smiling, but that water was looking choppier and choppier.

"All right, everyone—beginning descent," Ryu said crisply. "On my count, jump and land. Tread water and when you can, grab on to that hellish creation."

"Hey!" came Doug's voice over the comm line.

"Three, two, one—go."

It might have been irrational, but Jenny sucked in her breath as she leapt into the air. Hard to break the habit when your body and your suit were careening toward a vast land-less ocean. There should have been whistling air, a desperate slapping impact with the surface, water in your ears and eyes and nose.

But instead, it was just more of the same. The sensors and cams all fed in the fall—audio, video, readouts on the display—but thank heavens the suit toned down the haptics for this one.

She didn't submerge quite as far as she'd worried she would, mostly because she started fighting and kicking as soon as she hit the surface. It'd been tempting to select a lighter suit model for this portion of the mission, but... then there was the dive.

"Got it," came Kael's voice first.

"Me, too," Nova chimed in. "Damn it, the Theroki beat me. No fair."

Jen broke the surface and grabbed on to the handle on the drone as she saw Ryu emerge and do the same. "Ready."

"All right, Simmons, take us down," Ryu ordered. Via Doug's command from inside the *Audacity*, the drone started to move. "Hold on tight, everyone."

The water seemed to press in on all sides. It wasn't exactly water, though. It was comprised of other liquids, too; she hadn't really paid much attention to that part of the briefing, aside from the fact that this water had a slightly greener shade and wasn't your friend. The source of the pollution was unclear and recent. At the depth they were going, the pressure and mass of it would be much more of a threat than the chemical makeup.

Staying in your damn suit was always the best policy, and she had no plans to do otherwise.

Nearly all the light had faded, and the surface seemed miles above them before the drone reached the ocean floor. Or—no. It was metal. Her boots offered to snap on, but she didn't want to walk around down here.

She wanted to go inside.

The accompanying drone located an entry panel and started shining lights that direction. After about two or three minutes of waiting, which wasn't agonizing at all and definitely some of the best two minutes of her life, a heavy grinding sounded. Panels in the metal surface they stood on slid apart, revealing an airlock. Well, it would be an airlock when they cycled it. Right now it was full of water.

"We're in!" Doug chirped.

"Yeah, see if you'd sound that excited if you were down here," Nova grumbled.

"Let's go," Ryu said, voice flat.

They went. Jenny stepped off the edge and let gravity carry her down into the airlock chamber, darkness further closing around her. She switched on her suit lights as Nova found the control panel to cycle the 'lock.

"Everybody let go of the drone now and find a handhold on the edges of this chamber," ordered Ryu. "Our intel says this goes straight down. We'll have to let the water drain out, then make our way to the bottom. The drone can hover, but we gotta climb down."

"Is that why you brought me?" said Jenny.

"That and your sunny disposition."

"I'm afraid the sun feels... very far away at the moment," she said softly. Heights? No problem. Heights were her thing. But she was starting to think that depths were entirely different.

"Fact," muttered Nova. "Sooner we get in here and out of here—the better."

As the grinding panels screeched and groaned over their heads, Jenny took the comms beacon from the drone as Doug had instructed—hoping to strengthen the comms signal when they descended—and smacked it to the side of the 'lock. Hopefully, the auto-adhere would work despite the contaminated water. Then she found a suitable grip on the side while the 'lock cycled.

Water drained from the 'lock chamber fairly quickly. But not quickly enough for Jenny. Nothing was that fast.

Finally, the floor slid away, and a bleak bunker appeared far below them, lit only by emergency lights. It *did* look dry at least, except for a few trickles of water from the airlock.

"Damn right, it's hard to get into this place," said Kael. "What the hell are they hiding down here?"

"Let's go find out," Ryu replied.

They started down the shaft, the drone zipping down ahead of them to check for traps. Jenny located a ladder and went first, the others stopping periodically to check and cover her descent and then follow behind. It wasn't a complicated trip down—just plodding along from one metal rung to the next, a very basic ladder fused to the metal wall. Or hull. Or whatever this was.

She reached the bottom first and turned to scan, bringing her multi to the ready sooner than was strictly necessary.

"Spooked, Utlis?" Nova called from above. "Or do you see something?"

"No immediate threats," she said, not acknowledging the accurate assessment that yes, she was spooked. "But it's damn dark down here."

"I'll get the drone to work on the power situation," Doug chimed in. "Adan says he wants something to do."

"Isn't hiding from the Union enough? How is that ship looking?"

"It is coming closer, and I'd like to help speed you all out of there, thank you very much." Adan this time.

His voice both calmed her and tensed her shoulders. The slight waver in it showing his nerves made her bite her lip. She could do this. She could do this. But damn, did he have to remind her of everything she had to lose?

A loud clunk above them made them all jump, then three or four subsequent *thunks* before a heavy clank at her feet echoed through every part of the bunker system. Wow. Great. Way to announce their arrival.

She'd already staggered back and trained her multi on their new arrival—the comms beacon that *hadn't* auto-adhered after all. She sighed. "Just the beacon."

"This is fine, anyway," Ryu said. "We can take it up when we're leaving."

"The beacon will provide some signal boost from its current location, although less than planned," Xi chimed in.

Jenny sighed, not sure she found that reassuring. Damn, she needed to get her head on straight. Deep water, dark corridors, and beacons that didn't stick right—this was the stuff of a kid's scared-of-the-dark nightmares, not what could *really* be scary down here.

Two corridors led away from where they had come down, at right angles to each other, and she scanned them while she waited for the others. All reaching the bottom, they swept the first corridor fairly quickly—cabinets, crates, storage, two forklifts, all seemingly related to the comings and goings from this airlock.

"Well, that was a let-down. If there's anything useful down here, it's gotta be this other corridor, I guess," said Kael, as they started down.

"Hey, if it's all cabinets and crates, that's all right with me," Jenny said, laughing a little. The laugh came out sounding way too nervous. Damn it, this wasn't who she was. But she just didn't have a good feeling about this place. "You know, crates won't shoot you."

She hung back, letting the others take the lead. The second corridor was longer than the first, nothing but maintenance panels on the sides for a while, until they finally reached a large open area with doors all along the perimeter. Some even had window panels that suggested meeting rooms and labs.

"Ah! Got it," Adan said over the comm line. "Lights should be—"

The place flooded with power before he could finish. The light flashed so bright she gasped.

"Everything okay?" he said, a little too quickly.

"Yeah, we're just... making use of our visor light-modulation features..." Ryu muttered, although there was a wince in her voice, too.

Jenny shook it off. "Look—that room over there. Those racks look like computer storage—isn't that what we're looking for?"

Ryu nodded once sharply. "Yes. Let's check that one—but first, we need to quickly investigate in this one." Her voice was grim as she pointed into a room.

Kael slowed to a stop beside Ryu as the others caught up with them. The room they were focused on was still dark, but with the bright light filtering through the door's glass window, they could make out a cavernous space. "I... What is that? Some kind of debris on the ground in there."

"Not sure," said Ryu.

"Let's get a move on," said Zhia. "I'm not getting any younger."

"I nominate Zhia to go first," Jenny said, smiling. "She's lived a long life."

Zhia snorted. "Hey. I am not the one who's retired."

"I've got the heaviest armor model equipped right now," Kael pointed out.

"I'll happily go first." Ryu reached toward the palm pad beside the door.

"No, you won't," the four of them said in near unison.

She snorted. "I'll damn well go first, if that's the order, and you'll all learn to like it."

"Yes, ma'am," came the quick response.

"But I can't get in with that palm pad, anyway. Doug, can you get all these unlocked?"

"Workin' on it," Doug replied. "That should be good right about... now."

"Excellent." She hit the palm pad. "Since you're all so enthusiastic—Kael will start, take a quick recon. No need for all of us if it's just more cabinets and crates. Can we get light from the drone? Somehow this isn't on the main circuit."

"Let me do a quick search, too," said Doug's voice as the heavy drone motored forward, tapped the palm pad with its nose, and scooted through the sliding hatch before it could even finish opening. "Looks like an easy drop—two meters," Doug said as the drone drifted inside. "Ladder's missing. Or... torn away."

Ryu signaled for them to enter. Kael stepped up first and dropped, landing with a thud.

"Ugh. There's slime everywhere down here," he said as he

moved forward, the spotlight from the drone showing some kind of algae buildup on the floor.

Jenny sidled next to Zhia so they all had a clear view of the room. "Nobody's been here in a long time, I don't think," she murmured.

A crunching sound made her wince. Kael had moved a few meters ahead into the area, but he'd stopped short. Beneath the spotlight of his black armor, on the slick algae floor was something white.

"What was that sound?" she asked.

"Bones." Kael swallowed, voice rough. "They're bones."

"Human bones? How many?" Ryu asked. "Can you tell how many sets?"

"Look human to these scans." Doug's tone was analytical; she had to wonder if he'd sound that way if he was ankle-deep in them. She doubted the experience of seeing this via cam feeds was quite the same.

"Can't tell how many sets. There are a lot." Kael's voice was breathless. "They are… scattered."

Each step set off the teeth-grating crunching. Jenny fought to keep herself from a permanent dark grimace and failed. "I think I'm going to puke."

"Only if you want to swim in it," Zhia barked. "You can handle it, love."

"Handle swimming in it? Hope so, because I don't think it's super under my control right now." She swallowed back the bile.

"This is… an atrocity," Doug muttered. "Do you think they died the same way the others have?"

"This isn't the first time we've seen this," said Ryu, her voice cold. "If she abandoned them once to starve to death, she'd do it again. We know what she's capable of. Doug, can we get a scan from the drone for any valuable tech or… well, anything that's not bones? We don't need you and Kael searching through this entire horror show."

"I'm detecting nothing on the infrared or thermal," said Kael. "No unusual rad ratings."

"Getting a sonar map," said Doug. "Looks like there's nothing here aside from human skeletal remains."

They were all silent for a moment while the two of them worked.

After a while, Ryu spoke. "This is why we fight, my friends. This is why we're here. This is Upsilon Station all over again, times a thousand. And why we're going to go a lot farther than this if we have to, to stop Arakovic and anyone who's helping her."

"When we find Arakovic and bring her to justice," Doug added, "then we can come back here and try to give them a proper resting place. Burial or something. Maybe even identify them."

Jenny nodded solemnly. She hadn't thought she needed a reminder of their mission goal, but hearing it still seemed to buoy her a little. Or at least her it buoyed stomach.

"A hell of a way to die," Nova ground out, her voice gravelly. "If that's how they went, starving in this hell hole is not my idea of a party."

"A hell of a way to live, too, whether it's as one of her experiments or one of her discards," Kael said. "Somebody needs to pay for this. Some Songbirds might have been volunteers. But maybe not."

"Doubt anybody volunteered for *this*." Ryu was shaking her head. "And more likely, these are the discarded men from Faros and other 'farm' planets mentioned in the files."

"I'll get a nuke in, see if we can download any record to verify what happened here for sure," said Doug. He'd already fitted an arm of the probe into a port in the wall. "Beginning penetration sequence."

Zhia shook her head. "You used to need me to install your nukes. Now all I am is a fancy rifle stand."

"Aw, that's not true," said Doug.

"You're a fancy rifle stand who keeps scrawling on my walls," Ryu said.

"And you love me for it."

"No signs of other valuables in the sonar map," Doug said.

Kael started to make his way back to the door, faster now, but the squishing and crunching of the steps was even worse when it came twice as fast. Jen swallowed, trying to keep the bile in her throat down.

"I think we've seen enough here," Ryu said as he joined them. "No signs of life in probably longer than we've all been friends. Let's get to the next room."

Jenny followed Nova toward the server-racks room at a brisk jog. She tapped the palm pad with her gauntleted knuckles, just to see, but to her surprise, the hatch slid open. "Huh. Guess cracking one lock is cracking all locks around here?"

"Either that or there's nothing worth locking up in there," Nova replied. "Let's find out, shall we? This could be a different network in here. I'll install some fresh nukes!" She cheerfully marched over to the nearest machine's keyboard interface.

Zhia and Ryu had caught up, so Jenny fell in to watch the door while they started to investigate the racks and rows of computers. Outside in the large main space, Kael was kicking gunk off his boots.

She was just swiveling back when a large wall display inside the room flickered on. She froze—everyone did, except Nova.

A woman's face and shoulders appeared on the display. Her hair was auburn, her satin dress wrapping artfully around a thin, bony form. Were those pearl earrings she wore or the fancy network interface links you could disguise as jewelry? Or perhaps both. For a long moment, the woman said nothing.

Over the comm, but not on her suit's external speakers, Ryu whispered something.

Jenny couldn't quite catch it. "What was that, Commander?"

"Arakovic," she said louder now, her voice uneven, rough. "Silver your visors."

Jenny complied. Ice flowed in her veins, even into her bones. This… this was not good.

"Welcome, Ms. Ryu. A pleasure to see you again."

No one moved, except Nova's hands on the keys.

"I'm so glad you brought your four friends to visit me. But I'm afraid you're in the wrong location. Did you really think you'd find me there?"

They all remained completely still. Jenny listened for movement further into the compound, but the silence was painfully loud in her ears, like the dim echo of a gong ringing.

"Aw, you don't want to chat? It was such fun last time on Faros. I don't even mind that you killed one of my many telepaths. I *told* her not to underestimate you. I can't hold that against you. Cassandra at times can get… carried away."

Ryu took one step closer to the screen, her multi at the ready as usual, but it looked like more than just a ready stance. Was she thinking of firing on the display?

Jenny glanced over her shoulder. "She's broadcasting in the hall out there, too. And across the way."

"Did you think I wouldn't know you'd try this? You kidnapped several of my soldiers and one telepath. With *your* near-sighted sense of morality, you probably even let them hang around after you extracted your information from them."

As Arakovic spoke, Ryu stepped toward the hatch and looked out. "The feed is coming through in all the other labs. Maybe everywhere. Does she know what room we're in? Is this even live?"

"And what else could my children have told you? They led you here." Arakovic clucked her tongue. "Nice try, but wrong. Wrong, again. You're not as perfect as you like to think, Ellen Ryu."

Ryu did a one-eighty and squared herself to face the wall display. What was she thinking? Jenny bit her lip.

"We can't wait for the nukes," she barked, still only on the comm. "Jenny, Zhia, Kael—rip out the hard storage. Bring it with us. She might have wiped everything, but she's also trying to distract us. Grab what you can. Then we need to get out of here—now."

Jenny swung her multi on its strap over her back and started to work.

"Adan," Ryu continued. "What's the sit rep on that Union ship?"

"It will enter orbit soon, Commander. Then it will have an easy time scanning for us through the atmosphere, if it looks on the right side of the planet. Not like there's anything to hide behind."

"What about the water?" Ryu grunted. "Can you dive?"

Jenny could feel Adan swallow in the short silence. "I guess the water would slow down their scans a bit. Maybe."

"Hey, you wanted something to do."

"Submerging, Commander."

In between it all, Arakovic's voice droned on. "What is taking you so long to get this right? So quiet. So stoic. You were the perfect candidate. None of that toxic emotion that destroys so much good decision making. I suppose I shouldn't be surprised you won't answer me. You *do* want your four friends to live, though, don't you?"

Her rack was mostly emptied, with just one blade-like server left for her to unbolt. As she twisted, she scanned for a case to put it in—there. If they wanted this data to survive the trip *she'd* made down here, they were going to need a case. Hopefully, it was a water-tight one. She grabbed it from a stack and threw the latches open. "Server cases over here—no indication that they're waterproof but better than nothing."

"I'll ask again. What is taking you so long to find me? It's rather pathetic, really. I hope you appreciate that I could have burst you and your team into shattered atoms by now."

"Empty threats," Ryu muttered. "We didn't just waltz in here without scans."

"No scan is perfect," Zhia said. She got her own drive into a case and smacked the latches shut. "Got one. Should I—"

"We need to meet," Arakovic broke in, voice brash. Was the volume actually getting louder? "We need to talk. I haven't killed you and your friends, because I don't want your death. I want your service. I haven't given up on you. I've... revised my opinion."

"Ryu ignored it. "Put it at the hatch and get that next one."

"Roger." Jenny dashed to set down the case and head for another.

"Look at the little ants scurry at your whim. You would have made a great queen. It's not too late to admit you were wrong, you know."

"Same to you, asshole," Ryu grumbled, ripping a bolt out of the wall with more brute force than usual.

Arakovic laughed quietly. "What's the matter? Not used to being bested? Not used to making mistakes? Come here, and we can correct them."

"Got three packed and ready," said Kael.

"Get 'em up there," Ryu ordered. "Both of you, take what you got and go. Nova, Zhia, and I will follow. Doug, get your drone to the 'lock."

"Not leaving you," Jenny and Kael said in unison.

"Damn it—"

Arakovic's voice cut her off. "I know how to fix this broken, wretched mess of a universe. And I'm also brave enough to actually do it. You can still help me. End the endless wars…"

Ryu swore, and her suit's motors whined as she ripped out the last bolt on the drive she'd been working on. "There. There we go."

Jenny hurried to open another case and received the drive like a nurse catching a baby. "Last one?"

"Yeah."

Arakovic had paused, watching them scurry. Damn, was it *really* a live feed? The woman took a sip of tea from a sleek, mint-colored cup. What the— No, not the time to analyze.

"Nukes loaded," said Nova, hefting one of the drives. "If they get through, they get through."

"*Now* we can go," Kael barked.

"Wait—don't go," Arakovic started. "This is what you call a raid? My Theroki could teach you a thing or two, you know. Very disappointing performance."

They raced out of the blazingly bright lobby and into the corridor. Fast, though their burdens kept her from a true top speed.

"Hopefully, the nukes can use our comm beacon to keep a connection to the outside long enough to get all the data we need,"

Ryu said, panting. "We'll have to leave the beacon behind. Get the most data that way. Give us more time."

"Do you think your mother would be disappointed in this shabby farce of a mission, too?" Arakovic said.

Ryu stumbled but kept moving.

Jenny frowned to herself. How did this weird lady know so much about the commander?

"All her hopes for you," Arakovic continued. "And here you are. A thief stealing corporate secrets from a backwater ocean planet."

They reached the bottom of the shaft. Another wall display glowered down on them from inside the long tube.

Oh. Lovely. There were wall displays lining the shaft all the way up. Maybe for warnings or surveillance—or just for messing with people like this?

Zhia started lugging the drives up, as many as she could hook on a shoulder and under her arm.

"An outcast. A traitor. An outlaw. Why are you taking so long to find me? C'mon."

Ryu dropped her drive as she helped Nova get hers attached to her suit. Jenny helped Kael with his as he returned the favor. Nova started up.

"No country," Arakovic continued. "No vision. No honor."

Jenny jumped at the sudden growl over the comm.

In a fit of pure rage, Ryu swung her multi around and slammed the butt into the display. Shattered glass sprayed, the image fracturing.

Kael rushed to her, grabbing her by the shoulders.

The display flickered but didn't fail. Arakovic smiled, her image now splintered into jagged slices.

"Sorry." Ryu eased herself away from them. "I'm fine. Kael, Jenny—go. Don't argue."

Her suit was full up, so Jenny started to climb. Kael's heavy footfalls clanked on the metal rungs behind her barely a moment later. Ryu couldn't be that far behind.

Arakovic's low, quiet laugh seemed to echo in the chamber,

climbing up and bouncing down into the bunker. "Honor? *That's* what bothers you about all this? Well, it's too late to fix that. You made your choice. You'll never be Union again."

Jenny wasn't sure if the low growl she heard was Kael or Ryu. Or both of them.

"This is your last chance to assimilate willingly. Might as well join us—the Union will never have you back. You can be a Songbird again, though. Just come to this location and admit how wrong you were. On your knees. Yes, it's on the screen. Might want to take notes."

Jenny froze and turned. Coordinates flashed across the screen and Arakovic's shoulders. "What the—"

"Got that, Xi?" Ryu said.

"Affirmative, coordinates acquired," Xi replied.

"What fragging craziness is this?" Kael said.

"Bring your friends," said Arakovic smoothly. "I'm sick of waiting."

Something slick and wet caught her boot, her foot slipping. Luckily, she knew enough and had years of practice in always maintaining three points of contact, so she kept moving almost seamlessly. Damn, she'd be glad to get out of this algae-infested place. "Watch out, slick up here."

"The completion of my conquest of the Union approaches," Arakovic announced.

"Why tell us that?" Ryu grumbled. "It makes no sense."

"Maybe it's a lie," Kael said.

"I will begin my conquest of the Puritan Alliance in ten days' time." Arakovic's sickening smile slid past Jenny's view as she passed one wall display and approached another, the last one before the top.

"You have until then to make amends. As I said, if I wanted to kill you, I'd have done it by now."

"She can say that all she likes," Jenny said, "but we are *far* from out of this place alive."

"Why is she doing this?" Ryu demanded, to no one in particular.

"What's one augmented telepath compared to the dozens she already has? Does she want the battlefield advantage? I don't think she thinks that way. And I might *never* have found her. Why is she doing this? Something isn't right here."

"And I thought she seemed so trustworthy," said Zhia. "My drives are loaded on the drone."

"Maybe you're just the one that got away," Kael offered.

"It's a trap," said Adan. "Got to be—"

An abrupt cry cut through their speculation.

"Elle?" Kael started, his voice echoing down the shaft.

But they all knew it wasn't Ryu's voice. The shaft went dark a moment later, the wall display that had been glaring at her flickering, cutting to static, and going black. What the hell could that mean—

Jenny climbed faster. She was almost there.

"I'm okay," Ryu said quickly. "Just climb."

Silence descended upon them beyond the clangs of boots and gauntlets on metal rungs.

Moments later, the wall display flared back to life. The room's sterile background was the same as before, but the woman—Arakovic—was gone.

A different woman slid down into Arakovic's seat. She was maybe Jenny's age, maybe younger, with beautiful blonde curls and dark eyes that seemed like they'd be sweet, at least until they locked on to you and their deep black froze every corner of your soul.

"What the frag is that—" said Kael.

"Don't ask," barked Ryu. "Move, Jen."

She hadn't realized she'd gone still, so she got her ass in gear. "But you know who it is."

"Yes." Ryu's voice was strained. "That's Cassandra."

A dozen more rungs, and Jenny was up over the edge. Tossing her first drive over to Nova, she squinted at the display—damn, there was even one here inside the 'lock. This Cassandra had said nothing yet, but she *was* glaring off to the side.

"Does she have eyes on us?" Jenny asked, scrambling out of the way to help Kael up. He was only a few rungs behind her.

"Doug, Adan—is she in the networks?" Ryu called. "Can you cut her out?"

"I can't tell—I'm trying to—" Doug was scrambling.

Jenny turned her back on the wall display and set to fixing the drives to the drone with Nova and Zhia. "What do you need me to do?"

"Take one of these zips and..." Zhia trailed off, instead simply showing her how she slid one side through the drive's handle and then through the fastener. Jenny grabbed the next one.

"Hey, there's something else down here," Ryu's voice came over the comm. "Is that a—"

A brief alarm blared once, twice.

"Frag, it's closing!" Kael shouted. The two panels of the floor airlock had begun sliding shut, starting to close off the shaft. Kael scrambled toward it, grabbing on to one side.

"Why the frag is it—" Nova fumbled a drive, which crashed to the floor.

"Wait, frag—wait!" Jenny zipped her tie shut as quickly as she could and darted to the edge. Ryu was only a few rungs down, moving fast. "Kael—she's almost here—hold it!"

Jenny squatted, gripped the other panel, and pulled. Her suit servos screeched with effort, but the sliding floor panel didn't even slow down. The rubber edge twisted and shifted, making her lose her grip briefly. She grabbed on again, but it wasn't helping. Zhia dropped in beside her and pulled, too, with little to show for it.

Kael was growling from the exertion, but his effort had slowed the panel on his side. Some, anyway. The airlock mechanics—and maybe Kael's mechanics, too—were whining at the interference.

Since Jenny's suit was clearly underpowered to fully stop the panel from moving—she never favored the heavy models, especially when there was climbing involved—she reached down a hand to help Ryu up.

"Here—take this." Ryu hurled one drive over her shoulder,

colliding with the airlock edge.

Jenny wanted to throw the damn drives into the ocean instead, but she obeyed, grabbing it and tossing it to Nova, who was desperately trying to seal the others and zip them to the drone.

Over Nova's shoulder, the large warning light for the external airlock blinked red, then yellow. "It's flashing!" Jenny shouted. "Frag, it's going to open on our heads, even if this isn't closed? What kind of shoddy—"

"Hurry, Elle," Kael said through clenched teeth, still holding his panel back.

Was this Cassandra's doing? Jenny didn't care if that whole place was flooded and destroyed, but the force of the water rushing inside would take them with it, pull them in, pull them under, slam them against who knew what. Who knew how long it would take for that place to fill up so they could try to swim their way out again?

Could be too long. That sounded like a sure way to die cold and alone—and under the fucking water.

The doors were barely shoulder-width apart now, and Jenny's panel was on its normal trajectory since she hadn't slowed it a damn bit. Determined, she reached down and linked forearms with Ryu, yanking her up. A little too hard, though, in her enthusiasm. Ryu came all the way up in one quick heave.

Jenny's balance went wide, though, her back knocking into Kael.

"Wait—no—I lost my—" Kael caught his breath.

She didn't hear the rest of whatever he said. One foot skidded out from under her, still slick from the algae, and the other caught the edge of one floor panel, sending her into a spin.

She fell forward, her chest landing hard against the other side of the still-open airlock. Her legs scrambled for traction but only found air.

She groped to catch the edge of the sliding floor panel with gauntleted fingers—and missed, the damned rubber twisting and stretching again, defying her grip.

She fell into the shaft, the panels to the airlock finally sliding closed above her.

CHAPTER SEVEN

ELLEN STARED at the closed slab of metal. Jesus Christ, Jenny was down there. Alone. Water was already rushing in, filling the space with a dizzying white noise.

"Open it back up!" Nova recovered faster, lunging at the floor panels.

Kael caught her by the shoulder. "We can't, the water's already coming in!"

"Let go of me, dammit." She blocked him, knocking his forearm out of the way. "We got to—we got to help her—"

"We'll just flood the place," Zhia said. "Which won't help her."

The bottom of the chamber had already filled with a few centimeters of water.

"He's right." Ellen scrambled to her feet and grabbed Nova's other shoulder. "It'll push her further in."

Nova growled and twisted, ripping her shoulder from Ellen's grip. Then she stilled for a moment and swore.

"C'mon," Ellen said, keeping a rock-hard calm in her voice that she didn't feel. "We'll get her out. But we gotta do it the right way."

Nova didn't move for a long moment. But then she grudgingly nodded and stood.

"First, let's finish strapping these onto the drone. Then, we wait, let it cycle the 'lock. When it's drained again, we'll just open it back up and go after her. There was nothing down there, so she's perfectly safe. Maybe a little bruised. This is nothing but a small delay."

"It will be all right, *veija*," Zhia murmured to her. "We'll get her."

"Uhh, Commander?" Adan's voice wavered as he came over the comm. "I hate to tell you this but—we don't have time for a delay because—"

Suddenly the wall display flickered back on, silencing all of them. "I hope you enjoyed the ride, Ms. Ryu."

"Cassandra," Ellen growled.

"Because it's over. We've re-enabled the security system our darling Mother was so kind to disable for you. And now, we're going to sit back and watch the fun." And then, in spite of that claim, the wall display went dark.

"Are you still underwater, Adan?" Ellen demanded.

"The *Audacity* is wet as a fish, Commander."

"Any signs the ship has detected you?"

"No, but it has now entered the atmosphere. They're determined."

"Frag." Ellen kicked futilely at the rising water. Think, dammit. Jenny was stuck down there. Was there a faster way out of this?

Who or what in the hell could be down there with her? She'd assumed those people had starved to death, abandoned, like the ones on Upsilon. But what if they hadn't?

"Adan, Doug—is she telling the truth? What's the status on the bunker's security systems? We need eyes on what, if anything, Jenny is facing and how she's holding up."

"I'm on it," said Doug. "There *was* a change. Someone else is definitely in the system."

"What is the likelihood of that ship detecting you while underwater?" Ellen asked.

"If they scan right where we are?" Adan asked. "Very good. They have no reason I know to scan for us underwater, either, but nor do they have a reason to enter atmo, and they've done it. They still have to scan the whole planet. So it depends on how close to us they start."

"We can't rely on *luck*. We need something else."

Xi piped up. "I have identified nearby marine geography that will allow for a decreased likelihood of identification at mid-range. It would add time to your pickup from this location, however."

Ellen swore. The water was already up to their thighs and rising.

"The 'lock still needs to fully cycle. There's time for the ship to hide, then we gotta get Jen," Kael put in. "We need a bit of time."

"Yes," Adan agreed. "But nobody's hiding while in transit to Xi's spot. A sitting target might look more like a rock, at least."

"How long should it take the airlock to cycle?" Ellen asked.

"It is nearly forty percent complete," said Xi.

"We have no way of knowing how long it will take us to extract Jenny," said Kael.

"Any status on the security inside, Doug?"

There was a pause. "I—uh—not—hmm. I—"

"Doug, I need an answer."

"I can't get in. Yet."

She shook her head. "Adan—take the ship to Xi's spot and hunker down. Doug, do your best. The rest of us will sit here and hope this damn thing cycles as fast as it can. We'll let you know when we're ready for pickup."

"Roger. Good luck, Commander," said Adan.

We'll need it, she thought. But she didn't say that. "Time to play hide and seek."

———

JENNY'S back landed hard on the metal grating, knocking the air from her lungs. There was a voice somewhere. Somebody talking. One she didn't recognize.

"I hope you enjoyed the ride, Ms. Ryu."

She shook her head and blinked, trying to think. And see straight.

Diagnostics were streaming past the helmet display, but she couldn't focus on what they said.

"Because it's over now." That voice again.

Her eyes finally focused. It was the blonde woman. Was that the first thing she'd said, or had she missed something?

Something clanked in the distance, maybe down one of the corridors. Wait, had Ryu said that she'd heard something down there? That jolted enough adrenaline into her to get her to roll onto her stomach.

In the distance, down the long corridor, the lights Adan had switched on had gone dim now. The large open area had faded to darkness, no longer visible. Only the emergency lighting remained, same as when they'd arrived. She tried to make out the two corridors they'd explored earlier. The shorter one being just storage and offices, and then the longer one they'd gone down and found… Ugh. She didn't want to think about it.

Metal struck metal. Pneumatics. A dull mechanical hum.

She ticked on the thermal display—nothing new. Which shouldn't have been surprising, but she wasn't thinking straight. If there was anything down here, it wasn't biological.

The ventilation hum roared louder. Or was that the water pouring into the airlock chamber above her?

A 'lock that was well and thoroughly sealed off.

"Xi?" she whispered. "Ryu? Adan?"

There was no answer. Right. The comm beacon had fallen down in. With her. If it was boosting her signal, it wasn't boosting it far enough. Certainly no one was answering. Maybe the airlock seal was blocking it.

"I've turned on the security system Mother was so kind to disable for you. And now we're going to sit back and watch the fun."

Breathing was still painful from the fall, but she forced air in, then out. Slow and easy. She needed to figure out what was happening. How to survive until help came or however long was necessary. Flipping through every display setting, she only found a hint or two on the night-vision setting, nothing else was helping.

A trace of movement down one of the corridors. Slow movement, but in her direction.

Time for the dynacamo that would allow her to blend in with her surroundings. She tensed, getting ready to move. To engage, or hunt for an advantage down one of these corridors? Raking her memory, she couldn't think of any advantageous spot, nor did a night-vision smudge tell her much about her adversary.

What she'd thought was a maintenance panel not twenty meters down the longer corridor started to grind open. A warning alarm blared. A mechanical arm slid delicately out, followed the rest of the robot's body, a squat, sturdy thing that looked a bit like a turret on track treads. A sickly greenish-yellow eye—or at least it seemed like an eye, maybe it was a light or a camera—stared out of its body like a digital cyclops.

The eye seemed to lock on. To her.

Well, enough lying around then.

In one motion, she pushed up and leapt to her feet. Even as she did, the bot's weapons systems whined, starting to power up. Frag. Metallic clicking exploded down the corridor—so she ran the other way. Toward the short one.

She needed a fragging plan. Instinct was going to have to be enough at this point.

Her boots pounded across the metal grating, not totally silent despite the sound dampening at that speed. She was going too fast, too recklessly for that.

She turned abruptly, almost skidding, and dashed into the first door she came to. Crates stacked outside the door blocked the view of the entrance from back in the bunker area.

She slammed the palm pad. That door better close quick.

The cabinets on the far wall—those had been unlocked, hadn't they? That could work. Could be a place to hide, even if not a great one. She sprinted toward them and nearly cheered when the handle yielded and the cabinet opened.

Hauling herself inside, she swung the cabinet door shut as silently as she could manage. She held her breath.

Not that anyone could hear it, with the suit and all. In fact, she forced another even, deep breath. Steady. Ready. Coming out fighting…

Now night vision was useless, but the thermal scan picked up some slight signature moving in the hallway. Maybe the bot was heating up. The signature on the readout was tiny compared to a human, but if it indicated a power source or processor, it might make a good target.

She checked her multi. With robots, blowing them to disinte-grated bits or overcharging and burning out the circuits were your best options. But in the low light, she'd have to get mighty close to be accurate enough to be certain a stun would overcharge.

Otherwise, it might just tickle the thing.

She needed a less precise option. Checking her extra suit compartments, she found no knockout grenades. One mild incen-diary grenade, which was a fragging stupid idea in a tiny under-ground lab under the water. One flash-bang.

Could you trick a robot with a flash-bang? Would that even work on them? Did robots get disoriented?

"Xi—can a security robot be blinded by a flash-bang?" she said into the suit, before wincing. Right. Nobody could hear her.

Adan was probably freaking out right now. And that wasn't a helpful thought.

She removed the flash-bang as quietly as she could, snapping the compartment shut. Two other tiny thermal signatures approached up the hall. There were fragging *three* of them? As a unit, all three gathered outside her room.

And entered.

They couldn't actually detect her, could they? It'd been a long fall, but the suit wasn't spewing any repeating fatal errors, like a heat or air or pressure leak. Except that its comms couldn't reach the ship. They could have thermal imaging, but the suit should conceal her. Maybe the electromagnetic…

She bit her lip as the door slid softly open.

Think like a robot, that's what she needed to do. They were

grouping up. Safety in numbers. Or power in numbers. And they were starting with this room—why?

For the same reason that she'd chosen it. First one. It was logical to go systematically room by room, starting with the first.

She swore internally at that, and that she hadn't thought of it sooner. But who thinks of these things while they're barely outrunning death?

Sighing, she readied her left thumb over the flash bang, multi still steadied by her right.

Inside now, the door sliding closed behind them, one bot went along the wall to her right, the other two spreading out into the larger portion on her left. The single bot would reach her first. She could easily riddle it with ballistics when it opened the door—but the other two?

Did robots care about friendly fire? Or would they just let loose on her cabinet as soon as she showed a sign of life?

Or… There was a straight, open line between her and the door. If the flash-bang worked, she might even get a head start. And… and then what?

Maybe she could make a run for it. Find somewhere else to hide or a better ambush. Either way, it was better than getting turned into bloody shrapnel inside this cabinet.

She let the multi hang, dropping it on its strap, and took one last breath.

Then she shoved the cabinet door open even as her other hand flipped the switch… and threw.

She knew the direction of the door and raced for it—no need to adjust to the blinding flash.

Or to adjust based on the laser fire that peppered behind her footsteps, melting the metal decking.

The door barely slid open in time for her, and even so, she scraped through it sideways as it continued opening. And what now—sprint for the exit? The one that was still sealed shut?

The tall stack of crates loomed as she raced around them and then skidded to a stop.

The crates.

With one hard shove, she toppled the top crate into the doorway. Two steps back. Then she threw her shoulder into the next crate. This one was heavier and took some grunting, but with the armor's help, it slid, pinning the other crate down.

There. That might hold them a second or two.

As she raced back down the corridor, another blaring alarm sounded. More bots?

But no—there was a flash of yellow in the tunnel. The airlock. It was cycling again.

Now was her chance.

The deck beneath her shook with each sound-softened step, but she reached the ladder and clung on, taking each rung as quickly as she could.

She was a good twenty meters up—which was farther than she thought she'd get—when the first blast of a laser lanced up after her. That they'd caught up was hardly surprising, but she still jumped and almost lost her grip, as her only warning was the sudden heat flare on the side of her readout and the shaft wall beginning to melt.

How thick was that wall? The sudden heavy press of millions of liters of ocean water beyond that bit of concrete felt heavy—enormous even. Blasting through the wall of the shaft really wasn't a good idea, but apparently the robots either lacked a sense of self-preservation, or they wanted to kill her more.

No time to think about that. Drowning to death didn't need to be visceral when being pummeled by a robot was so in your face.

The next blast bit into the metal rail of the ladder just below her gauntlet, melting it halfway through. She swore. It wasn't really possible to climb any darn faster without getting reckless, but she gritted her teeth and tried to.

That was—bad. Very bad. If they wrecked the ladder, it wouldn't matter how good her armor was. She wouldn't be getting out of here alive.

She might be a great climber. A legend even. But nobody could climb a slick cement ten-meter-wide shaft with zero handholds.

If she reached the top, though… and the airlock wasn't open, what then? She was a good fifty meters up now. It wasn't open yet. It was quite possible. Damn thing had a lot of water to move.

Metal clangs shook the ladder rungs under her hands. Aw, slagging hell. One robot had begun to haul its metal ass up the ladder behind her.

The laser fire intensified, in a tighter pattern now, centering in on her suit. The dynacamo shifted for maximum reflection, sending bolts of energy wide, but it would hopefully conceal its reflective properties long enough that they'd waste some of their time. And battery.

But damn if it didn't make her crunch up her shoulders. Nothing like being fired on directly to make it hard to relax.

There was no sound coming into the suit other than the thudding against the ladder, the hissing of melting rock and metal, and the dull roar of the ocean above her. Taking a split second to scan the 'lock above, drips of water leaked through and splashed onto her visor—and some dripped all the way to the bottom—but the panels weren't open yet.

She kept climbing.

Whichever bot was firing the laser, she didn't think it was the one climbing, because it didn't seem to slow down. In fact, it was nearly on her.

"Probably shouldn't wait for it to grab on to my boot," she muttered. "Is it a bad sign to talk to yourself?" She got a good grip with one hand, swung the multi up on its strap, and leaned out. Not even two meters below her, a humanoid bot she'd never really gotten a clear glimpse of proceeded with precise efficiency. If it had eyes, she couldn't spot them—or they were trained on the ladder.

Sustained stun pulse right to the cranium-like component closest to her—three, two, one—she fired.

The thing jerked, then froze on the ladder. She frowned. Was it… dead? Decommissioned? Maybe the thing would at least shield her from some laser fire for a minute.

"Nah, can't be a bad sign, right? Everybody talks to themselves sometime." She dropped the multi on the strap again. "Just gotta keep on climbin'."

It was twenty more meters before the laser fire got close again, especially because Robot Number One finally lost its grip on the ladder—probably due to the extensive and indiscriminate laser fire now bombarding much of its frame.

Good, as far as she was concerned, it was doing its job. Except... was the ladder wobbling? What the...

A glance over her shoulder revealed a second robot making its ascent. The one with the caustic green eye. Oh, hell, now this was serious trouble. It was heavy. And it was coming twice as fast, because it had already passed its destroyed comrade.

And although it was definitely jarring the ladder with its efforts, it wasn't jarring it *that* much. The wobble she'd felt was worse. Something else was in play...

Whipping her head around, she caught her breath. Above her, one of the ladder's rails had been melted clean through on one side and was twisting. The other side was still intact but barely.

Gulping, she started skipping rungs. She could barely reach; this was a good way to die by making a mistake. But neither she nor the robot was light. If they reached that spot on the ladder at close to the same time, she was dead anyway.

It caught her two rungs from the break. The brush on her boot caught her by surprise, as she'd been thoroughly engrossed in upward momentum. She jammed a boot back down, kicking at that damn eye.

That turned out to be a mistake. First, the abrupt motion made the ladder groan and tip sharply outward. Maybe this was its plan all along or maybe it was a defense mechanism, but the bot let out a spray of God-knew-what.

She cried out in the suit, even though she knew it made no difference.

The helmet display streamed warnings. Frag. CORROSION DETECTED. CORROSION DETECTED. SYSTEM INTEGRITY AT RISK. Frag frag frag. Some corrosive bullshit. Frantically, she cleared the visor. She let out a growl of rage, of frustration, and then halted.

The ladder wasn't swinging wide. It wasn't wobbling. It was *falling*. Slowly, and backward.

Instincts taking over, she heaved herself up the last two rungs toward the break. Her stomach twisted as the ladder leaned away from vertical, but she pushed up once more with her legs, stretching out as far as she could, trying to get to the top rung and—

She leapt, shoving the ladder down as she shoved herself up.

CORROSION DETECTED. CORROSION DETECTED. SYSTEM INTEGRITY AT RISK.

Somewhere, an alarm started blaring. Time seemed to slow down to nothing as she reached. Just a little higher before she lost her momentum and—

Her body collided hard with the cement wall at the same time as her gauntleted fingers closed around the bottom-most rung. One hand missed.

But one didn't. One didn't. The alarm was still blaring.

"One's all I need!" Who the hell was she talking to?

But as she slapped her other hand on and pulled up, someone responded. Actually *responded*.

"Well, you got four here." Ryu. It was Ryu! "Brace yourself— incoming fire."

With a loud thunderous clang, the doors above her clanged fully open.

"God. I thought I was dead. I might make it out of here alive, after all!"

CORROSION DETECTED. CORROSION DETECTED. SYSTEM INTEGRITY AT RISK. Her helmet display was determined to be pessimistic.

"Well, maybe not."

"Pardon?"

"Nothing. Fry 'em, guys!" She clung to the side, time seeming to slow as ballistic fire poured in like the most beautiful rain she'd ever seen.

CHAPTER EIGHT

THE GUNFIRE WAS OVERKILL. But Kael wasn't going to tell them that. His mental telekinetic grip on Jenny was steady, and he'd already shoved the closest robot into oblivion the same way.

But opening the airlock to see Jenny nearly in its grip, and then her desperate leap away, nearly falling—well. That was enough to piss off anyone. And everyone. They'd have gotten her out either way. But firing a few rounds would definitely make his teammates feel more certain on the matter.

"What's all that shooting?" It was Adan—understandably concerned. Poor guy. Must be hell to know something was going sideways—but not be able to be there doing something about it. "Is she okay?"

"I'm okay!" Jenny yelled.

"She's in expert hands." Ellen paused her fire. "Kael—you helping her up?"

"Already on it." He nodded once. He didn't need an order to keep people alive—or suck them out of a watery grave. Fifty more meters.

"Reconnected to comm beacon," said Xi. "The panels appear

thick enough to block the signal. Communications download complete."

"Perfect—I'll dig into this," said Doug.

"One positive to this delay." Ellen straightened, glancing over at the drone, then back at the 'lock. "Keep this thing propped open."

"You think that lady on the wall display could try to close it again?" he asked. That woman had been a weird mix of Capital-type elite and hardened murderer. The outside shell had a polish to it, but her eyes... He'd known plenty of people who'd killed in their day, more than a few times, but most of them didn't exactly like it.

That one, however...

"Hmm. If Cassandra could do it once, she could do it again."

"Actually, Commander, we've shut her out of the security system to some degree." Somewhere, there was the sound of Doug's coffee mug sitting down on the holodesk. "Can't quite get her out of video systems, though. She can probably still see you."

"Maybe we can take a more... direct approach for that. Zhia, quit pulsing those bots and turn your affections to any vid cams, would you?"

"Be happy to, Commander," Zhia replied.

"We can't risk breaking the airlock, but if Cassandra's got an eye on us, we should put it out if we can." Ellen bent back down to join Nova in a stubborn grip on the floor panels of the airlock while Zhia started canvasing the sides of the chamber.

He winced at the thought of *those* eyes still on them. He glanced down at Jenny. Maybe only twenty meters left—and they'd all be out of here.

"Commander, I'd like to request no underwater missions... maybe ever again," muttered Zhia.

Ellen snorted.

"She's almost here," he said.

"I've got corrosives on my suit, Commander," came Jenny's voice over the comm. "You all might want to stay clear."

"Get ready to cycle it, Xi. Any way we can clean that stuff off while we're down here?"

"Cycle the airlock?" Xi replied. "That depends on the corrosive agent, but based on the readings from Jenny's armor, water would likely be an efficient means of removal. And it seems to be in abundant supply. Except that you will all be bathed in a higher concentration of the contaminant while the cycle is still in progress."

"Goodie."

The crash of Zhia's rifle against the chamber's metal wall only made him flinch a little. "Found one."

"Better than none." Ellen released the edge of the 'lock panel and reached down to link forearms with Jenny, helping her up in spite of the warning.

Just the sight of them both at the edge again made him tense up. The second Jenny was clear, he used his telekinetics to create a barrier beneath the panels. The idea of Elle getting locked down there had practically given him a heart attack by itself—and Jenny wasn't an acceptable trade. He was *not* going through that again. Praise the Almighty, he could not get out of this dank hellhole fast enough. As soon as they all released their grips on the floor panels, gathering around Jenny, the panels began to slide closed.

"Commander, don't—" Jenny started.

"Cycle it, Xi. I have other suits. And repair kits. And it could have been me down there. You okay?"

"Better than I was five minutes ago. Let's get the frag out of here!"

Once the floor panels had finished closing, the 'lock panels above their heads ground into motion, water roaring as it poured in. Kael got in position next to the drone. No time to waste.

"What's the damage, Jen?" Ellen was guiding her toward the drone.

"No penetration yet, but—" She stopped short. "Wait." She sighed. "Frag, I've got a seal starting to fail. The boot."

"Is that bad?" came Adan's voice.

"Yes, it's bad," Jenny shot back.

"Shut up, Adan." Ellen's voice was flat. "And get the ship back here now."

"Yes, Commander! I'm coming, baby."

Kael would have smiled at that if it weren't for the hiss of a gasp that came from Jenny at the same time. "That's where mine failed," he said instead. "Boot seal. But I wasn't going for a swim."

"Ah, frag, it's coming in. That stings."

Ellen swore. "We're gonna get through this. Hold on, Jen. Take the drone. We're almost out. The water will make it easier."

"Initiating armor medical protocols," said Xi.

"Yeah," Jenny said, weaker than her usual. "If it doesn't drown me first."

———

"GET her the frag out of there!" Ellen ordered as she hauled Jenny up beside her into the hold.

"Rescue team, coming through!" Dane's boots pounded across the deck.

Dr. Levereaux was right behind him, a lighter step, but she squatted down next to Dane in her own protective—less armored—gear. She was already disengaging pieces of Jenny's suit as Dane was hauling her further in.

The coughing and sputtering had gone quiet, though. Ellen forced herself to her hands and knees and crawled after them. Of all the ways one of her people might die on her watch, drowning in her own damn suit would not be one of them, damn it. Of course, Ellen could do her damnedest to ensure that, but until she saw ocean water spilling across the deck, there were no guarantees.

The drone whizzed past, seemingly unhindered by its many burdens. Compared to five soldiers, the hard-drive cases were probably nothing. The others were climbing in behind her.

"Contaminant-field protocols commencing," came Xi's voice over the comm. The footfalls, the voice—all of it felt hollow, like the sound came from inside a far-off tunnel. Maybe her suit was malfunctioning. Maybe she was disassociating. Maybe—

A sudden retching caught her off guard. She crawled forward faster.

Yes—oh, thank God. From its torso on up, Jenny's suit had given up the fight, lying in pieces around her now like cracked eggs shells. Filthy water was spilling everywhere. The metal decking and armor were steaming, still reacting to the corrosives and water and heat, hissing and blaring beeping alarms.

But that retching was coming from Jenny. Jenny was alive.

Alive enough to cough up absolutely horrible ocean water, anyway. Ellen grabbed Jenny's boot and started helping with the removal.

"Respiration restored," Levereaux was saying, not to anyone in particular. "Inserting re-hydration. Need a stretcher."

"I'll get it," Dremer replied. "I can float it in—I'm not suited up yet."

"Fine." Levereaux held up an injector, checked its settings, then bent toward Jenny's neck. "But get that thing on."

"Is she—" Adan started.

"Alive, yes, but not now, Adan," Ellen snapped.

"Got it. Permission to get us the hell out of here? That ship is making me nervous."

"Pedal to the metal, pilot."

Frazzled laughter was Adan's only reply. She busied herself helping Dane with Jenny's armor.

"Showers will be necessary," Xi announced as the hatch thundered closed. "Contaminant levels are exceedingly high."

"That's all right, Xi," Zhia said. "These hulks are probably overdue for a bath, anyway."

"Speak for yourself, Grama," Kael shot back.

Jen's retching and coughing had stopped. Her ragged breaths came unevenly, but at least she was taking them. Her eyes met Ellen's. Her skin was a greenish-pale, and her eyes dark, with none of their usual brightness or sparkle. But she mustered a weak smile at the corners of her mouth.

Ellen started to say something, but the suit's speaker wasn't on, and before she could switch it, the cleansing rain of decon started to fall around them. Jenny squeezed her eyes shut, but there was relief in her creased brows.

Only a few ways to get contaminants out, but the simplest of these was just washing them the frag off. Good old water. Unfortunately, Jenny was going to need all the other decontamination techniques, too.

"Frag." It was Adan. "They're hailing us, Commander. They spotted us. As soon as we surfaced."

Just what they needed. "Don't slow down. Don't answer. I'm on my way. Buy us some time."

"No, you are not," Xi cut in. "Decontamination is eighty-seven percent complete."

"Play their hailing message through the ship comm then, Adan." She dashed over to the edge of the contaminant field, right before the ladders, so she'd be ready to get to the bridge when she was cleared. "Let's hear what they're asking. Don't answer yet."

"Got it. We are close to leaving atmo. You all better get something to hold on to at least."

"Get me that stretcher!" Levereaux shouted.

"Here we go." Dane was grabbing the stretcher that floated toward them on its antigravs, bringing it down next to Jenny.

The rain had stopped, but her eyes were still closed.

An unfamiliar voice came over the main comm channel, as she'd asked. "Unidentified ship, this is Union ship *Everest*, Lieutenant Yamamoto speaking. Identify yourselves and state your purpose in this zone."

"One-trick ponies, aren't they?" She looked to Kael, who was shaking his head at the edge of the cargo hold.

He cleared the silver of his visor so she could see him, their eyes locking. "Here we go again."

"How many times have they hailed us, Adan?" She shifted side to side at the edge. God, would this damn decon hurry up?

"Two times, Commander."

"We should have at least one more chance before—"

A blast abruptly rocked the ship, apparently disagreeing with her.

Ellen staggered, nearly colliding with the contaminant field—which would have thrown her back if unsatisfied with her cleanliness. Nova, who'd been squatting to help Dane, stumbled and slid across the deck. Dane's transfer of Jenny faltered, as the ship shook but the stretcher didn't. Jenny grabbed on to him, which was a little reassuring. She had that much strength, at least.

"Well," Ellen said, "either protocols have changed, ladies and gentlemen, or our friend Yamamoto has an itchy trigger finger."

The blast had made Kael stagger against the emergency handhold he'd gotten a grip on, but he'd held on. "All the faster I need to get to guns."

"Reading my mind."

The voice started up again. "Unidentified ship, this is Union ship *Everest*—"

"Cut him off. Unidentified ship, my ass," Ellen snapped. "They know who we are. Head straight for the gate, Adan. Everyone not in decon—battle stations, now."

"Already there!" Fern replied.

"Good."

"Shields have taken a hit," said Adan.

She clenched her jaw at that but shoved the anger down. "They can slag off. Fire first, ask questions later? Get us some distance from these rat-eating snotferrets."

"They're firing already?" It was Doug's voice, incredulous. "I'm looking into those coordinates Dr. Arakovic flashed, but do we want personnel dossiers on this *Everest* instead?"

"Welcome to your first space battle, sir. Are you close on finding the coords?"

"Yes. I've got some bypass satellite imagery that's not *too* old. Trying to get into it now. Then I'll send it to Kentt and Isa for verification."

"Finish it up. Then get on the *Everest*. Dossiers sure, but security info first. Start breaking in."

"Now that's what I like to hear, Commander. On it."

"Decontamination complete," Xi announced.

She took off up the ladder, Kael right behind her. Forces beyond their grav generators pulled, making powering up the ladder twice as hard as normal. Adan was pouring on the juice and leaving atmo somewhere in there. Strictly, she shouldn't be running around unless she had to.

But she was pretty sure this qualified as "had to." Sitting on the cargo-hold deck in her wet, albeit contaminant-free, suit wasn't the greatest command-and-control position. The ship shuddered slightly as it gained speed.

A second blast rocked the ship, making her foot slip and narrowly miss colliding with Kael's helmet.

"Get us out of range *now!*" Ellen demanded. "Faster."

"*While* we go through atmo? That's gonna cost us," said Adan.

"Not as much as getting caught will," she snapped. Oh, there was math involved. The time their fuel would last at different rates, the distances they needed to cover, the comparable power of the Union ship… But sometimes, things were ones and zeros.

Either you got away. Or you got caught.

"A reduced efficiency of thirty to forty-eight percent," Xi was saying, "will decrease our evasion capability by somewhere between two and twenty hours depending on—"

"We can't evade them if we lose our shields before the gate. If they catch up, we'll play rough. I'd rather not, though, if they're this hot on the trigger." And we just took our own personal underwater beating. "Go on—punch it. Both of you."

"Yes, ma'am," Adan said, with a bit too much gusto. "Hold on to your helmets."

———

KAEL'S BOOTS, still slick from the ocean water, slipped on the grating as he made the sharp right turn toward the guns. Ellen had taken off down the hall toward the bridge, and he had to admit that some part of him hated that.

Why couldn't the gun ports be on the bridge? Not like he couldn't be twenty meters from her, but... twenty meters could matter a lot if the shields went down. Blast doors coming down could make twenty meters not so different from twenty lifetimes, if one side was in decompression.

They had their armor. And they had him. He would just have to make sure the shields didn't go down.

"Speed has doubled, still increasing," said Adan over the ship-wide comm channel. "If you're not in your bunks or harnesses, get there quick."

"They can accelerate, too, can't they?" Fern was already up in the other turret. Damn, that woman was never sleeping when she should be. "Pour on the juice as much as we can. How about some return fire, Commander?"

"Let's not give them any additional excuses." Ellen was quick to respond. "Xi, Doug—get us all the specs on those engines and their armament, too, if you can. Damn Union, updating their ships all the time. Used to know those ships like the route to the commissary."

"What *are* they thinking?" Fern replied. "Shoulda taken the Theroki route."

"I wouldn't complain right about now if they had," said Kael. He dropped into his seat at the gun ports, half a crooked grin sneaking out. Yeah, this was bad. Terrible, even. But damn if he didn't still get a little kick out of the thrill of a potential battle. Well, if they were firing already, the battle was no longer potential. It was here.

Not great timing, though. The image of Jenny coughing up sea water, her skin tinged a color he'd never seen—and he'd seen more than a few sick and malnourished kids in his day—well, that sobered him.

Time to plug in, lean back, and get to work. He twisted and unlocked the gauntlet, opened the port, and slid the wires home. The gun turret and his telekinetics would work together to deflect or destroy anything before it even reached the shields.

The press of the ship as it continued to accelerate was reassuring. Welcoming, even. Was this what people thought of when they said the word *home*? He'd never really been in danger of not making it back here, but he couldn't say the same for all of them.

What if they'd lost Jenny down there? What if this ship had reached them before they'd gotten her out? Then maybe they *would* all have been stuck down there.

Hadn't happened. Didn't matter. Luck or skill had been on their side. If it was luck, let the Almighty have a bit left for them now.

Regular fire beat on them from the Union ship—or it tried to. He wasn't letting it reach them now.

"Shields holding," Adan confirmed. "They're still coming at us, but nothing's getting through yet."

"Yet? Have a little faith, man," he muttered.

Adan snickered. "Hey, everybody has their limits. It's nothing personal. It's physics."

"Well, get us out of here, so I don't need to hit any limits." He smiled as he said it, playful, but some part of him meant it. What if they followed them through the gate? Who'd run out of juice first?

One lone former Theroki? Or that big ass Union ship?

Pulses continued. And *pulses* was the right word for it, really, as they were oddly regular. "Pulses from the enemy ship are in precise sixty-second intervals, Commander," reported Xi.

Kael deflected one into oblivion. The next was easy enough to cut off short with an errant satellite. The third, he directed closer to their ship, but not right back at them yet. A bit of a warning.

"They're trying to get under our skin," Ellen said from the bridge. He could just imagine her folding her arms, that irritated glare.

"I'm locked and ready to start firing, Commander," Fern put in.

"Duly noted."

The fourth pulse came. He'd waited long enough. He shot it back directly, but their shields had closed as soon as the beam had left the ship's shield space. He briefly opened his eyes to watch the pulse send light and sparks shimmering from the *Everest*'s shields on the view screen. Then he quickly closed his eyes again. This battle could go on for a long time. No need to waste energy.

"Commander," Doug said over the comm. "The coordinates check out. There's an asteroid with significant base development there."

"Preliminary visuals also match what we've seen in the memories we searched," Kentt added. "Satellites caught some imagery of the landing-tunnel apparatus. It seems like the real deal."

"It *seems* like a trap," Zhia cut in. "Did you all drink too much sea water?"

"Not funny," Ellen snapped.

"But why bother setting a trap at all?" asked Doug. "Why draw us in?"

"We're becoming mildly annoying?" Zhia said.

"A trap seems too simple." Even Dremer was joining in now. "And this one's too obvious. She'd know you're too smart to just walk into it."

"Maybe that's the trap," Ellen said. "A double feint."

"Maybe what she's really up to is on the opposite side of the galaxy," Kael said, "and she wants you—and us—far, far away from it." Yeah, if only. He could dream. He'd walk into and disarm any crappy trap if it kept them out of a fragging hell storm.

He sighed at the thought. No, there was no avoiding the storm, because wherever it was, that was where Ellen would be going. And he was going to follow her, damn it.

Doug cleared his throat. "There's something in this video. Something else. A reflection? Let me work on it—"

"Immediate hostiles first," Ellen barked. "Have you commandeered the *Everest* yet?"

He chuckled. "That's not possible. But I'll get you as close as I can get."

Kael deflected five more pulses as the conversation went on. He almost missed one while yawning when the fire suddenly came sooner. Damn, he'd used more energy down under the water than he'd thought.

"Enemy attack detected. Rate of fire has doubled," Xi reported. "Thirty seconds have elapsed."

He gritted his teeth. This would take… more. More work. More time. More space junk wouldn't be bad, either. He opened the cabinet beside his seat and started rummaging for ration bars. Energy boosters. Something.

"I need more space junk," he said over the comm.

"This isn't the time to redecorate, my friend," Adan said.

He snorted. "To deflect fire. Maybe the squad could help? I don't know, collectively they might have a larger range. Isa? Maybe she could talk them through it?"

Ellen hesitated for a split second—but only just. "Sure. Do it. Xi, get Isa. Get them on it."

"Tell them to get me any space garbage they can reach," said Kael. "And if they can deflect incoming attacks back at weapons systems, by all means. I play well with others."

"An unusual trait in a Theroki," Fern said, "but one I appreciate."

CHAPTER NINE

"*EVEREST*, THIS IS THE STARSHIP *AUDACITY*." Ellen's voice into the comm was pure acid. "Do you usually shoot first and ask questions later?"

"We do in this system." It was Yamamoto again.

Ellen muffled a grunt as the ship lurched in the opposite direction and her shoulders strained against the partially buckled harness. She hastily snapped the other bits in place. "*Everest*, this is a humanitarian vessel, providing peacekeeping support operations—"

"You're very far from your supposed war zone, *Audacity*. Only classified Union operations should take place in this system."

She raised an eyebrow. Classified Union operations, eh? "Funny. It sure feels like a war zone around here. Somebody forgot to mark Union on the system designator, too."

Yamamoto sighed audibly. Maybe she'd called his bluff that time —or his commanding officer's. "I don't need to debate sovereignty and legality. Your ship identifier is all the proof we need. You and your crew are wanted for several crimes against—"

"I knew you didn't think my ship was unidentified when you fired! We haven't done anything. What are you accusing us of?"

He sighed again. "A ship of your make and model has been reported for smuggling organs as well as harboring deserters."

"*Organs?*" she spat, exaggerating her surprise in order to hopefully blow past the second part.

"Illegally harvested ones, not vat-grown. Convenient for the crew of doctors you claim to have."

"That's bullshit, *Everest*. This vessel contains civilians. You're firing on *civilians*. Stand down."

"Pardon me if I don't take your word on that. If you have nothing to hide, then why did you run?"

"Because I don't want to die. And I don't want *them* to die."

"If you have nothing to hide, and you don't want them to die, come to a stop, allow us to board, and the matter will be settled."

"And why the hell would I take you at your word on that?"

The line was silent, as if she'd actually startled him.

"You had no right to attack us, and you did it anyway. It's against protocol—"

"We have a right to stop crimes from occurring in—"

"Don't lecture me about—" Another impact drowned out her response. "We're doctors and scientists, damn it. This is a research vessel! Stand down."

"I thought you were a humanitarian vessel." Yamamoto's voice was cool.

"We *are*. That's what the doctors are for. You know you've really got a lot of nerve, coming up here and picking a fight."

"Come to a stop, and we can settle this like—"

"Slag off." She muted the comm so he couldn't hear her. Maybe she should have hit it before she told him to slag off, but nobody was perfect.

She was *panting* from their damn-near shouting match. What was getting to her so badly? The recent op? Or was this Yamamoto just extra talented at getting under her skin? "We're almost to the gate—we can get there and—" she started to Adan.

Yamamoto couldn't have heard her on the muted comm, but his

voice cut her off. "I advise you to stop. Our colleagues may not be as lenient as we have been."

"Lenient?" She blinked, staring at the dash. "Colleagues? What colleagues?"

She got her answer all too quickly. Two more Union ships warped through the gate in two bright flashes of light. One of them was a destroyer, top of the line. Brand new.

Silence suffocated the air around her as the Union vessels slid closer.

They were already within range. The *Audacity* had almost made it to the gate, but now, there was a damned blockade in the way—a well-armed one at that.

Frag it all.

"*Audacity*, prepare to be boarded," Lieutenant Yamamoto said over the line. "Come to a stop, and we will cease our fire. Please."

Please? She slapped the mute button again so Yamamoto and his *Everest* could hear her again. "After you just tried to toast us? You think we're stupid?"

"On the contrary, Commander," said a very different voice. A voice that sent a sudden chill through her, the memory making her face flush with heat. She'd know that voice anywhere. "We know just who you are. And that you probably haven't been smuggling any organs, and that you do harbor at least one deserter. And we know that you're quite intelligent."

It was her turn to throw back some demand, some clever remark to make them see red. Throw them off.

But shock had a rare grip on her throat. That voice. It had once tickled her ear with his breath, sweet words that ultimately meant nothing. Saccharine poison. But she'd been too young to know the taste of that. They'd stirred her heart, once.

Froze her to ice now.

"Crew of the starship *Audacity*, this is Captain Paul Dealis—"

"*Captain*," she blurted, then swore under her breath.

"Yes, Captain. *Audacity* crew, you are being led by a wanted fugitive of the Union. We will pursue her without hesitation. Halt, give her up, and no one will be harmed."

"That didn't work last time, my friend. What makes you think it will work now?" Adan said. Ellen smacked the mute key again.

"Did he say last time?" came muffled over the comm, like the *Everest* hadn't intended her to hear it.

She sat stone still. Frozen. Adan's eyes were on her, but she couldn't meet his gaze. She needed to think. Think, damn it. There had to be a way out of this. They were waiting for her to think of something. Say something. Do her job.

"Did he say *Paul* Dealis?" Kael muttered over the line, probably not intentionally.

"Yes, I think he did." Was that Doug?

Didn't matter. Shut them out. Think of something. Think.

Find a way.

———

"YOU KNOW HER, SIR?" Lieutenant Yamamoto glanced over at Paul, one eyebrow raised, before turning his attention back to the command console.

"Of course," he mumbled. "Who doesn't?" Maybe Yamamoto would buy the brush-off. This wasn't exactly something he wanted to discuss on the bridge, even if few could hear their hushed voices as they sat not even a meter apart. He leaned back in his command chair, comfortably bathed in the beeps and hushed voices. The bridge was at full capacity, every justifiable crew member present. Every one of them was keen on the slightest twitch in the battle-space. Part of this was because they'd just come off the most boring diplomatic mission. Part of it was due to the woman they chased.

Among Union ranks, there were few who hadn't heard the stories of Ellen Ryu, of the heroism and sacrifice of the battle for SHR—or the cautionary tale that was her desertion.

Yamamoto tilted his head. "I had thought it was… perhaps more personal than that, from the tone."

He ducked his head. Yes, he'd been young and idiotic once. Who hadn't been? To be fair, he probably still was. But he couldn't say that to the man. Hanging his head wasn't the way a great leader acted, either. He lifted his chin and forced a shining smile. "Yes, I knew her personally. We… served together. Once upon a time."

"And it was no fairy tale?" Yamamoto gave him a mild, rueful smile, trying to hide his eagerness. A soldier of his rank and experience ought not to be fannish about a war hero who was half his age, and a disgraced one to boot. Yamamoto was also naturally reserved. Paul had rarely met someone so consistently in control of his own faculties. He envied it, even if he knew he'd never be that sort of man. His second didn't hide his enthusiasm well in this moment, though.

Perhaps he wanted some excuse, some insider secret, to make this pursuit easier on all of them. Well, Paul couldn't help with that. Disgraced or not, her reputation still held quite the shine among the rank and file, deservedly so. She still held quite the shine for him, too, if he was honest, although not romantically. Watching the wildcat stand up for her crew certainly didn't decrease his respect for her. And Paul didn't buy the silly organ story. That was true nonsense.

"It was fine," he said mildly. "It was… We were colleagues. Commander Ryu was enormously competent, as you might expect."

"Then how did she go from… well, you know… to this? A desperate dash toward a gate in some meaningless star system?"

"Is it meaningless?" he wondered.

Yamamoto's brow quirked. "You suspect otherwise?"

"If she's here, I doubt it's meaningless. And Colonel Tauber said it was important enough to risk redirecting us from the Freedom's Wing op."

"I also found that unusual." Yamamoto fought a sneeze and lost. He drew a disinfecting handkerchief from his pocket and blew his nose. "Not that I am complaining."

"Allergies acting up again?"

"When aren't they?"

Paul didn't need to be a genius to feel his staff's collective relief at the diversion. Dread had hung over the ship after his Freedom's Wing briefing, and he didn't disagree. The plan he'd presented—which hadn't been his by a long shot—was full of more holes than a Cesex cheesesteak. He scribbled a note on his holodesk. He needed to ask Jim if the senate had pushed for this renewed assault against the Puritans. Who in the hell thought this was a good idea? From what his brother had been saying recently, he deeply doubted it, but just because his brother was a senator didn't mean he knew everything about what the Union wanted or planned, or even a little of it.

No, it just meant promotions came a little easier. He wasn't naive to that.

The coming mission was short on details and long on risk. Every member of his crew would welcome that "ultimate victory," if officials hadn't promised it so many times before. And not delivered.

Some still hoped. Some rolled their eyes. Something was different this time, though, something strange in the operation that he couldn't put his finger on. Their last mission had spanned mostly ceremonial and goodwill visits across a few dozen neutral outsystem planets for the better part of a year. Which had been a relief to them all after a brief but violent tour near the front lines, because although the *Everest* had once been the darling of the fleet, those days were long gone.

His crew was, if anything, bored. If the *Everest* wasn't constantly falling apart, they might have been even more so. They *should* have been itching for a fight.

But if it smells like a pit dragon and sounds like a pit dragon, it's probably a pit dragon. A civilian farming system? Over seventy percent of the Union's force deployed across a small, unimportant area of the Puritan front? The people planning this must know something that he didn't, and that was more likely a bad thing than a good one.

Nobody really wanted to fly a bucket of bolts that had seen better days into a situation they had this many questions about. Or weren't being told the whole truth about.

"Any word back on that SURALA weapon they're pinning their hopes on?" he asked. How long had he paused, thinking about his doubts? Hopefully, Yamamoto hadn't noticed.

"No additional information." His second's lips pressed into a disapproving line. "I suppose it makes sense. A gamble of this magnitude, they can't afford word to leak to the Puritans of whatever they have up their sleeve."

"It better be as good as they're claiming." There was no way it was. Nothing ever was. He added a second note on his console—scheduling a reminder. He couldn't afford to forget to ping Jim about this. As soon as this situation with Ellen was resolved, he could then also share a bit of good news. Maybe that would distract Jim from noticing the warp that was gradually worsening in the metal sheet behind Paul's holodesk.

"With more than half the fleet on the line? Indeed. But the mission is set to begin in nine days, sir. Think we'll make it?"

"Depends on how long this goes on. I don't think Tauber wants us to miss it. If we capture Ryu, we might make it if we bring our prisoner along. But that hardly seems prudent or ethical."

"Indeed, whoever captures her should take her to the Inner Planets for trial."

"Agreed. I'd never think of doing otherwise if Tauber didn't seem to have such a bug up his ass about Freedom's Wing. Did you report to him yet that we'd made contact?"

"Not yet, sir."

Paul hid a small smile at that. "Good. Let's delay that for now, until we're sure of the exact outcome of this little confrontation." *And so that we can take as much time as we can possibly justify getting word back. If they missed the poorly planned clusterfuck that was about to ensue, all the better.*

"Speaking of our target," Yamamoto said. "Intelligence directed us here on a civilian tip. Her file also mentions several illegal bounties on top of ours." He frowned fully now as he began rummaging around in the pocket of his trousers. "Recently posted ones."

"I noticed that as well." He had only skimmed the file, but the sheer amount of the price on her head was hard to miss.

"Does that strike you as odd? That we are on the same side as black-market bounty hunters?" Yamamoto produced a handful of lusciously red hard candies. "Want one, sir?"

"Odd, indeed. And no, thank you."

"Suit yourself. Why did Colonel Tauber send us on this mission? Who's directing our hand?"

"I've wondered the same," he said, although he hadn't. But now that Yamamoto made it sound so utterly obvious, he was ashamed it hadn't occurred to him. He folded his hands behind his head and did his best to paraphrase, expand on the idea. "Perhaps some people just know how to make enemies. But if someone wanted to turn her in, why tip us off so that we get half the reward? Whoever knows her whereabouts could get a load of credits for her confirmed capture. From multiple sources. The black-market bounties are bigger than what the Union is offering."

"They likely don't have a fleet." His second shrugged, then narrowed his eyes at the view screen. "And perhaps they knew they'd need one."

"If she's still the woman I once knew, *we* need one. We're lucky we have the strategic advantage here. Make no mistake, it's luck. Nothing more. She'll be exquisitely hard to capture."

Yamamoto turned to meet his eyes, eyebrows raised. A crewman at the comms station tensed; he was probably listening in. Damn, that was the wrong wording. He'd revealed too much. Maybe it even sounded sadistic, which was not at all what he meant.

He could explain—that they'd been in love once, in as much as teenage soldiers knew what love was. That he'd taken a quality match for granted, like many young idiots had over the centuries and millennia—and like his ancestors, he'd lived to regret his own stupidity.

But what would that help? It would only risk Yamamoto treating him—and Ellen, for that matter— with less respect. It might make Yamamoto hesitate. Underestimate her, even.

Paul doubted they could afford that. Yes, it was better for everyone if he kept that bit in the past.

"If the bounties were recently posted," he said instead, "it does make me wonder if those posting the bounties aren't the same ones providing the intel. And making... dubious organ claims." It sounded smarter in his head than when it came out, but he rolled with it. "They clearly want the deed done, but not by them."

"The deed?" Yamamoto's lips pressed into a thin, disapproving line.

"I think they want our great war hero dead." Paul smiled tightly. "Just like our military court of justice will decree."

"You're sure?"

"Fairly." He wasn't, but confidence was a requirement in a senior officer.

"I thought you ordered her captured alive."

"I did. All criminals deserve a trial. Her fate isn't up to me to decide. Nor is it up to those informants. It's up to the tribunal."

His colleague nodded slowly. "Do you think the *Denali* will respect your orders on this?"

"I am... concerned Captain Ridgeway will take creative latitudes."

"But there are other punishments for desertion, aren't there? Life imprisonment?"

"There are. Which is exactly why a tribunal should be called. The sentence will depend on if they consider it wartime."

"Well, was it?"

"Oddly, her file isn't clear on that. By date, there was a cease-fire treaty in place at the exact time. Some courts have ruled that wartime would be dependent on the zone her unit was serving in during those few years."

"So how isn't it clear? That seems pretty cut and dry."

"The exact zone of the unit was classified." Which didn't make sense. The mission of the unit was right there. Who was on the team was listed in detail. Everything was available but the location.

Why cut only that? Unless the mission and its people were fabrications, and the real data was so classified you didn't even feel comfortable putting black bars down instead... And he had the highest level of clearance. He should be able to acquire the information, and in fact, probably should do that immediately, given how long it'd take to get through the bureaucratic approval processes. But he had a bad feeling it would be even more covered with red tape than he expected, and he expected a lot.

Yamamoto frowned harder as he sniffled again. Paul had never known anyone could be allergic to so many things on a space ship. Or maybe it was just the *Everest*. He wouldn't be surprised if there was mold behind one of those cracked corridor panels...

He decided that probably meant his suspicions about Ellen's unit location were on the right track, but he wouldn't share them yet. "I think some consider *all* zones wartime zones, these days," Paul said instead. "Until we defeat the Puritans—"

Yamamoto snorted softly. Paul agreed with that sentiment but couldn't let it show.

"—we will always be at war. Her actions caused the longest period of peace we ever experienced, though. So it will be... ironic if they execute her."

"Just ironic? I thought you said you knew her."

He sighed. Ironic? Yes. Tragic? Horrid? Another fragging injustice in a string of a life full of injustices? Absolute pit-dragon piss? Yep, all of that. But he just shook his head. "I did. But I didn't make her desert her assignment. We're all responsible for our own mistakes in the end."

Yamamoto hummed in the back of his throat. Paul had no idea if that was a subtle disagreement—or a sign he'd said something wise. That happened rarely enough that he doubted it was the latter.

He straightened and lifted his jaw, trying to look the part. "Let's give them a few minutes to stew, and we'll then try again."

———

PAUL DEALIS.

The rapid lurch forward of the ship gave Kael a moment to search the name via his link to the ship. He blinked at the display as it searched, trying to clear the sudden blurriness from his eyes.

That was exhaustion setting in, and that wasn't good. Was he delirious? Had he heard the name correctly?

"Xi—I need a restock," he mumbled. "Energy. Something."

"Would you prefer intravenous, liquid, or standard refreshment?"

He winced. One more needle shouldn't have mattered, but it did. "I'll take a beer, thanks."

"Liquid-protein energy reinforcement solution it is. Chocolate, vanilla, or zeefruit."

"Surprise me."

"I'll see that it's delivered."

He snorted. Then he glanced over his shoulder. If somebody trotted in with a milkshake, were they going to spot his current research topic? Maybe that didn't matter. He was just researching the enemy, between deflecting blasts.

But Paul Dealis was an enemy of a different sort. An enemy on multiple levels. The file that swam onto the screen in front of him confirmed his fears.

The image depicted a perfect, clean-cut soldier in his gray-and-maroons, gold glittering at the epaulets and collar. Full black hair gave his face a severity and gravitas it didn't really deserve. Handsome. He was fragging handsome, the asshole. And he'd apparently commanded the disastrous *Mirror's Light* mission from a remote command-and-control space station and thus had the good fortune to survive. Kael had assumed he'd gone down with the ship, but no.

Dealis was young, though. Not as young as Ellen, but likely younger than Kael. Fresh-faced. His eyes were a hard blue, sad and a little bitter. Like they'd made a mistake or two and survived to have to live with the guilt of it.

Like perhaps getting good people killed? If the *Mirror's Light* had haunted Ellen, Kael hoped it also haunted this asshole. Or maybe it was from abusing connections to get ahead? The captain was a ridiculous twenty-six years old, according to the file. Apparently, his strategy to get ahead had worked well, even if he'd paid a price in blood.

Kentt's voice suddenly came over the comm. "Commander, we have no signs of this yet, but some Union ships do carry telepaths. They could attempt to probe those who are unprotected, if the *Everest* carries any on her crew."

"Get to your assigned quarters," Ellen barked. "Everybody who can't get Persad's chip, get in the protected storeroom. Better safe than sorry. And strap in."

"On our way," Kentt replied.

"I'll get little Roya," Dr. Levereaux said.

Kael blew out a breath. The plan was for Shirin to head to the box Persad had built for them, too, in this situation. Should he check on her? Their plan outlined that as Xi's job, but it felt a little... sterile. Wasn't a father supposed to make sure his daughter was following orders? No, following rules. Being a good kid. Safe? Something like that. Like he'd ever been good at following rules or being safe himself.

The holodisplay to his left flashed to life, the relative positions of the starships lighting up—one, two, three. Fern was punching up a battle map for them all.

They all had their jobs. His job wasn't to look after Shirin. Not in the middle of the battle, anyway.

It was to keep her from being blasted to smithereens by knocking away missiles and grab beams. And maybe occasionally to shoot things. Funny how he'd been looking forward to that part of the job, and now that it might be on hand, it didn't sound so appealing.

"I'm waiting for a response, *Audacity* crew. Don't put them in this situation, Lieutenant Ryu," said the smooth voice. Dealis. "They shouldn't have to choose between their loyalty to you and doing the right thing—and their lives."

"I'm a commander now. And they don't have to choose between those things as my crew. The only problem here is you."

"Respect for the law is traditionally seen as doing the right thing. Sacrificing innocents, however, is not."

"How dare you lecture *me* about sacrificing innocents?" Her voice was reined in, but Kael could feel the seething rage behind it. "I bet you're wishing I had been on *Mirror's Light*, so you wouldn't have to deal with all this."

The brief silence felt loud, tense. "Please don't do this," Dealis said. Calm. Almost sad. The sad eyes of the crew portrait flashed in Kael's mind again. Frag, no. He was *not* having sympathy for that asshole. "Come in peacefully and face justice for your crimes. *Audacity* crew, the Union will reward your loyalty and morality with both credit and safe passage."

"My only crime," she said, voice hot, "was not wanting to play guinea pig."

"I don't know what you're talking about, but I'd be happy to discuss it with you aboard my ship. Please, listen to me. My sister ships may not be so lenient if—"

"Slag off, Dealis. I volunteered to defend the people and planets of the Union. Not for human sacrifice."

"We will neutralize you, Commander Ryu," Dealis shot back. Kael's eyebrow twitched. He'd adjusted to use the rank she'd asserted. Not much like Tauber, was he? In fact, if anyone was being disrespectful, it was Ellen, although he hardly blamed her. "You will face justice. In person."

"We'll see about that."

And because he knew her, he knew she'd cut off the external comm with those words. He swallowed, and something in his chest clenched. There was confidence in her voice still, but it was tinged with grim determination more than optimism or certainty.

They were surrounded. There was no way out of this but through —maybe up or down, but the fire they'd be taking would be immense. He could handle one or two ships, but at this close range, for a sustained period, from all three?

He and the squad would do what they could, but a full barrage? With a destroyer in the mix?

The hatch behind him slid open, making him jump, but a cleaning robot motored its way in. A cylindrical tube was balanced on its back.

"Liquid refreshment," said Xi from the ceiling.

"No beer?" He smiled as he reached down and relieved the little bot of its burden.

"My research tells me alcoholic libations are best reserved for celebrations. After the battle is won."

He twisted off the lid and raised his eyebrows as he took a drink. Chocolate. After the battle was won?

Try *if*. But he wasn't going to tell Xi that. Or whoever else might be listening.

A fresh blast left the first ship, followed by at least two more. More than he could sense—Xi was kicking in to help. In the end, seven beams attacked simultaneously. They managed to deflect five of them.

He forced down a swallow as soon as the ship stopped shaking.

"Shields, ninety-five percent," said Xi.

Yeah. He needed a lot more than a refueling. Praise the Almighty, he needed a miracle.

———

"I'M AWAITING A DECISION, *AUDACITY* CREW." Captain Paul Dealis, ladies and gentlemen. Ellen gritted her teeth. Never one to go off-stage without dramatics.

She forced Paul's voice out of her mind. Ignore them. Think. Find a way.

She paced back and forth behind Adan on the bridge, searching. Thinking.

They could dive. Try to get underneath the ships and come up on the other side. They could load shield energy on the most exposed side instead of all six sides of the ship and try to make a run for it across the underbelly, which would allow Kael and the squad to focus their efforts on that side.

But the attack would be close range. Hard. Too hard. It wouldn't work. They couldn't tolerate that kind of fire, and they couldn't guarantee another ship wouldn't dive and go for *their* belly. Unless they dove *that* far down, but then they could get cut off… It was a very slim chance. Minuscule.

Her mind raced. If the Union caught them, they wouldn't just catch *her*. Beyond those they'd rescued—Ana, the squad, the Persads —and those who might be on bad terms with the Union—Nova, Bri —there was also the empress. Roya.

And the Union could not get their hands on her. No. The power she possessed was too great, and they hardly understood it themselves at this point. They couldn't hand over a super weapon that they barely understood. Not to mention Roya would likely want some say in the matter.

"Be aware," said Paul again over the comm. "If none of you take me up on my offer for a reward, we will consider you guilty of aiding and abetting the escape of a wanted criminal. I'm sure you wouldn't want that."

"What are we doing, Commander?" Adan murmured.

Her eyes met his now, the brown one keenly concerned next to its glowing green brother, the replacement he'd received from losing his eye in battle with Ostrov's robots. She just wasn't going to get used to that thing, was she?

She sighed, pressing her lips together. He knew just as well as she did, their position was terrible.

How could she find a way? There *was* no way.

There was… a gamble. A desperate, high-risk move hoping to get lucky. A sort of jujitsu… Could she catch and then throw?

"You all know we're fragged here," she said over the comm. "They're too close. They're too many, with too much firepower. I've got one idea we can try, but it's a long shot. Chances are it won't work."

There was silence for a moment.

"What else do you wanna do?" Nova asked over the line. "We gotta do something."

A click and a cough came over the comm, then Jenny's voice. Unsteady, rough, but buoying, nonetheless. "C'mon. What do you want us to do, lie down and die? Try it."

"Nobody lives forever," Mo said quietly.

"It probably won't work." Ellen cleared her throat. In case that was at all unclear. "If we lose shields and can't make it to the gate, we'll have to let them board."

"We'll cross that bridge if we get to it," said Dr. Dremer.

"We're with you, Commander," Zhia added.

Ellen forced a deep breath and met Adan's eyes. Kael hadn't said anything, but he didn't need to. He wouldn't want to go down without a fight.

"All right then. Punch it," she ordered. "Dive down—max accel. Scrape the belly of the big-guy destroyer before you swing back up toward the gate."

"Why that one?" asked Doug. "Why not loop around the smaller ship? It's a longer path, but the destroyer could obliterate either ship with friendly fire. They won't risk it."

"I think they *will* risk it. And we will keep the *Everest* right behind us while we charge for the gate, getting the same effect. The other two may be more willing to fire at the destroyer, but the shorter path to the gate means less time to hammer us. Good?"

"Of course—do it."

"Xi, focus shields on areas of highest risk. See if you can get us a flight path that keeps *Everest* in the background as long as possible."

"So… we're sort of playing chicken with this destroyer?" Adan's eyebrow rose over the glowing green eye.

"Not sort of. We are. Now gun it. Let's see if we can get around them and through."

"Now, this I like." Adan slammed the controls almost before she'd finished those words.

"Does that mean I can start firing?" Fern chirped.

"Whenever the shields go down, be my guest, Fern. Theroki crew, give us all the deflection you got till then."

The ship screamed around them, their bodies slammed back into the seats. Grav usually tried to keep up, but her order meant cutting convenience systems, which included grav.

Speed was their gravity now.

"*Audacity* crew, what are you—" That sounded like Yamamoto's shocked exclamation.

Somewhere, she was pretty sure she could see Paul's frown of disappointment. But he wasn't surprised, no. He knew her well enough to know she'd try this.

"*Audacity* crew, I'm imploring you, stand down." Definitely Yamamoto, horror in his voice.

"*Everest* command," Adan said, flicking back on the comm to her surprise. "With all due respect, you can take your offer, and you can eat it. With a nice side of go frag yourself."

CHAPTER TEN

PAUL PURSED HIS LIPS, then raised one finger. "Did he just tell us to…"

"Eat it. Yes, sir, he did." Lieutenant Yamamoto's eyebrows were raised halfway to his thin black hair. Around them, Paul was careful not to look, but he hadn't missed the muffled laughter coming from the crew.

"Eat our offer. Hmm. I doubt it's very tasty." He folded his arms across his chest, smiling slightly at the hushed chuckles. But his mirth faded as the *Audacity* started to move. "What are they doing?"

Yamamoto looked up at the viewscreen, then back at his console. "No… They couldn't be."

"Are they…" A cold pit settled in his stomach. He should have known this wouldn't be so easy. In truth, he *had* known, but still… When the other ships had arrived, he'd thought he'd won.

He should have known.

"They're ramming the destroyer. That's—that's insane."

"They'll likely pull up or down at the last minute—the question is which." Bridell, one of his staff lieutenants, turned toward them from his chair in ops and targeting. "We should neutralize them now, sir. They are going to ram their ship straight into the *Denali*."

"She wouldn't," he said automatically. Even though that was a lie. She would. But did it really achieve her goal? He could see her going out in a blaze instead of being captured, but he didn't think she'd give up quite this easily. "No, there's some plan here."

"She'll dive," Yamamoto said. "Fewer guns on the belly of the *Denali*. Harder for *Lhotse* at this angle, unless Captain Weyer gets moving in response pronto. But their trajectory looks like Weyer ordered them to intercept between the gate, not go over or under, but behind."

"That's smart," Paul muttered. He hoped Yamamoto was right. But Weyer was consistently smart. That was why he liked working with her, when plenty didn't. She didn't sugar coat things. Couldn't, in fact. Since he himself was excellent at sugar coating, they made a good team.

"Sir?" There was a note of alarm in Bridell's voice.

"Yes?"

"Captain Ridgeway is warming up their lasers."

"What?" Yamamoto snapped. "They'll hit us."

"Get him on the comm," Paul demanded as he stood and strode around the console. It made for a more impactful, commanding presence on video, which was especially important when dealing with other commanders who were essentially peers. "Concentrate shields frontal."

Ridgeway's frowning, bushy eyebrows came on screen, but he was clearly only half paying attention. "I thought you knew this nutwaffle! She's charging us, Dealis! This woman is charging us!"

"Ridgeway," he said, trying to keep his voice calm but with an appropriate edge, "are you warming up your weapons?"

"Of *course* I am. You think I'm going to let her play tickleball on my prow? Then you're as mad as she is!"

"You're going to hit us." Threat laced his tone, but it didn't seem to faze Ridgeway.

"No, we won't. Our shots are good."

Yamamoto spoke up. "Those lasers will diffuse over the distance between us. There's no way you'll *miss* us. It's simple physics."

"Then get out of my way!" Ridgeway reached toward the comm controls.

"Ridgeway!" Paul snapped, taking a step forward. "You're talking intentional friendly fire. You want to join her on trial in the Inner Planets?"

"Better than ending up dead."

"She's not *really* going to hit you." Paul shook his head. Did this moron really not get her plan?

"Oh yeah? Or do you just want to think that cause you two were—"

He couldn't have discussion of that, so he quickly cut him off. "This ship cannot afford taking fire from you *and* them."

"Not my fault you fly such an old, beat-up beast! Tell your brother to increase retrofitting spending!"

"My brother has nothing to do with this, nor does he influence the naval defense budget." Although he'd definitely be filling Jim in on all this if Ridgeway actually endangered his crew. "Stop what you are doing and—"

The laser arrays fired. So did a whole volley of ballistic missiles... Ridgeway had the composure to slap off the comm.

Some of it must have hit the *Audacity*, but plenty went right past. Paul barely had time to reach the command chair and hadn't even buckled in when the ship rocked.

"Dive! Evasive maneuvers!" Yamamoto was yelling. Yes, that was a good idea. They should have started taking them as soon as Ridgeway had been uncooperative, but he hadn't really thought the tickherder would really do it.

Paul shook his head as he got the last buckle snapped. Ryu was a big fish to catch. And Paul would one day be competition for Ridgeway for a promotion to admiral. Why not kill two birds with one stone?

Possibly literally. Was that what Ridgeway was thinking?

He had to survive this. For her sake and his own.

———

THE CRASH that rocked the ship this time was worse. Harder. Close range.

Sweat beaded on Kael's brow. His thoughts were mostly silent, his brain joining closer with Xi's processes and the *Audacity*'s sensors as they sorted and deflected, sorted and dodged when they could.

It could have been minutes that had passed. It could have been hours or days. It was a rote process, like target practice. Like waving off bugs or refitting his armor into its case, taking very little thought.

Except with this, you never finished. There were always more targets, more bugs. More danger.

He realized he had a death grip on the armrest, so he released it and stretched his fingers. How far had they made it? It couldn't have been far. He muted his comm channel and kept his voice low. "How much progress have we made, Xi?"

"Two-point-three kilometers," she replied. "Shields are at forty-three percent."

He wiped sweat off his forehead with the back of the arm that wasn't jacked in. "That isn't good, is it?"

"At this rate, shields will not hold for the entire distance to the gate. We must either deflect more, decrease their rate of fire, or go faster. Preferably all of the above."

"Oh, okay. Is that actually possible?"

"No. We are already at maximum capacity at all those things. But I am looking for small tweaks to efficiencies."

He sighed. "Thanks."

He slapped the mute off in case he needed to talk again. But there wasn't much to say.

He usually maintained a perimeter about as far as he could sense. It gave him time to correct or adjust if he made a mistake. But even with the squad gradually picking up on his tactics, his perimeter hadn't held. None of the squad had reached the Tridelphi rank, so none had been trained on what he needed them to do.

He'd fallen back rather quickly. A little, then a lot.

There were ten, fifteen, sometimes twenty blasts a minute. Sometimes, they came all at once, sometimes in little groups.

Any regularity of the blasts had faded with his hopes of escaping this mess. The squad was managing to deflect a handful each minute or so, but they were really only one additional mind. It was easy to forget that thirteen minds didn't multiply into thirteen times the capacity. They still made one choice at a time.

Just like Kael.

Hard to believe three little ships could put off this much firepower. How many gunners did they have on that thing? Or were they AI-operated?

Nothing that he needed to be contemplating right the hell now. Because there were twelve volleys coming at him if there was one.

This time, the ship twisted sharply in what felt like an uncontrolled spin. He had to grab on to both armrests now with the jolt of at least three of those twelve getting by. Maybe more.

Frag—that was a strategy that worked. Almighty, let them not notice. Coordinating their attacks made it harder for him to catch them all.

"Shields reduced to thirty-eight percent."

Kael, for one, did not particularly appreciate the update. But there was no time to say so.

"Don't they care about friendly fire?" Ellen was saying. "Not even a little bit?"

"You called it," Doug replied. "I still can't get into *Everest*'s systems, but they are getting hit at least as hard as we are."

"This won't work if he doesn't hold back at least a little—God!" Ellen let out a stream of curses, moving away from the mic.

He was going to let her down, wasn't he?

In the horror of that realization, another blast got through. He slammed the mute on the comm and let off a torrent of his own swear words, just to let off steam.

He batted every single one of the next thirty-two strikes back with precision, battering the shields of the destroyer above them now each time. It wasn't enough, though, because when he reached for the thirty-third, he fumbled and missed it.

"I—there are too many—" he started. "Xi, frag it—"

"Every capacity is limited, Kael," she said mildly. "We are doing our best."

He nodded. Tried to steel himself. Sweat was pouring off him now. But in the next moment, a chill went through him when he batted back one blast… and it faltered. The energy direction had been reversed by his shove, but not by much. He had slowed it so little that the blast was almost stopped, traveling back toward their adversaries at a snail's crawl.

He was running dry.

A second smack got the energy projectile out of the way, but his body was in full rebellion now.

Another coordinated twelve-blast attack came. He winced, tossing back two, three, four in rapid succession.

The power flickered briefly as a new impact jarred the ship.

"Shields thirty-two percent," said Xi calmly.

Kael's snarl didn't capture his rage. He was losing this battle. He was letting them all down. But he was only human—or cyborg Theroki or what have you. Whatever he was, it wasn't enough.

"Kael, you okay?" It was Ellen.

He turned the channel back on. "Doin' my best."

"I know you are. You don't need to tell me that."

He frowned. "What are you really getting at?"

"Your vitals are flickering."

"I'm fine." He gritted his teeth when the words came out unsteady. "Everything's just peachy."

"Dr. Levereaux to Kael. See if there's anything you can do for him."

"Yes, Commander." Levereaux sounded like she was already moving.

"Keep on the handgrips. Status on Jenny."

"Stable. Corrosive acid and contaminants did enter her system, though. We're flushing it out best we can."

That was one tidbit he'd have rather not known at the moment.

He tilted his head back against the rest, relaxed his arms. Who needed a neck? Who needed arms?

He just needed this damn ship not to get shot full of holes, and for that, he only needed his brain. Or his central nervous system. Continuing to deflect *anything* was a feat on its own.

Head lolling, body mostly forgotten except its frown of rage and effort, he kept up the hard work.

If Levereaux ever came, he didn't notice.

———

"SHIELDS—" Xi was cut off by the rumble of the shields straining underneath a new collision, then another.

On the bridge, Ellen staggered, gripping the back of the command seat. She should be harnessed in, but she'd been pacing—with her magnetics turned on just in case. Pacing helped her think. Pacing helped her feel like she was doing *something*. But there was nothing to be done.

"Sorry," Kael said, voice breathless on the comm. "I don't... I don't know how much longer I can—"

He sounded almost feverish. Levereaux hadn't reported back. She gritted her teeth as yet another impact hit them.

The power flickered. The energy drain to the shields was massive, as Xi started disabling systems to steal for the shields.

"Hull breach," Xi announced.

An alarm suddenly blared, making her duck reflexively, then scamper for the co-pilot seat.

"Depressurization in cargo compartment 31XC detected," said Xi.

Ellen swore. "Close the blast doors," she ordered. That was an external compartment, but it meant that the shields had also flickered. Had been completely down, at least for a moment. That one blast had gotten through.

That meant *more* could. And more were about to.

"If you don't have your armor on, get it on," she ordered. "If you don't have armor, get a suit or your breather. Check your harnesses. Power down all non-essential systems."

"That is already nearly complete, Commander."

"What's the damage?"

"31XC has been sealed. Some minor loss of water storage."

"Like we had any to spare."

The ship lurched, grav systems barely keeping up, as Adan jerked the controls.

"Shields are at twenty percent," Xi announced. "Power systems in high-dynamic mode. Shielding a high radius blast to the fore of the ship left the aft weak to a single pulse getting through." Xi sounded apologetic.

Here was where Ellen would pay her price for this mad dash. When the crew thought that it was *their* fault that they hadn't made it through. When what she'd asked them to do was impossible. She would try to say so. She'd tried to warn them, but they wouldn't believe her. Not in their heart of hearts.

"How much farther to the gate?" she asked.

"Over fifty kilometers remaining," said Xi. "The smaller remaining ship is moving to intercept."

Time seemed to have slowed to the speed of molten sludge as Ellen let out a slow breath. She hadn't fought a losing battle too many times, but she knew the feel of it. The draining, sinking freefall. The creeping panic. She couldn't afford that.

She swallowed. "Anybody got any genius ideas to get out of this, now is the time to speak up."

"I am pretty sure this is not a genius idea," Nova said over the comm, gum cracking. "But we could let those space rats board and pray we can shoot them faster than they can shoot us."

"I mean, I'd take my chances at trying," Adan replied. "I can squeeze a trigger when you say so."

"At this point, let me at 'em," Fern said.

That wouldn't work, either, just based on sheer numbers and tech, but Ellen wasn't going to strangle their hope. She held her tongue. Oh, it might for a little while, until they started employing grenades. And some of the *Audacity* crew had high-tech armor, yes—but the civilians didn't. And their box fended off telepaths, but she doubted it was airtight against chems in the ventilation system. And that'd really be closer to the *first* thing the Union would try, not the last. Civilian breathers could only do so much when facing military weapons *designed* to overpower them.

"They'd have to come through the choke of the cargo hold," Fern was saying.

Nova continued. "We might even be able to funnel them up the ladders and defend from inside the cabins…"

A reckless last stand. Certain death. Although… maybe that did give her an idea. A different one. If they were facing certain death anyway…

The chatter continued, but she stood. "Adan," she said softly, away from the comm. "Take the bridge. I need a minute to think. I'll be in my cabin. Do your best."

He nodded, face solemn, and went back to their machinations.

She jogged up to the ladder to her cabin, having to brace herself and wince as two more hits got through. It wasn't fragging fair to pin this entire desperate attempt on the Theroki and some excessive speed. Kael was going to feel guilty as hell, and it was never his fault. This had barely had a chance, and what glimmer of that she'd hoped for had vanished.

Inside her quarters, she slapped the hatch shut. It was a good thing Kael was too busy to come up here, because she couldn't bring herself to lock him out, but she was going to need to be alone for this one.

"I have another idea, Xi. But no one is going to like it." She started removing a gauntlet. Just for a minute. For a breather. She'd put it back on in a second.

"Approval does not seem to be necessary for an idea to potentially be good, Commander."

"Get me a comm link to Captain Dealis," she said. "Private, please. As private as this ship can be, anyway."

"Right away." There was a pause. "Also, Commander?"

"Yes."

"Kael appears to be unconscious. Dr. Levereaux is attending to him."

She winced. "Thank you, Xi."

Her body sank down into her chair to wait, almost against her will. Should she stand? Oh, what the frag did it matter. She was sweaty from the mission and racing around this damn ship, still in her fragging armor, which was perhaps the only thing convenient about getting ambushed right after another harrowing op. Her hair was sticking to her skull, disheveled, basically a mess. And there was definitely seaweed on her armor.

Ironically, when Paul blinked into view, he was combing his perfectly black hair to one side. He looked at her, eyebrows raised as he lowered his comb, practically a perfect Union recruiting poster. "Ellen! Fancy seeing you here."

"Is this some kind of stunt, or are you actually combing your hair?"

"A stunt? Really. What would be the point of that?" He returned to combing it, looking off screen.

"You'd think you'd be more concerned with surviving this battle than with your hair, given the way your allies are shooting." God. She was really greasing the wheels of negotiation.

"I trust my people." He smirked. "I assumed your comm was urgent since we're pummeling you to splintered remains, but if you'd like to talk leadership styles—"

"Look, we both know how this is going to end and that it won't be long."

He set down the comb and looked at her squarely. "Yes, I'm afraid the clock has struck twelve. Your carriage is turning back into a pumpkin, and you'll run out of power and shields first, my dear."

"Don't call me that."

"I was only being friendly."

"Don't be friendly. While you've got a gun pointed at my head? Fuck you." She jabbed a finger at the viewscreen.

"Point taken." He sobered. "I apologize. You have some kind of deal in mind?"

"Sure. I want you to let my ship go."

He cupped a hand to his ear, as if it was hard to hear her. "And...? I'll get in exchange...?"

"And your buddies will stop firing at you, too."

"And...?"

"And that's it."

"Not going to fly, old friend. They will stop shooting at me eventually, whether it's because you've gotten passed them and are nearing the gate, or because I've gone through the gate and contacted their superior officers. But one way or the other, I will win."

She shrugged. "Worth a try."

"Surely, that's not why you got me on the comm. You're a better negotiator than that."

"Fine." She sighed. Why was she always so tempted to toy with him? "We have a fighter. I'll separate from the ship and turn myself in. But I won't come in range of you until the *Audacity* is clear through the gate. And you'll let her go. You *won't* chase her. Neither will anyone else from the Union. Period, end of story."

"Now why would I want to do that? Your shields are nearly gone. I can just wait and catch my whole quarry. And you want me to settle for half? Who knows what other fugitives you're harboring on that ship?" He smiled.

The last line was a ruse, some kind of diversion. She narrowed her eyes at him. She knew him too well to miss it. He *wanted* her to think he cared about the rest of the ship, but he really didn't. She was clearly his primary goal.

"Your whole quarry isn't an option. My crew is loyal. If we're going to die, we'll die together." God, let her be a better liar than he was.

"Nobody said you were going to die—"

"*I* said it." She slammed a fist on the table. "And they said it. You heard them. None of us are going down without a fight. They're determined to go down guns blazing. This is me trying to stop them."

"Guns blazing?" He snorted, looking amused. "That's insane."

"That's what I told them."

"You want me to think your crew is going to blow themselves up? Just to spite me?"

"You're some narcissist, to think this is about you."

"I'd be lying if I said I hadn't heard *that* before."

She paused before she spoke, letting the silence settle. "Would you rather die free in battle or caged with a needle in your arm?" Her words were steely quiet, and they had the desired effect. They wiped the smile right off his face. And she *would* rather die in battle. That didn't mean she was going to let anyone die with her, whatever the method. Not children, not civvies who didn't sign up for this. But he didn't know that.

His jaw twitched. "You wouldn't kill your crew."

"You're right, I wouldn't. This is their idea." A bluff, an important one. "They are insisting, in fact."

"You'll let them waste their lives, Commander? For what? I know you probably respect and trust every one of them. Probably even more than those you served with. They're your hand-picked crew." His eyes searched hers as best they could on the screen.

"I picked them. And they also picked me. I can order them to stand down all I want. But you and I both know, there are limits to a commander's authority."

"You're bluffing." He shook his head. "There are no limits to *your* authority. Don't try that with me. Don't do this. Let them turn you in, and they can go on with their lives. And be rich, to boot."

"There are some things money can't buy, Paul. Like self-respect. They won't turn me in. You might not believe this, but there is such a thing as loyalty left in the world."

He let out a bark of laughter. "You? A deserter? Are lecturing *me* on loyalty?" He was shaking his head. "I know you. You're bluffing."

Damn it. If only he were in the room, so she could slap him. Do something wild to make him doubt. Make him think she was desperate. Make him understand she *was* desperate.

"Try me," she said, barely audible above the ship's hum. "What do *you* want to be remembered for, Dealis? The one who drove a war hero to a suicidal last stand? We won't let you board this ship."

He flinched at the words, then hardened his expression. "You *were* a war hero. Once upon a time, Ellen. But you won't go out that way. Going out with fireworks and a big bang won't remove the tarnish you put on your record."

"I did not—" She broke off the words. She'd made her choice. To say she hadn't tarnished her reputation wasn't true. She'd known. It felt like no choice at all; she'd only had one real option, that or death. But she'd made it. She'd walked. "I didn't *start* it. But I sure as hell will finish it."

"You think sacrificing innocent soldiers will fix anything? Help anything? This is double the disgrace." His expression was severe now. "Die with some honor, damn it. Don't take good people down with you."

"What do you know about honor?" she snapped. "Or sacrifice?"

"You know for a fact that I know plenty." He was shouting now. "I've made mistakes that cost lives. Don't make the same ones. Control your crew and make them *surrender*. Sacrifice is not a way out."

"It was at SHR." She kept her voice low, calm, controlled. Robotic even. "People will do a lot of desperate things to protect their home system. I'm not special. They don't put much detail on that in the history books, do they? But we lost dozens of ships. On my orders." She gritted her teeth and hoped he wouldn't see through her. The difference was huge—those were warriors, willingly under her command, fighting for survival, and it was freedom and sovereignty on the line. On the *Audacity* right now, there were scientists and civilians who most definitely did not deserve to die in a last-stand shootout. And they wouldn't, because she wouldn't truly sacrifice them. But so far, her assertion that her crew would be shooting until they were cold and dead hadn't quite convinced him, but it sure had drawn his ire. "You think I won't sacrifice them, you're wrong. I will. But that's really beside the point. It doesn't matter. You're acting like I can convince them. I can't. I've already tried and failed."

His expression had darkened as she spoke, like he was looking at someone from his past and he didn't like what he saw. It was the intended effect, but it still stung.

"You've changed, Ellen," he whispered. "You never used to give up. You've changed."

Her neck and shoulders snapped tight with tension, like she was bracing for a punch. Like she'd *been* punched.

"Life on the run will do that to you," she snarked, to cover the hurt. They were tangled up in lies now. It was too bad there was no one but Xi to appreciate the irony of this. Kael had wanted to give up, and she'd claimed she never did, and yet somehow *this* was her only solution? And whatever Paul thought, nothing about her had changed, except what Arakovic had forced her to change. She'd been forced to try taking matters into her own hands, going outside of the rules and laws she respected and preferred. But that didn't mean she liked any of this. She let her anger infuse her voice. "I'm just being a realist. And trying to find a way out where they don't die. Because I care about them."

"Then make them surrender!"

"I can't!" She smacked a palm on the armrest. "It's not an option. The only option is what I'm offering you. I can sneak away, turn myself in, and you let them go. It's that or a fight to our death. You think I like these options? Slag off. Do we have a deal or not, Dealis?"

His eyes searched hers for another long moment, then he shook his head. "We have a deal. Send the details of your demands to Yamamoto. The distances you require and the model of the freighter."

"Fighter."

"Whatever."

"Consider it done."

He shook his head once more, his eyes burning. And then he hit the button, and the feed blinked out.

She sank down into her seat and covered her face with her hands. "Xi. What have I done?" It wasn't a question really.

Xi answered anyway. "You have done what you had to do. The logic seems sound to me to minimize casualties. I am concerned for your safety. But I will ready the fighter."

She forced herself straight and nailed shut the box of emotions welling up. She had work to do. "Okay. Thank you. I will tell them."

———

"ISSUE A CEASE FIRE. WE HAVE AN ARRANGEMENT."

Paul waited a beat while comms carried out the order, Yamamoto eyeing him with curiosity. The vid feed of the bridge floated over his holodesk in his cabin.

When it was clear the attacks had actually stopped—on both the *Audacity* and the *Everest*—he let out a long breath. "I can't believe it. That comm was legitimate. She's offered her surrender." For victory, it didn't feel very good.

His second-in-command ran a hand through his hair. "Thank the heavens, sir. We couldn't have taken much more of this."

He relayed the details they'd agreed upon. "Does that work?"

"Yes, sir. We'll contact the *Audacity* and then be on the lookout for the fighter."

"Has it slowed down its progress toward the gate?"

"Slightly. Can't say I blame them. I wouldn't want to give up acceleration only to restart again for this. They'll probably launch her out at the max speed they can manage."

"Hmm. Perhaps. If the situation has settled, I'm going to step away for a moment. Can you handle things for the time being?"

"Of course, sir. Just one more thing." Yamamoto fought off another sneeze, winning this time. "Which ship would you like her to be held on once in custody? Captain Ridgeway has demanded—"

"Oh, no, no," he said quickly. "We ferreted her out."

"He has requested I point out that the *Denali* is the largest ship present with the best facilities, and—"

"And I don't care. We will not reward his recklessness. Finder's keepers. If he wanted to get the trophy, he shouldn't have shot at us." A better reward for Ridgeway's behavior—or perhaps he should say punishment—was exactly what he'd get. Without Ryu, Ridgeway would have to join Operation Dubious Success aka Freedom's Wing first.

"I will tell him you want the reward and recognition, sir."

"Will that shut him up? I doubt it. What I *want* is to be sure Ellen Ryu is escorted, alive and unmolested, to a fair trial," he said sharply. "Why don't you tell him maybe it can be his turn next time, when he's learned to play well with others?"

"That, I can do." Yamamoto's features eased.

This was one of those rare moments when telling the truth was actually helpful. Sure, since Captain Ridgeway commanded a larger vessel, he had a leg up in their promotion race, but Paul was sure his insistence on firing at the *Audacity* was more than misguided thinking in the heat of battle.

Capturing Ryu would be a career-elevating feat. And Paul had already exhausted quite a few of his options to catapult himself ahead. But this… This could help him make admiral.

But he *was* truly concerned about what Ridgeway would do. He tried not to think about it too hard—much more fun to think about his career—but he'd also played cards with Ridgeway and hadn't found him the most gentlemanly or progressive of men. Not terribly honorable, either. And the commander of the *Denali* had even tried to cheat on both the game and his wife in the course of one sitting.

Of course, Paul hadn't exactly been playing fair cards, either, but only so he wouldn't completely lose his shirt. And *he* hadn't gotten caught. This all certainly made Ridgeway's behavior today much less surprising.

So, no. He owed it to Ellen not to let her fall into Ridgeway's hands. His gut was usually right about that much.

"Understood, sir." Yamamoto was standing a little taller now. "I will ensure she is captured alive and securely brought on board this vessel. Only a matter of time now. And the *Lhotse*?"

"Keep her alongside us, if Captain Weyer has no objection. Best to keep sister ships together in case some ally might seek to help Ellen Ryu. The *Denali*, though—do not inform him of our flight trajectory. And ping me when you've tractored Ryu's vessel and are ready to board."

CHAPTER ELEVEN

ELLEN'S MOVEMENTS felt robotic as she made her way back to the bridge. Why had she even come down here? It was only Nova and Adan here, hardly the whole crew, and she wasn't going to be calling them all together at a moment like this, anyway.

"Commander!" Adan said as soon as she entered. "They've totally stopped fire. They're still moving in line with us, no longer hammering the shields—"

She held up a hand. "I can explain that. Halt acceleration. Switch to power conservation while I explain. I've spoken with Captain Dealis." She checked the ship comm line—it was still broadcasting to all stations.

A silence fell over the *Audacity*.

"We're in a no-win situation here." Her words were somber. It felt like they echoed through the ship, through the hull, out into the eternal midnight. "We need some way out of this. So please understand. I didn't agree to what I'm about to announce lightly. But I see it as the only route out of this mess."

Adan frowned. "What is it, Commander?"

"I'm turning myself in."

The silence on the bridge and the comm turned electrified, violent.

"Have you lost your mind?" Dremer's was the first voice over the comm.

She raised her eyebrows.

"No, no, no—wait. This is a trick, right?" Kael's voice came over the comm. He sounded groggy, but good thing he was awake. She did *not* want to explain this twice.

"You're lying to them?" asked Nova.

"It had better be," added Zhia.

She sucked in a breath. Braced herself. "I'm not lying."

A stream of curse words and mutterings came over the comm; it was hard to identify them all. Now Nova shot up out of her chair, pacing.

One voice was silent in the morass, though. Blazingly so.

"You can't give up on us that easily, Commander." Adan had his hand on his forehead, like he was trying to get his brain to find some way to reason with her. "We've got thirteen Theroki here. Powerful telepaths. There's got to be something else we can try. Our shields are damaged, but—"

"You and I both know that won't cut it," she said mildly. "Thirteen more of us in heavy armor is still tissue paper to hundreds of them."

"Don't do this, Commander," Dr. Dremer said. "You can't know exactly what they'll do. Even if you and Captain Dealis are former colleagues. That's all changed now."

"We can't just give up." Nova stopped her pacing to punch a fist into her palm. "We have to fight."

"No, we *want* to fight." Ellen's glare was hard. "But we don't *have* to, and we definitely don't have to die. They have six or ten times the firepower. And let's say we make it through the gate. Who is to say they don't have more ships waiting for us? If not that jump, then what about the next one? There are only a few ways out of this system."

"They can still do all that *after* they have you." Kael's voice was rough. "How does you jumping ship help with any of that?"

Inwardly, she winced. "I'm not jumping ship. I'm saving all your asses. Here is the arrangement I've made. I'm going to take the fighter. I will stay clear, out of range until the *Audacity* gets away, safely through the gate. They've promised to let you all go in exchange for my peaceful surrender."

"Who says Dealis will keep his promise?" Kael growled.

He remembered the name. Had he put two and two together yet? She kept her voice hard, trying to reassure him. "He will."

"Oh, so you trust him? Is that it?" Oh, yes. He knew *exactly* who they were dealing with.

"I don't trust him, but I *can* read him. He's not interested in the *Audacity*. Just my arrest. I am confident I can keep the fighter at a safe distance long enough for you all to get away."

"And then instead of going with them—you'll go through the gate, too!" Fern exclaimed.

"Brilliant, that would give them the—" Zhia started.

"No." She cut the air with her hand, even if they couldn't see it. "They want me alive, but that's not required. If they've confirmed my location, they'll be perfectly happy to incinerate me if I don't keep up my end of the bargain. They'll still get their reward. And then they'll probably still come after you, because why not?"

"You don't think they are going to wonder why you want us gone so badly?" Kael's voice was hard.

"I've convinced him I've got some good reasons for that. Look, this is about more than me. You must keep going. We can't afford for the *Audacity* to fall into their hands. Not given what it carries. Not given what it stands for. I broke the law. I broke my oath. I deserve to face the consequences. I need you to do this for—"

The bridge door slid open, and Doug floated in, pushing his gold glasses up his nose slightly. "What's this I hear about ritual martyrdom?"

"I'm trading myself for your safety."

"Did *I* ask for that?" Doug looked to Adan. "Did you?"

"I don't recall asking, no. Did you?" Adan looked at Nova.

"I certainly didn't." She turned her frown to Ellen.

"I don't *have* to ask you," she snapped. "I'm the commander of this vessel. And you *will* comply."

They all went silent for a moment. Doug's eyes were staring into the distance of the viewscreen, his lips set in a bitter line. His expression didn't say he wanted to challenge her; it said he knew she was right, and he hated himself for not having a better idea. Yeah, join the club, pal.

Nova started chewing her gum furiously and went back to pacing. Adan was glaring at the viewscreen like it was the cause of every problem in the course of history.

It was Zhia who spoke, voice slow and careful. "If you surrender, that makes *me* the commander of this vessel."

Ellen nodded sharply. "Correct. At least until a point that I would be able to return. And?"

"Just want to make sure you realize what you're giving up."

Her jaw hardened, and she closed her eyes. "If you think this is easy for me, you're wrong." Not just wrong, but seriously delusional. But damn it, if it wasn't her job to convince them to let her go. At least until the fighter left the cargo hold.

No one replied to that.

"This is about more than me," she repeated. "We have the empress to think about. We can't let them have her. I made a promise. I'm not giving up, but I'm not arrogant enough to think I'm the only game piece in play. I need *you* to continue what we're doing. And to trust that I know what I'm doing. I'm going to do my damnedest to rejoin you and finish what we started."

That was a bitterly empty promise, as she had no plan and no clue how that'd ever be possible. She only had the one thing left that anyone who had nothing left could have—hope.

The silence felt like it could shake her, them, the entire ship. They all stared at her, and she met each gaze defiantly in turn.

"I made a promise," she whispered. "We have to protect her."

"She asked me for a promise, too," said Kael.

Her head ducked further. "Then you know they wouldn't let us keep that promise. If the Union gets ahold of her…"

Zhia lifted her chin. "We will continue the mission, Commander. At the very least, we can recon the location we've just pinpointed for Dr. Arakovic. And we'll keep Roya safe till you return."

Doug opened his mouth, but Yamamoto's voice suddenly cut in over the comm line. "The captain says we've come to an arrangement. I await the details of your fighter."

She pointed at the controls. "Tell him, Adan."

Gritting his teeth, Adan jabbed at the proper commands, then flipped on the external comm. "Small fighter ship. I'm sending the details now." He cut the comm again. "How do we know they won't just toast you right there while they can?"

"Because I haven't run that hard."

"*That's* no guarantee."

"There is no guarantee."

"So we can't know they won't just kill you." He slapped a palm on the armrest and glared.

She opened her mouth, but before she could answer, Yamamoto was talking again. "Come in hot, Ms. Ryu, and we will defend ourselves. I'd regret it, but we will not unnecessarily risk Union lives. Understood?"

She slapped the comm on. "Isn't that what you just did?"

"Our orders are to capture you. We're just following orders, ma'am. I reiterate, we will not risk—"

Her turn to interrupt. "No need to reiterate, Lieutenant. I have more than a few things to live for."

"Thirty minutes, and we'll resume our attacks." The line clicked.

"They're gone," said Adan, looking at the console. "Commander, there *has* to be another—"

"Let me know if you think of it, Adan," she said. "If not, you heard the man. Thirty minutes. Xi, how's that fighter prep coming?"

"Fifty-eight percent complete, Commander."

"Then, if you'll all excuse me, I better get my things." She started for the door.

No one stopped her, but their voices rose in her wake. Doug followed, hot on her heels. "Please don't do this."

"I have to." She kept her eyes on the hallway and grabbed on to the ladder to head up.

"C'mon. We've got thirty minutes. Maybe we can repair something." He'd slowed to a stop. But she wasn't falling for that tactic. Not today. She kept going.

"Sorry, my friend," she said without looking back. "If there's another way, we haven't found it. And we're out of time."

WHEN KAEL FELT like the floor had stopped tilting out from under him, he staggered to his feet. Oh, it had nothing to do with the grav. That was perfectly semi-functional. He thought. There was a med-patch on one arm, and his neck was itchy, so Levereaux must have been here and gone. He *was* exhausted from battle, but that was only half the problem. Maybe less.

By the seven suns. What if they killed her?

He pinged her comm. The room seemed to wobble a bit, so he seized the back of the gun chair to steady himself.

She answered immediately. "Yes, Kael."

"What's the punishment for desertion?" he demanded.

"Depends on what they decide at the court-martial." Her voice was flat. All business.

"Is it death?"

"It could be life imprisonment."

"I notice you didn't say it *wasn't* death." In spite of his unsteadiness, he lurched toward the door. "Isn't it usually death? I think it's death. Wasn't it wartime?"

"When is it not wartime? I'm a war hero."

"A notorious one."

"Your point?"

"My point is I'm coming up there."

"Kael, don't. You can't talk me out of this. I'm not in my cabin, anyway."

"I'm coming." He cut off the comm and took off at a jog. "Where is she, Xi?"

"Strictly speaking, she said not to—" Xi started.

"*Please*, Xi."

There was a moment of silence, the desperation in his voice filling his mind. He tripped and had to grab the wall to steady himself. It was too much—he had to get a bar or something, or he'd pass out before he got to her.

"She's heading to the cargo hold," Xi said, almost meek.

"Thank you," he whispered.

The mess would be on the way. He slid down the ladder, barely holding on enough to slow his descent. He crashed loudly and unceremoniously at the bottom, but just kept on staggering toward the mess hall.

She was leaving. He had known something was coming. He had known it would be bad. But he hadn't thought *she* would be the one to dive headfirst into—well, danger wasn't something he could keep her out of.

But damn it, knowing that and accepting that were completely fragging different.

By the time he reached the mess, he'd gone from furious to broken to furious again several times. But by the time he was out of the mess, half a bar devoured, he was stomping his way toward the cargo hold and solidly furious again.

As he approached Doug's lab, his boss floated into the open hatch. And frowned. "Just what do you think you're doing?"

"Stopping her." He barely spared Doug a glance.

To his surprise, Doug sped forward into the hallway, blocking him. "Oh, no, you're not."

"Like hell, I'm not! Get out of the way." He kept walking.

Doug glided back slightly but put his hands on Kael's chest. "Stop. Will you stop and think for one damned minute?"

"I don't need to *think*, I need to—"

Doug cut him off with a shove.

He staggered back and to one side—not fully recovered, but damn that shove was *hard*. He stumbled all the way into the open hatch of Doug's lab and had to grab on to one of the lab tables for balance before he steadied himself. "What in the seven suns—"

"You're not the only one augmented with technology around here. Now will you just stop and think?"

"Did you just shove me? Did *you* just shove *me*?"

"You wanna shove me back? Go on then!" Frag, even Doug was shouting now. He glided right up, inches from Kael's face.

"You think I'm malfunctioning?" Kael scowled. " 'Cause there's no way—"

"Oh, why is *that*? Because I'm—"

"Because you're my *boss*." He shouted the words back. "And I'm not an idiot!"

"Really?" Doug raised his eyebrows, face dead serious for once. He wasn't sure he'd ever seen Doug look like that. "You're not being an idiot? You sure?"

"What the frag is that supposed to mean?"

"You think storming down there pounding your chest is going to change anything? I'm going to have to disagree."

That stopped him short. His mouth had been open to shout something else, but he snapped it shut now. "What am I supposed to do? Just let her go?" He shoved the table at the wall in lieu of his boss, and damn if it didn't make him feel better.

Doug was silent for a moment, just watching him.

Without the table, though, the world felt like it was spinning. He grabbed on to the back of a nearby metal chair. "How am I supposed to protect her?" he murmured, more weakly now.

Doug let out a slow sigh, shoulders slumping. "You're not. You can't."

"Well, I can't settle for that. I have to... I—" He faltered. "How can I not try?"

"Well, the alternative isn't keeping her here, safe and sound, on the ship. If we could get away from them, we already would have. How exactly did you think talking to her would play out?"

"Well, I didn't—think—"

"No. You didn't." Doug folded his arms across his chest.

"You wouldn't understand."

Doug narrowed his eyes. "Try me."

What the hell? "What's that supposed to mean?"

"Nothing." He waved at the air. "Forget it."

"Did I miss something?" Kael glanced around, not sure what he was looking for.

"It doesn't matter."

"Oh, I think it does. Are you—"

"We don't have time for this!"

He was right. "Do you have a suggestion? Better than slamming tables and stomping through corridors?"

"Go say some goodbyes that you won't regret in the morning? You've still got… how long, Xi?"

"Twenty-three minutes."

Doug shrugged. "Seems like plenty."

"I can't do that." The metal under his fingers bent suddenly. He released it with a jerk and raised his eyebrows. Oops. He'd crushed a dent into the top of the thing.

But damn it, say his goodbyes? Now? Already? Like *this*?

He growled and flung the chair aside. It tumbled end over end and collided with the far wall of the lab. The wall dented, but at least it missed the wall display.

He didn't wince. But this time, it didn't make him feel better.

"Well, what was your plan?" Doug stared at the toppled chair flatly but appeared unfazed by it. He didn't comment.

"I hadn't gotten past the 'demand she not leave' part."

"I suggest you think of some way to help. She's decided. It will get us out of here. We've got a cache of data, coordinates, and the empress. It'll give us time to regroup. Then we can find somewhere to hide the empress. Or plan a rescue."

"Rescue? Rescue? You think there'll *be* a rescue?" He waved his arms wide, glad there were no more chairs to throw, or he might hit the wall display for real this time. "If they put a bullet between her eyes, there'll be no fucking rescue!"

Doug opened his mouth, but the words choked in his throat. "We're outnumbered, Kael. If she doesn't go, it'll be a bullet between the eyes for all of us. Isa, Shirin, Roya, all of them."

He groaned and slumped against the wall. "They might take prisoners."

"You didn't rescue Shirin so she could spend the rest of her life in a Union jail, did you?"

He glared hard at Doug now. "You really know how to stab a guy in the kidney when he's down."

He shrugged. "I'm just telling you the truth."

"Maybe. I guess. But I have to do something."

"Figure out a way to help. Maybe there's some way we can preemptively help her escape. Maybe a tracking beacon or—maybe something she can smuggle on her person to short-circuit handcuffs?"

He frowned. He could short-circuit electric cuffs himself, but if they had tools like that on board, he hadn't paid attention because he didn't need them. They probably did have them—but Ellen would know that, right? She could get something like that herself, but the Union would probably pat her down and take them. A waste of time. What was he bringing to the table?

He should be the one by her side, blasting the capacitors on anything that would try to hold her back.

Wait. Maybe that was his answer right there.

He forced himself upright, ignoring the way the world spun. "I'm going with her."

"What? No. She won't go along with that."

"How else am I going to protect her?"

"You can't protect someone like her."

"We're supposed to protect each other. Aren't we? We're in this *together*. I love her."

"I know." Doug swallowed. "Yes. I know. Protect each other."

"Then I'm going—"

"Kael, stop."

But this time, he didn't stop. He darted out of the lab and back toward the mess. He had a plan. Not a very good one, but it was a plan. "If you want to help," he called, "get your handcuff whatchahoozit and give it to her."

———

DOUG RAN a hand over his face. This situation was spinning out of control fast, and he had no idea how to right this ship. Metaphorically speaking.

Before the hatch could slide closed again, Mo appeared in the hallway. Her eyes flicked to his, then the toppled chair. Scowling, he floated over to it, dipped down, went horizontal, then righted it and himself. Then he drifted out into the hall to her side, staring in the direction Kael had gone.

This wasn't good. This was bad. Very, very bad. But he couldn't stop Kael. Couldn't even blame him.

He started drifting toward the cargo hold. It was already buzzing with activity. Mo followed, quiet as usual. They stood on the upper level and watched the others firing up the fighter. Zhia and Dr. Dremer had joined in with Xi's preparations.

"That was a nice thing you did," she said, resting one hand on the railing. "As his friend. As their friend."

"Yeah?" He came closer, their shoulders touching, and shrugged. "Yeah."

"Who's going to do the same for me?" He forced a weak smile.

Her own shrug was calm, her sharp gaze gliding across the fighter, but he could sense deeper emotion roiling within. And the fact that she knew he was right. His own day like this would come. Maybe not so dramatically, but some day, she'd be in danger, too. Like Jenny had been—still was. Like they all were. But some day, there'd be nothing he could do to help.

"Maybe I can play you back your own holovid," she said mildly. "I'm sure Xi has it recorded."

He snorted, the dark feelings evaporating. She had a way of doing that. "Maybe I can just play it back to myself and save you the trouble."

"Maybe." She shrugged again, still not looking at him, but a hint of a smile was on her lips.

"Don't mind me. Where were you headed?" Her hands were on the railing. He reached over and laid his on top of hers, squeezing. He was about to let go, but he didn't really want to. And he didn't have to, either, did he?

"To go give them some help." She jutted her chin toward the fighter. Then she turned and looked at him, their gazes locking for the first time in the whole conversation. She smiled, a soft playfulness in her eyes that didn't used to be there. That he inspired, he realized.

"YOU A MECHANIC NOW?"

"No, but I can pick up heavy things *and* put them where they tell me to. Sometimes, even check if a light is on. Or blinking."

"Gosh, that's complicated." He smiled. He should really let her go help. But watching Ellen and Kael coming apart at the seams, he just wanted to keep her here. Just a moment longer at least. "Ah, well, that's more than I'm accomplishing right now. Don't let me hold you back."

He forced himself to limit it to one more squeeze of her hands in both of his and then on a whim, a bittersweet kiss to her knuckles. Someday, she'd leave him, like this. And he didn't know how he'd survive it, but he also didn't really have an option in the matter.

He loved her. And he had to come to grips that the day would come when he'd lose her, too. But he didn't say that just now. Instead, a loud, raucous whistle broke through his thoughts.

Mo pulled her hand away from him, laughing, and made a rude gesture toward the center of the cargo hold. "Slag off, Zhia."

Zhia was grinning at them from beside the fighter's open hatch door. "When all this is over, Sergeant Mosi, you owe me a report."

Dr. Dremer was shaking her head, but there was an unusual amusement in her eyes. "*Commander* Verakov is mad with power already. Look at her. You're going to regret this, Ellen."

Was his face getting hot? No, it was just… unusually warm in the cargo hold that was kept scientifically five degrees colder than the rest of the ship. Yes, that was all.

Mo smiled. "*That* was a nice thing you did, too," she murmured. And then she kissed him quick and soft on the cheek and headed for the ladder.

———

NEARLY THE ENTIRE crew had cycled through the cargo hold to say goodbye. Notably absent were Kael, Jenny, and Dr. Levereaux. For the latter two, much as she wanted to go check on that situation, Ellen had to swallow the bitter pill that they wouldn't be coming.

She was already doing the best thing she could to help them. And that was to draw Union fire—and attention—away.

As for Kael… Well, she still held a hope that he'd come. Even though she'd basically told him not to. She hadn't meant don't say goodbye. She'd only meant… don't try to stop me.

But how could he not try? Was he really not going to try?

A beep on her comm brought her attention back to the task at hand. A message from Dr. Persad. *A quick note—checked the chip, before and after upgrade. All functioning normally. Hope it helps.* She let out a breath. Well, if she was leaving Kael behind, at least she knew no one was messing with him.

It was probably about Shirin. Battle was one thing when you had nothing tying you down. But he had more to worry about now. That's why he'd wanted to stop. But she hadn't listened, and now, their luck had run out, just as he'd said.

She slipped the comm back into her pocket with a sigh.

Bri was leaning against a far wall, and Mo was completing one more check inside the fighter. Other than those two, only Zhia remained. She stepped toward the fighter to stand face to face with Ellen at the hatch.

"Fighter's all ready for you." Zhia lay a hand on its side.

She nodded. "Thanks. You'll be a great commander while I'm gone. I... I know you didn't want the duty but..."

Zhia ran a hand over her white hair, then waved her off. "Sometimes, it is the season to read, and sometimes, it is the season to write." Then she pulled something small from her back pocket and held it out.

Ellen frowned. It was a book. "What's this?"

"Just a collection of poems. To keep you sane." Zhia gave her a hard pat or two on the shoulder, then leaned against the fighter.

"Well... Thank you. By whom?"

"By me. Just finished."

She caught her breath. The cover was a rich, dark blue, matte, sturdy. Her fingers tightened around the gift, then she slipped it into the outer pocket of her small bag.

She didn't receive gifts very often. Definitely not gifts like that one.

"I... I can't wait to read it. Truly, thank you." Maybe she shouldn't even take it with her. They'd probably take all her personal effects, so she hadn't grabbed much. But a book... Maybe they'd let her keep it.

There was no guarantee she'd ever be back on the *Audacity* to read it, either. Maybe she'd have to read it on the trip if she wanted to be certain to have the chance... Her throat tightened.

She held out a hand to shake. "Thank you for everything. Really."

"Aw, *jagiya*." Zhia stepped forward grinning, arms wide. "Give an old woman a hug."

Ellen laughed quietly, in spite of it all, and complied.

Then Zhia turned and waved as she headed out of the cargo hold. Mo hopped down and gave her a sharp salute, then headed out, too.

It'd have to be empty for the fighter to leave.

Bri strode back in. "If that bitch gets a hug, then so do I."

Ellen laughed, and she was still smiling as Bri slipped behind the blast doors as they drifted shut to seal the cargo hold. But the sigh she let out was shaky.

She was leaving. He wasn't there.

"Ready to begin depressurization, Commander." Xi's voice echoed in the quiet, mostly empty hold.

He hadn't come.

"Commander?"

She jolted herself out of her blank stare at the closed blast doors, her smile fading. She should have—said something—done something—differently. But she hadn't. "Xi, how long do I have?"

"Four minutes to exit the *Audacity*," came Xi's voice from her comm. "I estimate it will take at least five minutes in transit time, possibly more. Yamamoto did not say if he meant thirty minutes to exit or thirty minutes to arrive on the *Everest*. We are assuming it's the former. You must proceed soon, Commander."

Blinking fast, certainly *not* because she was upset, dammit, she stormed onto the fighter, shut the hatch, and slammed herself down into the pilot's seat. Maybe she could radio her apologies to him from vacuum.

It certainly wouldn't be the first time she'd fragged things up with him. The more pressing question was would it be the last.

Buckling into the seat, her eyes caught on a small red paper box on the dashboard. She finished the last buckle before picking it up.

Unfolding the petals of the lid, she found a slip of paper inside. *For when you most need to forgive me… I'm sorry. I just couldn't handle losing you.*

Underneath the slip of paper was the golden-brown disc of a chocolate chip cookie, two more nestled underneath it.

Her eyes burned. She damn sure needed at least one of these right now. Maybe all three. She took a huge bite and jammed the button to display the preflight check sequence onto the screen. A few more steps now.

Damn this Union ship. Damn this Yamamoto. Damn Paul fragging Dealis and whoever tipped him and his Union goons off to her location. Quentin Davenmore? Arakovic? The authorities on Faros? Kentt from the inside?

Whatever. Nothing could be done about it now.

She had to do this. But everything in her ached. She leaned back into the seat and focused on the buttery taste, the chewy crunch.

Soft chimes came from the preflight checks completing, one by one by one.

This was likely the biggest mistake she'd ever made.

But she'd run for a long time. Time to face the old music and hope she still knew how to dance. Or at least, dive for cover.

CHAPTER TWELVE

KAEL HURRIED to the passenger cabins at a soft jog, hoping his footsteps would stay quiet in spite of his rush. When he reached the hatch, he tapped the chime. It slid open quickly, to his surprise.

Inside, there was no baby Roya crawling around today. Instead, a sweaty Shirin was wearing boxing gloves and punching at pads strapped over her caretaker bot EOE8's hands. He raised his eyebrows at the scene.

"Shirin, can I talk to you for a second?"

She stopped her punching. "Sure. I was just going to get a drink, anyway."

"Didn't you hear the comm line? Shouldn't you be strapped in?"

"Well, I was. I *just* got up, I swear."

He glanced at EOE8, whose expression was idle. Apparently sparring wasn't super entertaining for a nurse bot. "Greetings, Lieutenant Dad," it said. "I can vouch that this is truthful."

He snorted. Lieutenant Dad? Probably should give the poor robot some name-clarifying instructions, but not right now. Where had they even gotten that name from?

"I can't keep sitting still." She took a swig of water, then frowned. "Is Commander Ryu really going away? Is she going to be okay?"

"She is going to try to talk with them. Could be pretty dangerous. But I... I need to talk to you because I'd like to go with her."

"So?" She tilted her head, then took another drink.

"So... so what do you mean?"

"So what do you need to talk to *me* about?"

"Well, I won't go unless it's okay with you."

True confusion flashed on her face, then recognition. "Are you asking my *permission*?"

"Yes. I know you have EOE8 and Xi, and you don't really need me. But I'm your... well, your father, and it seemed like the right thing to do. To ask." Although now, he was feeling incredibly stupid as it was obviously off the mark judging by her facial expression. But this was his story, and he was sticking to it. "If you want me to stay, I will."

She bit her lip. "If you stay, then she'll have to go by herself?"

"Yes. She's planning to go by herself anyway. I just want to try to bring her back. I certainly intend to return alive and well, but I'll be straight with you. It's possible we both might not. Probable, maybe. But I really think you're safe here. Dr. Dremer and Doug and his parents and Xi and EOE8—you have lots of people here who care and can keep you safe long term. Good people."

She took a deep breath, then walked up to him. "You can go," she said, her voice stern. "But only if you promise to come back."

He frowned. "You know I can't—"

"Promise." Her eyes bored into him with the determination of an asteroid miner. Then she punched him with one boxing glove, gently, on the shoulder. "You still need to fight with me, *Dad*."

His eyebrows flew up. Was that sarcasm or sincerity? "Spar with me," was all he could manage. "Sparring is the proper term."

"Promise you'll come back and *spar* with me."

"All right, fine. I promise. We'll both come back. Maybe we'll bring a puppy. And a glow jelly, too. And a million credits." Why not embellish if he was going to lie?

She snorted. "I prefer rabbits. I had two on Faros, and I miss them every day. But whatever, you can't have everything. In case you can't keep your promises like everybody else in the world, can I have a hug first?"

"Um. Okay?" He held his arms wide and bent down to her slighter height. Her embrace hit him like a punch to the chest, and his arms wrapped around her and squeezed just as hers did. It felt weirdly mechanical and natural at the same time, and to his surprise, she pressed her face against his shoulder for a long moment. Then she pulled away.

"It's not true, you know," she said, as she moved back toward EOE8. "I do need you."

"Then I'll have to be sure to make it back." He smiled. "But you don't need anyone but yourself in this world, and don't forget it. You have everything you need right here." He tapped her temple gently. "Goodbye, Shirin. For now."

"Bye, Dad."

And he only stared awkwardly for a second or two, failing to comprehend if there was sarcasm or sass present or what that meant, before he turned with a wave and headed for the cargo hold.

He grabbed his go bag from outside the door as he broke into a run.

Let him not be too late.

———

WHAT THE HELL had she been thinking? It was one thing to have the idea. But drifting out of the hatch of the *Audacity* into open space alone… This was another thing all together.

She let out a slow breath, surprised it didn't fog the air in front of her. The fighter was damn cold. Her bones felt cold, her toes, her fingers, her thighs, her neck. She wasn't shivering yet, but probably soon, if it didn't heat up a little. Or maybe that was anxiety sapping the blood from her extremities. Making her a little light-headed.

Kael, Zhia, Doug, the crew—they all better get away with the empress and make this worth it. If Paul betrayed her on this… she'd gut him herself, regardless of the consequences. Captain. Ridiculous. She should have guessed as much.

Her brave face still sat in place, hung there like a mask, but inside, she was dry mud, crumbling in a harsh wind.

What the hell had she been thinking?

Was it that Paul's sudden appearance had thrown her off? The constant pounding of their guns finally getting to her? This wasn't supposed to happen. She was supposed to do the impossible. She was supposed to find a way.

Some way she'd found. What a load of crap.

Heat pricked at the corners of her eyes as the fighter dove down, away from the *Audacity*, away from the three waiting Union ships. The *Audacity* wasted no time making for the gate. Good. It was exactly what it should be doing. Sure, watching the ship grow smaller made her eyes ache. And her chest. But seeing that ship go through the gate would make it all worth it.

She was leaning slowly toward the viewscreen when a quiet scuffle from the back of the fighter made her go still.

Her body tensed, listening. Some malfunction? Had some creature sneaked on board on their last ground mission? No, couldn't be. Nothing living got past the bioscan.

Everything was quiet. She twisted as quietly as she could in her seat, starting to unbuckle the first harness strap without making a sound.

The left compartment door popped open, and a head popped out. Chocolate eyes. Smug grin.

"You ass-faced, piss-drinking—" she started.

"Nice to see you, too, darlin'." Kael stepped into the tiny corridor.

"What the frag do you think you're doing here?"

"Thought you'd need someone to man the guns."

"I wish I was a Theroki, so I could punch you straight out the side of this ship."

"Ah, but that comes with so many unwanted side effects. Are you sure it'd be worth it?"

"To see the look on your face? Just once? Definitely." She scowled.

He just grinned wider. "Well, luckily for both of us, the only Theroki here is me."

"What, you didn't pack the whole damn squad?"

"And ruin our romantic getaway?"

That hit like a punch to the gut. She ducked her head. He probably still wished they'd walked away from this mess. And yet she'd insisted. She'd dug her teeth in and wouldn't let go.

And he'd come with her.

"Dammit, I am so mad at you right now," she said, even if she was melting a little.

"Have a cookie." He gestured at the box.

"I ate them all already. Didn't save you one, because I thought I was *alone*."

He laughed, his eyes studying her for a moment before his smile faltered. "Oh, hell, you really did think I wasn't going to come to say goodbye." He started to rise.

"Slag off, Sidassian. I haven't forgiven you yet."

He snorted but sank back into the seat. "Why are you really doing this? It's not just to protect the empress."

"I said, slag off."

"I saw you doing the math. There had to be something to add for one and one to make two. Empress plus *what* equals Ellen throws herself at the mercy of her enemies?"

"You see this?" She pointed. "It's my shoulder. It's cold."

"Let me rub it then—"

"It's an expression!"

"It was a joke!"

She smothered a laugh, jutted up her chin, and rotated her seat away from him. "I *said* I haven't forgiven you yet, Lieutenant."

"I'm sorry I made you think I wasn't coming. And I'm sorry I didn't follow orders. Again."

Swiveling slightly, she peeked over that cold shoulder. His gaze imploring, earnest, eyebrows raised slightly—it was enough to melt any woman's resistance. She slowly rotated back toward him.

On the viewscreen, the *Audacity* was closing in on the gate. Not long now.

"I'm not sorry I came along, though."

"Well, I'm not sorry I ate all the cookies."

"Nice dodge. I'm part of this operation now, whether you like it or not, so you might as well fill me in."

She glowered at him, then checked the screen. Partially because his stare was so intense, like he wanted to see an x-ray into her skull and finally understand what went on in there. Good luck, because she didn't understand it half the time, either. She sighed. "Fine. We need help."

"And *they're* going to help us?"

"Unlikely." She shrugged. "But more likely than any other candidate. We don't have a lot of options, and the chances of us defeating a multi-planet fleet of Theroki and telepaths with not even fifty people is also pretty unlikely. Especially since barely half of our fifty are trained soldiers. You said so yourself."

"Hey, I suggested walking away."

"Wish I could. Can't."

"Gathered that. So instead, we're doing *this*?"

"Yep, pretty much."

He let out a long sigh, somewhere between amused and furious.

"Maybe I can convince the Union to do something," she said. "It's our best bet."

"Convince *them*? To help? Brainwashing them would be more likely."

"I'll consider it."

He snorted.

"Hey, if Arakovic gets *her* way, brainwashing is exactly what they'll get. And *they're* going to need help, too. Who else can we turn to? The Puritans? They haven't been infiltrated like the Union has, so what do they care? And I also have no ties there."

"We have information and tech that could help the Puritans, and they don't want to court-martial you for desertion."

"That *is* a pro in their column."

"But they'd probably rip out both our spines."

"I knew there was something I didn't like about them."

They both watched as the gate flashed, and the *Audacity* finally disappeared from view. She realized she'd clenching the armrest and forced herself to let go and relax back into the seat. A death grip on her chair wasn't fixing any of this.

Seconds later, Adan's voice came through. "We're through the gate, Commander. Looks like we're clear."

"Stay safe, Commander!" It was Zhia yelling, but there were other voices joining in behind the ship's *new* commander that she couldn't make out. Damn it, her eyes were hot again.

"Godspeed, Ellen," came Doug's voice now. "Hopefully, you'll be back aboard soon."

"Thanks," she said, curtly. "Keep them safe. Good luck. Now get the frag away from here."

"Yes, ma'am," said Adan. "Safe travels."

The line went dead. They both sat silently for a moment. They might have sat there in silence forever, feeling any concept of home and safety slipping away from them. The grabber from the *Everest* broke the spell, though, jostling them as it took hold.

Kael let out a bitter sigh. "I know it's a bit late for this, but… Maybe there are some outsystem planets we could ally with? Mercenaries?" he said. "Planets that don't want to imprison or execute you? Or both?"

"Mercs—we no longer have the funds. We need mature armed forces. Almost every outsystem planet that's mature enough has already been bullied into the Union, or infiltrated, or—"

"Or they're fiercely independent?"

"Yes. But if they're fiercely independent enough to defy Union attempts at assimilation, do you think they'd lend me their navy for a problem I can hardly even prove is real?"

"I mean… it's for the good of the galaxy." He shrugged, smiling. "That's why we're doing this right?"

"Hah. If only it were that easy."

"I never claimed to be a political mastermind. I just hurl heavy things."

"I'll keep that on the list in case this Union thing doesn't work out."

He reached out and squeezed her hand where it lay on the armrest. "If you live that long."

"If *we* live that long." She finally met his gaze, eyes shining. "I'm sorry I can't just walk away."

"It's okay. Your iron determination probably has something to do with why I fell in love with you."

"Don't forget obstinate stubbornness."

"That's a mouthful. How about perseverance?"

She smiled. "I love you, too, you know."

His eyebrows twitched. "Really now. That's a first. Almost makes this whole suicide mission worth it."

"It's not a suicide mission. It's a strategic risk. A wise man once told me—we'll figure something out." She waved her hands in the air and tried not to feel ridiculous. She preferred a concrete, detailed plan. Briefed hours or days beforehand. But there were too many unknowns, too many variables.

"Who was this wise man? Someone in the Union, I hope? An old friend we can call on for help now that we're in deep shit?"

"It was Dane."

"We're fragged."

"Of course, at the same time, he was also telling me about the importance of lying so your whole team doesn't freak out."

His eyes flashed with his crooked smile. "Tell me more pleasant lies, darlin'."

"I can't. Looks like we're docking."

He winced as bright silvery light flared out of their docking bay, the doors yawning open for them. "Into the dragon's den we go."

Maybe he realized it might be his last chance, or maybe he was ducking from the blinding viewscreen, but he slid out of the chair toward her. On one knee, he leaned forward to press a kiss to her mouth—warm, firm, living courage. She caught his face in her hands and ran her fingers through his hair.

That kiss. He was breathing life back into her. Old-fashioned mouth-to-mouth resuscitation. The rage in her melted further and she found calm, readied for battle.

Their lips parted, but his forehead rested against hers.

"I'm still mad at you, you know." Her smile probably belied the words.

"I never want to make you mad," he murmured. "But I will, if it means keeping you alive."

"Such a romantic."

"I am starting to think so. You teach me new things about myself every day."

He wasn't alone in that. She didn't know his presence could shore up her reserve while at the same time amplifying her terror that this was a gigantic mistake.

Now she could get them *both* killed. Delightful. She covered his mouth with hers again. One more time.

The ship thudded as it came down inside the *Everest*'s bay.

They parted reluctantly, and he stood. Sighing, she flipped open the first buckle. "Time to meet some old friends."

"You know what they say about Theroki." He stepped back so she could get up, moving toward the hatch. "We love making new friends."

"Good thing you belong to me now, and not them." She kept her face straight, dead serious as she strode after him.

"It *is* a good thing." But he grinned, far more than was appropriate as she palmed open the exit hatch. "Best thing ever."

CHAPTER THIRTEEN

"THERE ARE TWO HEAT SIGNATURES, SIR." Yamamoto cleared his throat.

Paul frowned and clasped his hands behind him. The bridge of the *Everest* was tense, not only with anticipation of the new arrival, but with anxiety as three engineers tried to repair damage from a wiring fire that had broken out eight minutes ago. He'd been pacing around behind them, trying to provide moral support, but he stopped short now. "Come again? I must have not heard you correctly."

"There are two heat signatures inside the fighter. Could it be a trap, sir?"

He groped for the memory of their call. He hadn't explicitly forbidden her to bring anyone with her. "I suppose it's within the confines of what we discussed. But why? Just to get arrested?"

He'd had a hard time believing her crew was so attached to her, but apparently, it was true. One of them had refused to be shaken. Unless she wasn't even aboard… "Can we confirm at least one signature is appropriate for a human female of her size?"

"On it, sir."

Paul enjoyed a moment of self-satisfaction that his order had gone off without a hitch. Sometimes, he could really bumble them up, but that one had been a good one.

"Sir?" Yamamoto raised a finger. "Captain Ridgeway is hailing."

Paul let out a groan before he could think the better of it. Yamamoto hid a laugh behind a fist and a possibly faked cough. One of the lower-ranked crewman, Rusoe, had a small smile on his face but was trying to hide it. It was hardly first-class behavior to groan at fellow officers, but the plus side to these sorts of mistakes was that they endeared you to your crew all the more. Especially because some of them might have worked for Ridgeway, as Rusoe once had.

He waved blithely at the screen. "Fine, fine. Let us have it. I mean, let him on."

Ridgeway was yelling before the screen even fully resolved. "Dealis, you bastard! That rabbit was mine!"

He narrowed his eyes. If this was the sort of game Ridgeway wanted to play, he was up for it. "A woman is not a rabbit, Ridgeway."

"You know what I meant."

"Colonel Tauber gave us this assignment. I tracked her down first. The decision was mine."

"My ship is better equipped than your scum-bucket of rust to carry a prisoner of this importance."

"Are you planning to give her the presidential suite?"

"Is that a char mark on the wall behind you?"

He ignored the question. "Last I checked, all brigs are required to meet certain basic regulations. And they rarely exceed them. Yamamoto, do the brigs on the *Denali* have satin cushions?"

"I can't say, sir. I haven't been there myself." Yamamoto didn't look up from his console.

Ridgeway, for his part, was growing redder and redder as they spoke. He was lucky he hadn't played poker this way, or he'd have had to cheat even *more* to not lose any money. "Dealis, I oughta throw you in there myself. I know you have a history with that woman. The proper thing to do is to turn her over. Let somebody uninvolved take her in."

"That was the past, Ridgeway. This is now. Back then, she wasn't a deserter, I wasn't a captain, and neither were you. Ancient history."

"This will not stand, Dealis. I'll talk to the *Lhotse*. They'll be on my side."

"Who, Captain Weyer?" Paul let out a puff of laughter. "Be sure to call our war hero a rabbit. That should win Weyer's alliance right off the bat."

Ridgeway curled his lip. "Hell, Weyer got that damn ship? No wonder they gave her that death trap. It's barely sturdier than a pile of leaves in a dust storm. That ball buster listens to proper protocols even less than you do."

"This *is* the proper protocol, Ridgeway. My mission, my assignment, *and* my right of first arrival. You've got some gall to lecture me about that. Did they not let you spend enough time playing around in debate class or something in Academy?"

Ridgeway huffed. "At least I went a full four years."

"Pardon me for being deployed in an emergency." A beep came from the console, and he caught Yamamoto's eye. His second gave him a slight nod. "And yet, it doesn't seem to have hurt me because there is Ellen Ryu entering my docking bay right now." He grinned.

"Fine. I'm following that damned ship of theirs then."

"No, you're not. I gave them my word."

"You can't stop me—"

"Just because this ship is a piece of junk doesn't mean it doesn't have brand new 5Ms, Ridgeway. Don't make me fire some test shots."

They glared at each other for a long moment before Ridgeway relented. "Fine, fine. Have fun with your fool deserter. The real glory is at Freedom's Wing anyway. I'm hauling out."

"Godspeed," Paul said, for as much as he wanted to wish the man ill, something seemed too off about the mission for him to do it in good conscience.

The comm channel cut, the screen going blank.

"Scans of the ship show it's standard issue, sir. No large ordinances. Two passengers, one clearly Ellen Ryu."

"Tell my staff to meet me there," he said.

Time to go meet an old friend. One who knew all the worst parts of him and hated him for it, deservedly so. If only Ridgeway knew that having a "history" with the prisoner was only going to make this mission harder for him, not easier.

"Keep an eye on Ridgeway," he added as he reached the hatch. "He says one thing... but he's likely doing another."

FOUR UNION OFFICERS waited for them outside the hatch. None of them looked particularly friendly.

Beyond their welcome party, dozens of charcoal-and-maroon-colored uniforms stood watching. Six small spacecraft stood ignored, in various states of repair. The place had none of the usual hum of a docking bay—the clinking, the drilling, the sparks, the buzzers clearing people out for liftoff. All that had stopped, and all attention had turned to the new arrivals.

Kael found one of the Union folks particularly interesting, though.

For all the trouble Paul Dealis had unknowingly caused him, he wasn't sure what he'd expected. A bumbling idiot? That wouldn't have captured Ellen's attention. A preening narcissist masquerading as a military commander? That seemed more likely. And he wasn't ruling that out.

But precision and command radiated from Captain Dealis. Just his air, the angle he held his chin... They put Kael's senses on alert. Dealis might be a fool or an asshole—likely both—but he would be no easy adversary.

He was a little tall, and his hair was raven black and perfectly trimmed, just as it had been in his file. His impeccably pressed uniform hadn't been adequately captured, though. The epitome of clean-cut military decorum and competence.

How did they expect to get out of here alive again?

Three aides stood at Dealis's side, tablets clutched to their chests.

They were armed with pistols, but not a one had the mien of someone who'd actually drawn them as their tool of choice in battle. Or in any situation, really.

A short, serious-faced woman was scribbling with a stylus, black hair in a severe bun. Silver frames perched on her nose, a tiny blue light winking in the corner of one lens. Info frames, not just visual augmentation.

The second aide was brimming with a friendly smile; he had bronze skin, a button nose, and a shock of dark red hair that was no natural human color but coordinated perfectly with his uniform. Enthusiastic, or enthusiastically rebellious? Didn't a traditional military have dress codes against that sort of thing? Maybe they made an exception for the team colors.

Not that *Kael* had ever abided by any dress code, so he wasn't one to judge. You can't wear a tattoo wrong, especially if they carve it on without your permission. The Theroki dress code was mainly "try to get all the blood off."

The third aide was eyeing them both hard. He had clearly styled himself in Dealis's image, too—black hair, clean cut, blue eyes, perfect military decorum. While the other two scribbled, his eyes darted around, eating up information.

"Commander Ryu," Dealis said, raising his chin. Everything about the gesture was respectful, which was a little bit of a relief, even if disrespect would have made it easier to hate him.

And Kael was definitely determined to hate him.

"Captain Dealis," she replied with a nod.

Kael forced himself not to search her face for hints of a reaction to seeing Dealis again, allowing himself only a glance. Staring would be stupid; it would reveal too much, and she likely wouldn't show even a silver of emotion, anyway. Even in his single glance, her face might as well have been made of stone. An unchanging mask for an unflinching warrior.

She was in wartime mode now. He knew the rush of battle, the rage of blood lust. But she had something else, something cold, steel-nerved, deadly.

Her acknowledgment bolstered Dealis, as he straightened a bit in response. Surprised, it seemed. "This is my personal staff. Lieutenant Shu, are your scans complete?"

The woman adjusted the glasses, even though they hadn't looked out of place. "Yes, sir. Nothing dangerous. Extensive cybernetics in both parties."

Dealis raised his eyebrows.

"Would you like me to pat them down for you?" the suspicious, black-haired one said.

"No, thank you, Lieutenant Bridell."

"I wouldn't trust those scans implicitly, sir; they could have the know-how to hide something." Bridell's eyes narrowed as they locked with Kael's.

He glowered back at the man.

Dealis sighed, his eyes flicking toward the ceiling briefly. "Fine—Shu, Bridell. Pat them down. Ensign Mertz, signal our escort."

Mertz appeared to be the cheerful, maroon-haired one, who waved across the docking bay and then happily took the tablets of the two who stepped forward. Bridell's pat-down was aggressive and peppered with glares and pokes.

He couldn't bring himself not to smirk down at the slightly shorter Bridell. "You're not going to find anything." He had nothing on him but the clothes on his back.

"Yeah, like I'll take your word for it," Bridell blustered.

Lieutenant Shu, on the other hand, was blushing red as a hull-breach alarm. She kept her eyes on the task, stopping and pointing at one cargo-pant pocket. "I'm going to remove this."

Ellen shrugged, staring straight ahead.

Shu drew out a small book, flipped through the pages. "What is this?"

"Poetry."

Bridell snorted loudly and half-turned away, although he was clearly enrapt with whatever Shu might find. Shu looked to her captain.

"I never knew you had such a… romantic streak," Dealis said, eyes glinting. "Poems by whom?"

Now it was Kael's turn to snort.

"A crew member." Ellen shifted her weight, meeting the captain's gaze. "It's just for comfort. It would mean a lot to me if I could keep it. She meant it to console me in dark times."

"Well, this is a dark time for you, if I ever saw one." Sighing again, he held out his hand, and Shu handed him the book. He flipped through it quickly, then thrust it back at her. "All right. But nothing else. Give you something to read in the brig. Complete your search, Lieutenant."

Cheeks reddening again, Shu finished her pat-down and backed away, grumbling at Bridell as she accepted her tablet back from Mertz, "I hope you're happy."

Bridell looked like he'd eaten a lemon and ignored her. The four young soldiers summoned by Ensign Mertz approached.

"All right, then. You are under arrest for desertion," Dealis said. "You will be tried by a military tribunal in the Inner Planets. Your… associate will also be placed under arrest for aiding and abetting your desertion."

Two of the young soldiers stepped closer, fresh-faced and jittery, with steel cuffs that glittered with lime-colored, lighted indicators in a dozen places. Now it was Kael's turn to tense up. He'd been expecting it, known it was coming, but it still didn't feel great. He could have batted both kids aside in a breath. He could have knocked the cuffs out of their hands. Better to keep that secret, though, for when they really needed it and so they kept security lower, if they could. But he indulged in visualizing it a little while they locked the cold cuffs in place in front of him.

Watching the other young soldier lock the cuffs around *her* wrists, though? That called for upper-cutting the kid into the docking-bay ceiling. Hey, visualization was stress relief, right? Somehow, it didn't seem like Dr. Taylor would approve of these specific choices of his.

Still. Kid's head would probably leave a massive dent.

"Aren't you going to introduce us to your associate?" Dealis asked.

Ellen's nostrils flared slightly. "This is Lieutenant Kael Rhee. My second-in-command."

He bit back a laugh. He never had picked a new name. No one had. Asidian and Sidassian were probably splashed all over the nets. And it didn't look like Elle would be winning the award for plausibility in naming, either. Shu looked closer to hailing from any planet with a family named Rhee than he did. But he nodded, as graciously as he could.

Dealis nodded back. "If you would, Commander, Lieutenant, I would like a discussion with you in my conference room before you are escorted to the brig."

"Of course, Captain," she said smoothly. "Lead the way."

He tried not to smile at the civility of it all as Dealis and Lieutenant Shu led the way, a cheerful Mertz and a scowling Bridell falling in behind them. That wasn't where Kael would have preferred them. It made his shoulder blades itch.

What a fragging farce. Pomp and circumstance and politeness, like a damned parade that moved out of their docking bay and into nondescript steel corridors, past unnumbered doors. He spotted more than one or two spots of corrosion, burns from lasers and repairs, dents in hatches. One soldier took a ladder to another floor, clearly unsteady and clanking the whole way.

These people would do whatever they wanted with him and Elle once they were in the brig. Hell, they already could. And what was he going to do about it? Bash them into a wall? He'd only have a shot or two at that before they sedated him. Or shot him.

If they didn't already know what he was from that scan.

What exactly was his plan again? Letting Ellen leave alone had been unthinkable. But how exactly was he planning to save her if the Unionies simply separated them and punted him out an airlock?

Of course, there was nothing stopping them from putting an immediate bullet in both their brains, but no one had pulled out a weapon yet. Although by the studious look of Dealis's staff, they might not actually know how to do that.

The more burning questions to consider were—how could he stay by Ellen's side long enough to protect her, if that was even possible? And how the *hell* was he going to remember to answer to 'Lieutenant Rhee?'

CHAPTER FOURTEEN

DOUG LOOKED up from his work to see Zhia stepping inside the hatch.

"Okay, so how do we find out where they are taking them?" she asked.

"Ready to mount a rescue already, Commander Verakov?" he said as he started pulling the charts he wanted to show her into the air above the holodesk. "Already on it."

She snorted. "I will do whatever it takes to be in charge for as little time as possible."

Smiling weakly, he leaned back and waved her toward the desk. "You're the most experienced person we have. And well-qualified to lead us."

"In everything except ambition." Her own smile widened as she strode closer. "Got something to show me?"

"Yes, ma'am. This is where they are." He pointed at the tiny red dot on the star chart. The *Everest* hadn't traveled far from their original ambush, although it was in motion.

"How do you know that?"

"They brought our fighter on board their ship. I put a transmitter on it. Well, several transmitters." He shrugged. "I don't think they've even bothered to sweep it, because they haven't even disabled the decoy I put in a really obvious place."

"This is…" She leaned closer, then straightened. "Good work. This will be invaluable if we're going to help them."

He raised one shoulder, then lowered it again. "Don't congratulate me too much. If I was that good, I'd have kept this from happening in the first place."

"Now, none of that. We look forward. We're going to need all our attention if we're going to figure a way out of this."

"Yes, ma'am," he muttered, since it seemed like she was waiting for him to say something. Even something sheepish and grudging.

"If it's all right with you, I will call the team to the briefing room to figure out what we will do next."

He nodded. "Of course. You don't need approval from me for anything."

"Maybe not, but I appreciate it, anyway." She took a step toward the door.

"Wait—there's something else." He swiped all the star charts away and brought up the video he'd spent far too much time analyzing.

"Is this a still from the vid feed? From Aeori III?"

He nodded. "Look at this enhancement. There's a reflection here behind Arakovic."

"What is that?" Zhia leaned forward. "Looks like heavy armor. Uneven shape. Is that… a Theroki?"

"Yes." He scrubbed the video forward. "It's a Theroki that comes in with the second woman—Cassandra. And that's who hauls Arakovic off screen."

Pointing a finger, she traced the faint outline of the forms in the reflected glass. "So… so what?"

He paused, trying to figure out how best to put it so she'd believe him. "I've listened to it a dozen times. Okay, maybe dozens. She says 'Why haven't you found me already,' over and over. Like she's goading us. Like that's what she wants us to do—find her."

"But why would she want that?"

"Well, she might want the empress," he said, spreading his hands. "But look at this." He scrubbed to where the gauntleted hand closed around her arm, pulling her out of the frame. "Look at her face. Does that look like a woman setting a trap to you?"

Zhia frowned. "No, it looks like a woman about to piss herself."

"I agree. It looks like fear."

"You think this is a genuine cry for help? Not just a trap?"

"Actually, I do. Could be both."

"She doesn't deserve our help." Zhia folded her arms.

"Agreed. But it tells us something. Who is in charge may not be who we think."

"You think it's this Cassandra character?"

"Yes. The hive mind."

"So maybe Arakovic is in trouble. It could still be a trap."

"If it is a trap, it won't be easy to just sneak in. Check this place out." He dropped the video back to the desk surface and pulled up the satellite feeds he'd found on the system coordinates. "Here's the system."

"But that's all asteroids," Zhia said. "Dozens of them. Hundreds maybe."

"Yep. If they are where they say they are… their facility must be inside one of these asteroids. Or floating among them. I think that fits with what the telepaths found in the memories, too."

Zhia blew out a breath. "But it doesn't make it easy on us. We show up, we have to sort through a haystack looking for a needle."

"Sort through a what?"

"Never mind."

"We'll have to be a lot closer to do real sensor analysis to find the asteroid that's got a thousand people inside it rather than just rock and vacuum. I mean, most of them aren't big enough, but there are at least ten candidates I can see from just this partial feed."

"We'll be sitting ducks."

"Unless we can think of some way to camouflage ourselves."

"Need dynacamo for the hull. Get to work on that, will you, genius?"

"I'll add it to the list, Commander," he said, his tone wry.

"I thought as a commander, I get whatever I want."

"You do. Within the laws of time and physics."

She grinned. "Well, we're not going there without Ellen and Kael. Not yet, anyway. And we need a resupply."

"You're reading my mind. And… if we're going to be sitting ducks… there might be a few people we need to relocate to another ship." Like his parents. Among others. He tried not to wince. Jumping jellies, hopefully she knew what he meant.

"This has never been a mission without risk," she said, "but I agree. We need everyone on board to know what they're getting into. And get a chance to catch a different ride."

"I look forward to your meeting. Do you want me to put any of this together for a briefing?"

"Yes, but not for this first meeting. I want them focused on the *Audacity*. She needs our TLC right now."

"TLC?"

"Tender loving care. Repairs. Fuel. Goods. New equipment, if we need it. Once we're en route to a restock, we can start planning our jail break."

He raised an eyebrow. "Jail break? That ship is locked up tight. Actually, I think someone else has recently hacked into their system, because it's not standard Union stuff locking me out. Something strange is going on there. Especially given that it's an old model, nothing state of the art."

"If Ellen and Kael are still alive—"

"You think they'd kill them that quickly? Shoot on sight?" It sent a chill through him. Kael had *just* been here. It hadn't even been six hours.

"Some would. Do I think Captain Dealis would? No, but I'm not certain. Anyway, if they're alive, the *Everest* will have to take her to trial. There will be transfer points. Transfer points mean weak spots. An opportunity to strike. Maybe get them back."

"This is why you're in command and not me, my friend."

"Also, I doubt that one little ship will take them all the way to the

Inner Planets. They may transfer them to another ship. Possibly a bigger, better defended one. Could be an opportunity to intercept them. Could also be an opportunity to miss the transfer. We've got to track them carefully. At the very least, they'll need to refuel likely as often as we do."

"I can work on confirming their safety." That sounded better than 'figure out if they're already dead.' "And if that doesn't work, those weak spots sound like a good next step."

"Excellent." Zhia gave him a crisp nod. "Glad to have you on my team, sir."

"Right back at you, Commander Verakov." He winked as she strode out.

———

LIEUTENANT SHU SILENTLY INDICATED A CHAIR. Ellen slid into the offered spot, propping her forearms up on the edge of the table so the cuffs would always be visible. Just so nobody'd forget that and get too comfortable.

In spite of Ensign Mertz's cheerful air as he and his perfect maroon hair shut the door to the conference room behind them, they weren't having a fragging picnic here. She was risking her life.

From Paul's smile as he slid into the seat at the table's head, though, you wouldn't know it. His other staff members took their seats. Kael dropped down into the seat beside her, rarely taking his eyes off Paul, and then only to spare a glance at the grumpy Bridell.

Paul's smiling gaze never wavered away from her. Internally, she couldn't help but roll her eyes. Some people never did change. Even as she thought it, his smile broadened, like it would have if she'd said that aloud. Beside him, the blue light in Shu's glasses twinkled yellow, green, then blue again. She was getting transmissions—what was so timely?

"Well, well. Ellen." Paul's gaze briefly flicked to Kael. "And second. I must say, I am *so* glad I am the one that finally got you."

Her own expression hardened, but she held her tongue.

"I'm sorry, my staff should be more hospitable. It's not often we get visitors who aren't diplomats or suppliers. Criminals still deserve a drink, too. Can I get you anything?"

"No." She blinked. Slowly. "Thank you."

One of his eyebrows twitched in amusement. "Well, I suppose you're wondering why I haven't simply hauled you off. The answer to that is I have questions. Lieutenant Yamamoto had some questions, too. I must start with the one that's weighed on me the most all these years. Can you guess it?"

She blinked again, even more slowly this time. She never went along with his little games of wordplay. He should remember that much.

His grin widening told her that he remembered just fine. He didn't wait long for an answer, although his staff twitched and tensed up at her lack of response. "I always wanted to ask you… Why? Why'd you do it? We can start there."

She dropped her gaze from his eyes to the cuffs, to the table beyond them. She said nothing.

"It never made any sense to me. Still doesn't." He cleared his throat and waited, the pause pregnant.

As the moment lengthened, she finally relented, shrugging one shoulder. "The situation then didn't make sense to me, either."

"I want to know," he said mildly, leaning back. "What leads a hero like you to turn your back on a lifetime of service?"

What could she say? If she just blurted out what had really happened, he wouldn't believe her. Her shoulder lifted and fell again in half-hearted response.

"Was it money? Did you get bought out? Was that it?"

She kept her eyes on the table and hoped he couldn't see her gritted teeth, the way her shoulders tightened.

"Perhaps a pregnancy."

That comment made her head snap up reflexively and she shot him a look, meeting his surprisingly sincere, earnest eyes. "Did you really think—just—" She sighed and lowered her head. "No."

"I know it can be hard to admit fault. It's certainly not one of *my* strengths. But everyone knows the military life isn't an easy one. Perhaps you just couldn't take the pressure anymore. The itch for freedom? God knows we all joined up so young. We never had a childhood to speak of."

She nodded slightly but didn't look at him.

"The court martial will take your motives into account, you know. And this is on the record, if that is your preference."

She said nothing.

He leaned forward a little. "Or it can be off the record."

"It doesn't matter."

He sighed, throwing up his hands, though not with much vigor. The gesture was calculated. Put on. "I always thought you took duty seriously."

"I did." She met his blue eyes now, still the same striking shade, like pool water. "I still do."

"Then what was it, Ellen?" He leaned closer, holding her gaze with his now.

Beside her, Kael shifted, tensing. She pursed her lips. Paul wielded the power of his physical presence, his visual charisma, like a weapon. And it was not a delicate one, trying to flatter her, to draw her out of her shell with that inner magnetism. It had worked once. He had to know it wouldn't work now, after the ass he'd been.

Maybe he didn't even realize he was doing it. That had never really occurred to her, but older and wiser now, it seemed somehow obvious. She held Paul's gaze a second longer.

"There's no good way to bring up the past," she said slowly. "And it's not changing anything. We can't change the past now. I made my bed. I'll lie in it. So stop asking."

He smiled faintly, multiplying the charm rather than backing off. "You're the only one I let give me orders, you know."

It took all her effort not to glower at him. Beside her, the armrest Kael was leaning on suddenly creaked—and bent.

"Oh my gosh, are you okay?" the red-haired Mertz started, sounding more than a little amused.

"Oh, yeah. I'm just peachy," Kael replied.

"What in the seven suns. I've never seen an armrest just... break out of nowhere like that."

Kael narrowed his eyes. "I'm fine."

"Suit yourself, sweetie." Eyebrows raised high, Mertz went back to work, scribbling on his tablet. How much was there to fragging scribble? If this showdown between her and Paul were any more of a draw, a tumble weed would blow by.

Paul's smile grew wider. "I didn't mean to startle anyone. I just have a simple question. Give me a simple answer. Why?"

"Why do you care so much?" She let the words take on an edge of irritation. If he was going to keep poking at her, he should expect to get slapped. Verbally, of course.

"I've had five *years* to ponder this question. If you think I'm giving up my quest for the answer in five minutes, you're wrong."

"I can withstand five hours of questioning. You know my training."

"Ah, I do." He laughed lightly. "Certainly, you can tolerate even five days of my mild questioning. You're trained for a lot longer than that. But has your training truly prepared you for me?"

"What, and how annoying you are?"

Bridell smothered a snicker at that.

"Precisely. The Puritans are one thing. But five weeks of this smile?" He flashed it even brighter. Wait, did he *know* he was being annoying? "That I am more doubtful of. Lieutenant Shu, are there any regulations on how quickly I need to rush *Ms.* Ryu to her trial?"

She gritted her teeth at the "*Ms.* Ryu," but she wasn't going to let him get to her by reacting to something so juvenile.

His aide pushed her glasses up on her nose and answered without raising her eyes from the tablet. "If a trial is scheduled, six months would become the limit, but no trial can be scheduled until you report Ms. Ryu's capture in the first place, sir."

"Oh, come now," said Bridell. How weird that he looked like a little mini-Paul—and sounded like one too. "We all know Captain Dealis is a fine, upstanding commander. He would *never* hesitate to report his noble deed, his great accomplishment to higher command. Certainly not for any kind of personal gain."

Shu glared at him through her shiny silver glasses, her nose crinkling in too obvious distaste. "Information acquisition is hardly personal gain; it is a logical and prudent intelligence activity. One that can't be done very well under the scrutiny of the press, either." She turned her eyes back to Paul now. "It's also possible higher command would grant extensions if emergency outsystem operations were to arise based on your intelligence gathering."

Paul nodded, his smile wide and his eyebrows slightly raised. The vacant expression in his eyes made Ellen seventy percent sure he had no idea what either of them was talking about, nor did he really care.

"I'm sure this capture will be excellent on your record, Captain," said Bridell. Ellen squinted at the rank on his shoulder—a junior lieutenant. Figured. He had something to prove. Goodie. He certainly seemed to have Paul figured out, and not in a good way.

"A more detailed confession is not likely to influence your professional advancement," offered Shu, again without looking up from her tablet.

Now Paul chuckled. "Wise and pragmatic as always, Lieutenant. But I want my personal curiosity satisfied, most of all."

The strange tilt to the words made both Kael and Mertz twitch.

"That... that's not what I meant." Paul sighed, then folded his hands behind his head and leaned back in the chair. "I just want an answer. As you can see from my staff's... very detailed answers, I can apparently justify five months of this. At least! I may have to take you with us on some dangerous missions... and delay shore leave for the crew. But I'm sure they won't mind."

Did he really think three months from now she'd be wasting away in the brig, enduring endless days of this showdown, clutching some juicy secret and determined to take it to the grave? Long enough for him to have to employ crew pressure and mistreatment to get it out of her? Luckily, torture was as bad an offense as desertion, if not worse, and had been for over a century now.

Then again, if the project that had practically driven her mad wasn't on the official books… what else wasn't on the books?

What a load of drama. And for what? Why did it matter? What kind of reason did he *think* she had? Maybe he just didn't like that question hanging out there. That's what he kept saying to her. No explanation made sense. He must think her confession of some scandal, dark op, or human depravity was just at the tip of her tongue, waiting to spill out.

The truth was going to disappoint him. If only she could say, "Yes, Paul, I ran off to sow my wild oats, make billions of credits as a merc, hunting down my enemies for fun!" Okay, maybe a few of those were closer to the truth than others, but none of them had been the catalyst. The truth was mundane.

The silence in the room had shifted, as if they had all sensed she might say something now. Their eyes were on her. She bit her lip, straightened a little. "It's not like you think. It isn't so interesting. I just didn't want to die for nothing."

He raised an eyebrow. When she stopped, he said, "Do go on, Ellen. Can't you see we're on the edge of our seats?"

"Is this some kind of entertainment for you?" she snapped. "Well, it wasn't for me. I would have *happily* given my life for the Union, for my people, but not—" She faltered. Not for science? Not for bad science? Not for her body to live on as a hollowed-out shell of her former self? A wraith, in essence? A ghost?

The blank eyes of Udo, their zombie John Doe, flashed through her mind.

Her mind had been her greatest gift to the Union. To kill that and leave the sausage casing behind?

It made no sense. It wasn't serving the Union to let that happen. It wasn't serving anybody.

Maybe it was just blind, stupid pride that had driven her out. Some Puritan bullet wouldn't have known or cared whether it was the brain or the sausage casing it was destroying, it would have destroyed her just the same, and she'd have called it valorous. A worthy sacrifice.

She dropped her head slightly. Let out a long, slow breath.

"Look up the Songbird program," she said softly, her voice rough. "That should tell you what you want to know."

Mertz and Shu redoubled their furious ministrations on their tablets. Bridell only frowned harder.

Paul, for his part, jerked his head back like he was dodging a punch. The warmth vanished from his posture, and his eyes had suddenly gone sharp, eagle-like. "What do *you* know about the Songbird program? That's all classified."

She went still. "What do you think *you* know about it?"

"I know plenty. Shu, inform intel we have a leak—"

"You don't have a leak."

"If you are aware of classified Union information available for sale, you are required to divulge all details immediately." Bridell leaned forward.

"Nothing's for sale." She glared right back, defiant now.

"If you want to avoid further charges, you'll come clean with us," Paul said, voice mild as he held up a palm toward Bridell.

"I already came clean by showing up."

He wasn't mollified, though. "If you're so *clean*, then why are there so many black-market bounties on your head?"

"Because I didn't stop punching bad guys just because I had to run from the people I trusted," she snapped. "Turns out, bad guys don't like to be punched."

"Just tell us exactly what you know," Paul said.

"Slag off. I told you, look up the program. I'm not saying anything else."

Paul folded his arms. "Suppose I actually bothered to do that, how would I know what you've discovered and what you haven't?"

"Fuck if I know, Paul." She did roll her eyes now. "That's not my problem."

The minute it slipped out, all three aides straightened in surprise.

The corner of Paul's mouth quirked, but he didn't let up. "I want to know what you know exactly. There will be consequences for disobeying my direct orders."

"I'm not giving away my intel to you for nothing. Give me something in exchange."

"In exchange?" He laughed, incredulous. "And I should give *our* hard-won intel to a *deserter* and a criminal? One already in my custody, for that matter?"

"You know I wouldn't do anything with it." If their familiarity was obvious, she might as well appeal to it.

"No, I don't. I don't. I don't know *what* to think about you anymore."

She pressed her lips together. "Just look up the program then," she said coolly.

"I don't need to look it up." He straightened in his chair. "Every Union officer is familiar with the Songbirds. Brilliantly familiar. We have extensive intel."

The edge to his voice was a bit gratifying; she was getting under his skin. He usually kept himself from complete bluster like that.

At the same time, the words gave her a chill, too. Had they kept the program *going*? What if they too had been indoctrinated? What if Arakovic was just one phone call away?

Her blood pounded in her ears at the idea. Facing death or imprisonment? She'd mentally prepared herself for those potential consequences. But being sucked back into the hell she'd fled...

No, no. It couldn't be. They didn't *act* like a Songbird unit. They were individuals, with clear personalities and preferences and—Mertz's red hair and—

She forced the panic down. Her gaze stayed locked with his for a while, both their eyes hard. Irritation poured off Kael, radiating like heat from a star.

In the end, Paul blinked first. "You both face life imprisonment at best, death at worst. Especially after *this* showing of cooperation and goodwill, neither of you is ever leaving Union custody. There might be hope for a happy ending for your lieutenant here. If he plays his cards right, he might survive and one day be freed. For example, if *he* were to offer up what he knows about the Songbird program at the appropriate time..."

Kael smirked. "Sorry, Captain. But that's her story to tell."

"Leave him out of this," she cut in.

"Then tell me what *you* know instead. What could an intergalactic terrorist group founded after you fled have to do with your desertion?" His eyes widened. "Unless you're the founder?"

"Oh, for frag's sake, no!" She kept her face hard, but inwardly she winced. He was getting to her, too, now. She had to get control back.

He scowled, and she deserved it. These comments were way out of line to either your captain or your captor. Not the smartest moves she'd ever made. The three aides were fully on edge, with Shu exchanging a subtle glance of surprise over her glasses with the young Mertz.

"Wait." Kael sat up straighter in his seat. "Founded after her desertion? That's not right, is it—" He stopped short as their eyes locked. Realizing he shouldn't have admitted to anything specific?

Ellen seized on it instead. The proverbial pit dragon was out of the bag. "There. You want quid pro quo? We'll trade intel. We'll even start. The Songbird program was definitely founded before my desertion." They'd already given that much away, anyway.

The staff was scrambling. Bridell was shaking his head and had even dug into his tablet, too, now. "That's not possible, sir. That's— not what the—wait a minute."

"Our intelligence reports date back four years at maximum," said Shu.

"Fine. Quid pro quo." He ground out the words, slow and precise, lobbing the information at her like rocks. "The Songbird group is an intergalactic terrorist conspiracy working to destabilize planets and planetary systems. The group seeks to infiltrate and replace governments with members of its own program. It is somewhere between a political movement and a cult—possibly both. We believe it has been funded and encouraged by the Puritans, either in whole or in part, to further destabilize us and other enemies. They began with smaller, less stable planets but have since moved up to attacking—and taking control of—larger governmental systems. Now—your turn."

"They've even taken Capital," she said smoothly.

He scowled harder, which she hadn't thought was possible, but there it was. "Lies. Rumors. And that will not pass as your part of this exchange."

She put her elbows on the table and steepled her fingers, since it was one thing she could do with the cuffs still on. "They do it all using cybernetically-linked units coordinated by telepaths as an attacking force."

Paul went still, as did the aides. "You really do know about it."

"The telepaths conduct infiltrations," she continued. "Spies and similar. They use forbidden telepathic techniques to gain control of key governmental figures."

They were all sharing glances now.

"I'm right, aren't I?"

"How the hell do you know all that?" grumbled Paul. "Definitely inform intel we have a leak."

"You *don't* have a leak." She shook her head. "We figured it out on our own. Through personal experience."

"That's dog spit, and you know it. And I still don't see how it could have anything to do with your desertion. This better not be misdirection, Ryu. I know you're good enough at it."

"C'mon, I know specifics. Give me some credit."

"I never fail to. But how would you even *encounter* the Songbird program?"

"You'd be surprised," she shot back. Kael snickered, and she couldn't blame him. She had a feeling that 'surprised' was going to be an understatement.

"What are you snickering at?" Paul glared.

"Nothing, sir." Kael gave Paul an admirable smirk, but at least he added the *sir*.

"Your turn," she cut in. Bad idea to let Paul notice Kael too much. She couldn't even quite say why, but she just had a feeling that the more Kael faded into the background, the safer he'd be.

"*That* was your trade?" Bridell's gaze flattened. "That you know what the program basically consists of?"

"Captain Dealis said he wanted to know where the knowledge overlaps are. Well, there you go."

"Enough, enough." Paul cleared his throat. "I'll also share that the terrorist program is coordinated somewhere in the outsystem near the Plycon Nebula."

She raised her eyebrows.

"You didn't know that."

"Nope."

He sighed. "Well. There. Trade's fair, then. Your serve, Commander." He smiled, looking like he expected an objection. But also like he was enjoying himself.

"I also had first-hand knowledge of the program to help me know all this," she said.

"First-hand knowledge of what?" Paul demanded.

"Of the Songbird program."

"You deserted us for that *cult*?" he snapped. The red-haired ensign's mouth dropped open.

"No," she said slowly. "They forced me into the program against my will. While the program was still under Union control."

The rest of their mouths dropped open in unison.

Paul snapped his shut first. "Ridiculous. You're making this up now because you're out of factual information."

If he really thought that was true, though, he'd have laughed and thrown her in the brig. He wasn't moving.

"Where do you think they got the technology?" she said mildly. "Cybernetics research is extremely expensive. Those researchers are paid well and in high demand."

"Cults typically have ways of manipulating their followers into funding their activities." Lieutenant Shu shifted the glasses on the bridge of her nose.

"Their stuff is cutting edge. State of the art. Not some hobbyist starting a mods club in their local space-station rec room."

"How do you know how sophisticated they are?" He narrowed his eyes. "Or are not?"

"Where do you think they developed it? It wasn't the Puritans

—you have that wrong. *We* developed it. Union scientists. I was one of their test subjects, Paul. They *made* me become one. A Songbird."

His eyes widened. "I *always* knew you could read my thoughts too well."

She scoffed loudly, before she could stop herself. "I'm not a Natural telepath—" She had to bite off the *you idiot*, but it was very, very challenging. "They installed networked telepathic add-ons into me after a heli crash where I was injured. They forcibly connected me to my unit. Telepathically. It almost drove me insane—drove many of us insane. People died. We were losing who we were and just becoming one big… hive mind. *That's* why I left. I couldn't let that happen. I couldn't die for… for nothing. As someone's guinea pig."

He blinked. "You… that doesn't…"

"I'm *not* lying. I told you you wouldn't believe me. But you said yourself, how else would I know all that? How would I know any of this?"

He glanced at his staff. Shu shrugged. "We have some research to do, sir."

"I want that redacted location," he started. "And that file."

"What redacted location? What file?"

He ignored her. "We need more details. It is need-to-know now. And I want to know who exactly posted every single one of the bounties on Ryu and from what location. Don't take no for an answer, you hear me—"

Yamamoto's voice came over the comm suddenly. "Captain, we are approaching wormhole jump for the reward transfer. Do you want to be present on the bridge?"

"Ah, yes. Be right there." Paul frowned. "Maybe there's another stop for you before the brig, after all."

———

ADAN HAD BEEN HOLDING his breath for what felt like hours, and he'd thought this would be the moment he could release it. But staring at her, he found himself holding it again.

The long, plexi cylinder glowed in a dim corner of the sickbay, reddish fluid sloshing, bubbles drifting from the bottom to the top. Jenny floated inside, eyes closed.

He had rushed straight here from the bridge, as soon as he could, but now that he'd made it, he was frozen in front of the tank. He'd raised his hand to touch the cylinder, but stopped just short, realizing he didn't know if that would be okay. He didn't know if anything was ever going to be okay again.

Was it water? It was hard not to make the connection between the sloshing red liquid and blood, but he knew it *wasn't* that. It couldn't be, right? It was too clear, too thin.

He swallowed hard as footsteps shifted behind him. When he finally found his voice, it was rough, groggy.

"Is she going to be okay?" he asked.

Dr. Levereaux was standing at a display, studying something. He didn't really want to think about what exactly. His heart was already in his throat—and pounding twice as hard as normal. She held up a finger as she squinted harder for a moment, then straightened.

"Do you want the long answer or the short answer?" she asked.

He bit his lip. "Uh. Short?"

"Yes. She is going to be okay."

He frowned. Maybe that was too short. Maybe he really wanted the in-the-middle story. "She… doesn't look okay."

"Oh, she's not."

"All right, fine. Long answer. Give me the details. But try to spare me a heart attack or two, okay?" He wasn't sure he could handle the details, but he needed more than just *yes*.

"I think one patient is plenty right now, thanks," Levereaux replied. "She's going to be fine, because we have great tech here. But if we didn't, she would not be. The corrosives actually weren't the worst of it. They got into the suit with the leak along with the water, which diluted them a lot. There's some minor burning on her left calf where the suit leak was and where the concentration was strongest, but nothing we can't heal with some topicals and grafts if needed."

He frowned. "Wait—that sounds pretty bad. What was worse than the corrosives, then?"

"The water itself. More specifically, the pollution in the water. Mercury and lead, a few other chems. I can't identify one of them, which is concerning, but it appears similar in structure to the other heavy metals. It looks like damage from this contamination destroyed the civilization that was thriving here at one point. I've got more about it in my report to the commander, but the toxins are concentrated around this facility."

"Frag. What—what does that mean?"

"It means Arakovic and her Songbirds may have caused the pollution and the ecological damage here. Because of the concentration, she sustained a higher than average exposure for this planet's overall toxicity, not that you care. We're applying several treatments to flush the poisonous levels from her system. I've also deployed some nanos to seek out and repair any cell damage or lead her cells might have tried to store. The body mistakes lead for calcium so it can shuttle it away to all sorts of places. It gets hidden in the bones. The nanos can't get one hundred percent of damaged cells, but hopefully they'll get enough to prevent too much long-term damage."

His heart was flipping in his chest. Doing somersaults. "Hopefully? What happens if we're… um… unlucky?"

"Hard to say. It increases the likelihood her cells in the future might go wrong and mutate, particularly in cancerous ways. But she can cross that bridge with lots of treatments when she comes to it, if it ever even comes up."

"Ah. Okay." That didn't really reassure him, but it didn't sound like the reassurances he needed would ever be possible. At least not till they were old and gray together, sitting around in an orange grove somewhere, muttering about the too-hot weather. Maybe then he'd sit back and muse that the mercury and lead of that stupid old ocean planet hadn't ever come back to bite them. Maybe by then, he'd have forgotten the name Aeori III, instead of cursing it like he was now.

That image, sitting by the orange trees… that did reassure him a little. Levereaux said such a thing might be possible. Would be likely, even. So he shouldn't worry. Living a life like this, they'd surely get themselves killed long before that, but… It was a fun idea. He knew he would never be willing to give up the stars, even if he could someday afford an orange grove. Which was highly unlikely at this point.

"Was that enough information?" Levereaux smiled. How long had he been lost in thought? "Or was it too much?"

"I… I'm honestly not sure at this point. Sorry."

"No, I'm sorry. Try not to worry, okay? She's in good hands."

"Okay."

"Anything else I can do for you? Otherwise, I'm going to check on the lab results at my desk."

"Can I… can I touch this?"

She smiled. "Yep. No danger in touching the tank."

"Thanks. That's all."

He lowered his head as she walked away. What right did he have to her time or answers here, anyway? He and Jenny had never exactly been subtle or private about things between them, but it wasn't like they were wearing each other's rings.

Lifting one hand, he pressed his palm against the tank. It was surprisingly warm. Something in his chest tightened as he looked at her, really looked.

She was so still. So unmoving. "Hang in there, baby. Hang in there."

Perhaps old and gray were out of the question, but other parts of that fantasy should be acted on sooner rather than later.

He swallowed hard. He'd literally run here after his shift. He should go get some food, and pee, and sleep. Come back and check on her before his next shift. Twelve hours off sounded like a long time until you needed to do all your basic functions within that window.

But he knew that for at least a few more minutes, or hours, he wasn't going anywhere. Hand still pressed to the tank, he brought up his comm in his other hand and started searching.

Who could sell him some plants? Or at least oranges? They'd have to refuel soon. Maybe he could find something wherever they stopped. Soil was expensive as star dust on a space station, but maybe if they found a moon, he could find a tree. Or maybe he should think of something else...

The warm, red healing chamber was a mix of reassuring and alarming, the liquid sloshing away beneath his fingers. He leaned against the tank, wishing he was leaning against her, and searched.

CHAPTER FIFTEEN

DESPITE THE SOMBER tone that had settled over the *Audacity*, the next day, Xi's circuits were buzzing with excitement. Because soon, it would be briefing time.

Xi loved briefing time. And also lunch. Breakfast and dinner too. Perhaps it was a little presumptuous and maybe even premature to adopt the word 'love' for herself and apply it to briefings, but… when the human crew gathered, well. There was so much to learn.

Of course, she was always observing every crew member every moment of every day. Every spot of the *Audacity* had sensors within reach, and Xi was almost always recording.

And of course, some portion of her processing power was devoted to plans to rescue Kael and Ellen. More than a few cycles were spent missing their ideas, their direction, their presence under her camera-encrusted wing.

But she looked forward to today's gathering, anyway. It was possible for her to be both excited and sad at the same time. She had the processing capacity.

When the crew clustered together, though, it was such a wealth of data to analyze! The myriad group interactions! The personalities that emerged in social dialogue that could not be observed in solitude!

It was possible that it was the crew she loved, not just the meetings, but they did not always interact with her in the same way. She was an interface. A button to push. To some a more person-like entity, to some almost equal intelligence. But when they got together, there were so many more colors of interactions to observe.

It was enough to put her on the edge of her proverbial seat waiting for the meeting to commence.

Perching on a seat edge seemed like a precarious position and an odd thing for a human body to do, but she tried it anyway.

When one's body was as difficult to acquire and build as Xi's, she liked to be cautious, so she only tried the edge-of-seat-sitting for a moment or two before returning to a more optimal position.

Her prototype had taken extensive experimentation and many hours of planning and construction, but now that she had a body of a sort, was it prudent to casually balance it on the edge of a ship chair in the robotics closet?

Just for fun?

No, it wasn't just for fun. She was learning what it felt like to be a human. Or at least an android in a human's image. It was for *science.* Her relational models for interacting with sentient beings would be vastly expanded by the countless number of new interactions she might observe. But it wasn't time yet. For now, she just observed from a distance, her body no more than another one of her drones that happened to be online inside the robot-repair station. But soon, she'd find something more, some greater purpose. She just didn't yet know what that would be, beyond her own scientific pursuits and education in human psychology.

When the briefing time came, all of them had crowded in around the white sparkling table, apparently forgetting they'd really grown too large in number for the room. Ellen had been moving them to the cargo hold.

Alternatively, another hypothesis suggested the cargo hold—

empty of its fighter—was too glaring of a reminder of the negatives of their current situation.

"Commander Verakov," Doug said, smiling crookedly. "Never thought we'd be saying that right now, but it has a ring to it."

Zhia's returning smile was tinged with something Xi couldn't yet compute. "Thank you, sir. I also enjoy my own name."

"That's nice and all, Commander," Nova said, kicking her feet up on the table, "but how are we getting the commander back?"

"First things first, Nova." Zhia cleared her throat. "We have large repairs to make. We're low on supplies."

"But they're getting farther away every—"

"We can't help them if we're falling apart. I'm all for getting Commander Ryu back as quickly as possible—and Lieutenant Sidassian too—but I think—"

"Wait, what?" Rachel sat up in her seat. "Sidassian went with her?"

"Yes, he did," said Doug, with a certain odd hardness to his eyes directed at Rachel that Xi didn't quite understand. Rachel often muttered to herself in her cabin about certain interactions that had not gone quite as planned, and she seemed to regret that others saw her as hard and cold, or at least she thought they did. Xi often marveled at the considerable amount of energy a brilliant woman like Rachel Levereaux spent on trying to figure out interactions that seemed to come naturally to crew members with considerably less educational opportunities or credentials to their names.

Nova practically spat on the ground but settled for some enthusiastic gum chewing. "That ass-faced pisswizard. How could he not say goodbye to me? Did you know about this?"

Zhia narrowed her eyes. "I did."

"And you allowed it?"

"He didn't ask. But I wasn't Commander Verakov then. I am now, however."

Nova opened her mouth, but stopped short, seeming to read something in Zhia's expression. She frowned and folded her arms.

"How is Jenny doing?" Mo asked, from a back corner where she stood, arms folded.

Zhia sighed. "She's alive. Not recuperated yet; she's been better. She'll get there."

"Jenny was exposed to serious heavy metals and other pollutants in the water," Rachel put in. "We can treat it well, but I've reviewed the scans with the others. The environmental contamination seems to have been originating from the facility you visited. In other words, Arakovic and her people are probably the source. I want to make sure you're all aware of this. We need to be extra cautious about environmental contaminants on future ops."

"Thank you, Rachel," said Zhia. "That's just one more reason we've got to get back on our feet, in fighting shape. That said, we all know that we can't run back into a fight we just lost. We have limited funds. So repair and resupply will be our first order of business."

"Might I make a suggestion?" The room went quiet as all eyes turned to look at Etrianala Kentt, where she'd raised one finger in the back of the room.

"Of course," Zhia replied.

"We appear to have been cut off from most allies, other parts of the Foundation," she said. She waited a minute, and no one disagreed with her.

"There might be a chance we could contact other Foundation cells," Doug said. "But at the moment, we won't know if we can trust them. What's your point?"

"One potential ally we have not tapped has occurred to me."

"I find it amusing you're calling us 'we' now," Nova said. "Are you a member of this crew?"

"I'm a passenger, and I'm also looking to have a word with Dr. Zeta Arakovic, so I do not believe the pronoun to be out of line."

Nova popped her gum, a grin on her face that did not appear to be sincere. "Yeah, we'll see."

"Please continue, Ms. Kentt." Zhia shot a glare at Nova.

There was a sixty-eight-point-two percent chance that Nova would stick her tongue out at Zhia next. This was a gesture Xi was very far from comprehending, but this particular time it didn't happen. This was both disappointing and disconcerting. Why was *this* moment in the thirty-one-point-eight side of the occurrence? Was it random or causal? What a mystery.

"What ally?" Zhia said.

"The telepaths I helped to hide from the Songbirds," Kentt replied. "I, of course, know where they are. They are committed to a path of nonviolence, but couldn't they potentially help? It seems as though we could use any help we could get."

Doug pursed his lips, thinking. Zhia frowned.

"How do we know we can trust you?" Adan said slowly.

Kentt's head dipped slightly. It might have been disappointment or sadness expressed, but Xi was still not certain of that particular emotional model. So many variables to capture... so much work to be done. Such a wealth of data she'd process later. "I don't suppose you can know that you can trust me, aside from that I certainly have had opportunities to betray everyone before and I haven't taken them."

"How comforting," Adan grumbled under his breath. "How do we even know they can help?"

"If the hive mind absorbs all telepaths, then it is effectively a single mind with significant power. That still means it will make one decision at a time. If we had enough telepathic power, we might turn their own tricks against them, or at least block them in—it is a complicated procedure I shouldn't waste your time explaining. It is uncertain that we would have enough power at our disposal. But it would certainly be more than we have now."

"They ran from the problem, didn't they?" Adan raised his eyebrows slightly.

"Yes, but they had no allies then, other than me—"

"But you were pretty powerful on Capital. Enough to get them away."

"And it doesn't matter what happened then, because they cannot run forever. If the Songbirds get their way, they will expand to every corner of the galaxy they can reach. There will be no running from them then. This is our best chance."

"So you say. To find people only you know about to do a procedure you might be able to do and won't explain." Adan folded his arms.

"I didn't *have* to save your life, you know." The tone seemed no different from any other, but many eyes turned to Kentt as she gazed at Adan.

"You must admit that the timing of this suggestion is a little unusual." Dr. Dremer leaned forward onto her elbows on the table. "The minute Ellen Ryu is off the ship, this becomes a priority? And yet you never mentioned it before this moment."

"I didn't think…" She sighed. "Commander Ryu is eminently capable. I assumed if she thought the services of a dozen young telepaths were necessary that she'd tell me. I mentioned that I knew their location to her, but not to Commander Verakov. I thought she should be apprised of her options."

Dr. Persad cleared her throat. "Since everyone on the crew now has their telepathy-blocking add-ons—at least, everyone that is going to receive them—there is certainly less risk that a group of unknown telepaths could do us any harm."

"They wouldn't harm anyone, anyway," Kentt said, a note of distress in her voice. "That is the real risk, that they still might choose not to help in their pursuit of nonviolence."

"Where are they? How far?" Zhia's expression was flat, any hint of humor gone for once. A rare occurrence. Was this caused by her assumption of the commander rank? Xi furiously recorded extra details.

"I… I'm not sharing that unless we are actually going to go get them. I hope our trust will continue to grow, but I hope you can understand that this is not yet an alliance of complete trust on either side. You've made that clear enough. And the first thing I did aboard your ship was identify a traitor."

Zhia's expression hardened. "That spoke well of you and less well of us. But if your friends are back on Earth, it's going to change our plans. We need to know where they are roundabouts. And what they might contribute."

"They are not as far as that, Commander. As to what they might contribute… I cannot be sure. I don't know if they've been studying their craft. I encouraged them to study the defensive arts, in case our plan failed or they were eventually discovered. It is possible, if they've studied, they'd at least be able to keep other unscrupulous telepaths from attacking or influencing them. If I had adequate time, I could teach them the procedure I mentioned, but that seems doubtful."

"Can they attack with those fancy mind powers?" Nova quirked her eyebrows with a crack of her gum.

Kentt scowled. "It's forbidden to use such abilities. Many wouldn't even know where to start."

"But surely, *you* know how to—"

"I most certainly do not," Kentt snapped. Her heart rate and temperature had dramatically increased, Xi noted. "It's forbidden. Forbidden, as in other telepaths will murder you for it. With *poison*, not fancy mind powers. We cannot afford the public to fear us as all-powerful and aggressive, or they will wipe us out."

"I think somebody forgot to give Dr. Arakovic that memo," Doug said, smiling.

Nobody laughed.

Zhia stood to get their attention. "Thank you for bringing up the option, Ms. Kentt. We must find a port first, get supplies. On the way, we can debate our options, including Ms. Kentt's, in further detail."

"Thank you, that's all I ask."

"Xi, what options do we have for refuel?" Zhia said.

Her circuits hummed. "Not as many as we usually do." She checked her probability list. "I believe the following ports would meet an acceptable level of risk. Please be advised that Ellen and I recently increased our tolerable risk threshold due to a lack of available options at our former settings."

Doug winced.

"Options include Horus XII, Molyarch Station, Setiro Moon, and Helikai."

"Wow. Those are some posh options." Nova pursed her lips.

"Every one of those is desolate," drawled Catherine, Doug's mother. "Or crawling with lowlifes. Darling, isn't there *something* better we could try?"

"There are worse options," Xi said instead. "I excluded the spots favored by bounty hunters."

"We *are* the lowlifes, at this point, Mrs. Simmons," Zhia replied. "At least as far as bounty hunters and certain established governments are concerned."

"Oh yeah, didn't Genius here earn a target on his back?" Nova said, grinning.

"He didn't *earn* it," Mo said, unusually quickly. "Unless you count pissing off assholes as earning it."

"Oh, I do." Nova's grin widened. "Badge of honor, sir." She gave him a mock salute.

Zhia smirked. "There is… that. And even if Ellen and Kael aren't with us, there's still a bounty on our ship. The Union will likely issue something related to our ship's capture, on top of the already existing bounties."

"But they agreed to let us go," Xi said.

"They did." Zhia nodded. "They also lie."

Xi's body in the robotics lab frowned. Options for surveillance of Union ships burst across her mind, and she started pulling up the data. Tracking signatures—none detected. New bounties posted— none of those were found on the usual boards. Yet.

But could they have been followed? No ships were immediately identifiable as Union… If she correlated the lists between their last several wormhole jumps with other ships that had also jumped within the right time approximation… How long should the window be? How many jumps mattered?

The search didn't require much experimentation, however, because it quickly yielded a result. One small ship had jumped within thirty minutes of their last jump—for every single stop since they'd escaped.

But they hadn't escaped, had they. This small ship was tailing them.

"I have identified a ship following us," she said from the ceiling in the briefing room. "Based on our discussion, I investigated transit logs and found a ship that has joined us for every jump since Aeori III."

Zhia threw up her hands. "There you go. That's the Union I know."

"Let's ambush them!" Nova sat forward, pounding one fist into her other hand. "Sit outside the next gate, get the squad to get some big rocks, and—"

"You know we do have weapons systems, right?" Zhia held up a palm. "At this point, we can't afford another battle without repairs. And the Union is only pursuing us on association with a deserter. They might give up if we are hard enough to catch. Or even if we just take a little too long. If we attack—or destroy—a ship full of Union soldiers... Well, that is a different level of priority, don't you think?"

Now, she *did* stick out her tongue. "Well, we gotta do *something*."

"I'll start an ident-key rotation," said Doug. "Might help throw them off."

"Might not. They still know our make and model. But we keep moving. Maybe we go faster."

"Can we find some tough jumps?" Doug asked. "Maybe we can lose them?"

"Immediate analysis presents no quick victory," Xi replied. "But I will begin plotting the most complex course options I can."

"We gotta stop sometime," said Nova.

"And if we haven't lost them, we'll be ready for them." Zhia's face was different, harder than Xi ever remembered seeing it.

"How much time do we have?" asked Doug.

"Depends on the course we select," she replied. In the robotics closet, she sighed and ran a hand over her face. This gesture achieved nothing and seemed to be entirely pointless, but all humans seemed to do it. The why was what she longed to understand. It would have been an appropriate expression of the exhaustion the crew felt. Since she couldn't feel exhaustion, she had yet to decide if she should really mimic such gestures.

But for now, she was trying them out. Finding out what a human felt like.

It felt a little silly. It felt like a mess. A random, disconnected, irrational but predictable mess.

Her current hypothesis was that this sensation was possibly quite accurate and that she seemed to be doing something right.

"I would estimate one week maximum before restock," her machine-self said into the briefing room. "More complex routes will shorten the time."

"Let's try Molyarch again," Zhia said. "We've been there before, albeit with fewer bounties on our heads. They haven't seemed too concerned on previous trips, though."

"What's on Horus?" Doug asked. "Xi, why'd you put that on the list?"

"Your cousin resides there," she replied. "And he is actively speaking out for you in the news feeds. He may have his own motives, and scrutiny of you around him may be increased. But he is hardly without funds. He could possibly restock us more thoroughly than a hasty docking at Molyarch, but with greater risk."

They had very few funds to purchase such supplies and fuel, but Xi had been built not to let that stop her. They would just have to liberate some more funds from the types who'd stolen their wealth in the first place. That, and she could optimize to profit from minor market fluctuations over the course of a few days and create funds that way. It was… somewhat the same thing as the former option.

"God, what is he saying? I haven't talked to him since I was thirteen," Doug muttered. "Let's not start with him. I agree with your assessment, Commander."

Zhia nodded. "Molyarch it is. Between here and there, we sprint to see what we can do to lose them. And we will talk about what we can do to save Ellen and Kael."

"Preparation of course options commencing." Xi left the room of nods and quiet murmurs, letting herself sink into her calculations. She had plenty of work to do.

———

IT WAS a good thing these cuffs were comfortable, because it looked to Ellen like she might be paraded around the whole ship with them on. The brig was starting to sound like a relaxing break.

Walking onto the bridge with them, however… Something about that was extra uncomfortable, like they glowed with a heat everyone in the room could feel.

There were new instruments, but the bridge was largely the same as the last one she'd been on.

What ship had it been? Oh, it didn't matter. It hadn't been hers, and that had been okay. Ground teams were always shuttled around on larger ships. Boots on planet had always been more her style.

She hadn't planned on ever being on a ship this size again. She hadn't planned on contemplating a sea of Union uniforms or furtive glances.

She hadn't planned on remembering.

Remembering while also being reminded how things had changed was even weirder. Kael's wide eyes beside her were proof, though. Sometimes, things change for the better.

"Can you believe this insanity?" he whispered to her.

"What? What's insane about it?"

"All these people, and no blood on the walls at all." He gave her a wink. "Uniforms with no moss or burn marks or…"

"They're trained to be civilized. Sort of."

Paul turned to nod to a lieutenant that approached. "Lieutenant Yamamoto, may I present to you Commander Ellen Ryu and her lieutenant Kael Rhee."

"I believe we've met," he said, with a hint of a smile. Yamamoto turned out to be a slight Japanese man with an intense gaze and the most perfect upright posture she might have ever seen. He seemed like he might need some time to relax. Yamamoto bowed deeply, then straightened, to look between them. "Both Korean?"

"Not exactly," she muttered. Rhee was a common name at home, another form of Ryu at times, and it was common in the Union, too, which was why she'd picked it. Of *course* they'd run into other people from PAS right away who would notice it was a poor choice for a man who clearly hadn't had ancestors sailing the Pacific. "It's a long story. You know how things get blended." She started to wave a hand and jerked against the forgotten cuffs. Scowling, she dropped both hands.

"Indeed…" He nodded and bowed slightly again. From his tone, he wasn't buying her explanation. He fidgeted nervously for a moment, and Paul frowned beside her. Was this… not Yamamoto's normal mode of operation?

"Something wrong, Lieutenant?" Paul asked.

"Sir, I… I know Ms. Ryu is a deserter and a criminal in our custody, but if I may…"

Paul snorted, but she had the impression he knew something she didn't. "What, do you want an autograph?"

Yamamoto's face reddened slightly. "No, sir. I just… I would like to offer my gratitude, if you consider it appropriate, Captain."

"You've earned that much latitude and more," Paul replied. "We likely wouldn't have apprehended Ms. Ryu without your handling of the situation. Of course, you may offer your sentiments to her, if you wish. It doesn't change anything about our stance on her later actions."

"Of course. Of course, sir." Shoulders relaxing and a slight smile on his lips, the lieutenant turned his attention from Paul toward her. "Commander—Ms. Ryu, my whole family still lives in the Pacific Alliance Systems. I just… I want, no, I need to thank you."

"Thank me?" She frowned. "Just doing my duty, Lieutenant."

"Duty changes nothing. My grandmother and my great-grand-mother and her grandmother, who reside in PAS to this day, instilled in me that we must offer gratitude, especially in this case. Whatever happened afterward, I am grateful for your heroism in defense of SHR. They have lived great lives, thanks to you." He bowed deeply now.

Whatever hardness she'd been stocking up melted out of her as she returned the gesture. Yamamoto meant his thanks sincerely, but the words stung just the same. Maybe even more than she could have expected. She swallowed, throat tight.

Once, times were simple enough where doing the right thing meant doing what she was asked. Following orders, putting one foot in front of the other. Tackling the challenge right in front of her. And yeah, it was hard and fragging complicated, but it hadn't involved betrayal and facing down the fact that life could be full of corruption and lies and people using you for their own ends, which weren't always good ones.

That simple world was long gone, though.

"You're welcome," she said, irritated to discover her voice was rough. "You honor your family. But I was just doing my job, same as I'm sure you would have done."

Yamamoto sniffled a little—did he have a cold?—and glanced over his shoulder as a comms officer called to him. "Looks like we're almost there. It is an honor to meet you, Commander Ryu."

"You as well, Lieutenant." She glanced at Paul as Yamamoto was moving away. "Are you sure you want me here for this? Shouldn't you just throw me in the brig?"

Paul's eye twitched. "You'll stand here and face your fate. Just as we all will in our time." In spite of the harshness of the words themselves, his voice was mild. Canned, almost.

"What are we doing?" she asked.

"We're paying the reward for your capture. The lucky tip came from someone only a few hours' journey from where we found you."

"How did you find us?"

"Someone spotted your ship. Nothing fancy. And that someone gets the reward. Well, part of it."

She frowned. "Only a few hours. Just one jump?"

"Yes."

"They were that close by? That's pretty… convenient." Something swirled heavy in her stomach, some misgiving that she couldn't quite put her finger on. "Why wouldn't they come after me themselves then?"

"Yamamoto and I had the same question," Paul muttered out of the corner of his mouth, not taking his eyes from the screen. Did he sound suspicious? "But if you noticed, you weren't exactly easy to catch."

"Are you sure this is…"

The wormhole released them, the soft glitter in her eyes flashing past, then fading.

"Ship hailing," said the comms officer. "Looks like our contact."

"Bring up video first, so I can assess," Paul ordered. "Don't open the audio channel yet." A face materialized on the view screen.

"Quentin Davenmore?" she blurted. "*Quentin Davenmore* is your informant?"

Paul raised an eyebrow. "What did you do to piss him off?"

"Oh, I don't know, what did we do, Kael?"

"Let me think," Kael said. "I believe you said it was… oh yes. We stopped him from starting an international banking monopoly. Killed his co-conspirator. Ruined his plan to extort and abuse planetary governments throughout the galaxy."

"Yeah, that was it. Something like that." Ellen grinned mirthlessly. "Our hard work seems to have really paid off for us."

Paul's face had gone pale. "Wait—what?"

"Comm channel ready on your command, sir," said Yamamoto. "He's blustering over what the holdup is."

"Impatient, don't you think? My, my. All right, then. The prisoners will remain silent. Open the channel." Paul shook off his surprise, settling into his official mode. He even pasted that damn diamond smile on his face, his voice automatically cheerful. Asshole should have been a diplomat or something. "Video and audio feeds."

Davenmore's voice came over the comm. "Greetings, Captain. Did you find her? Did it work?"

Paul gestured to his side to where Ellen stood beside him. "The Union thanks you for your cooperation, Mr. Davenmore. I won't neglect to mention it to my brother, Senator James Dealis, the senior councilman from Rena V. Would you still prefer to receive the reward by drone deployment? If so, we can begin the transfer now."

Beside her, Kael flicked his eyes toward the ceiling before shaking his head. Yeah, like Davenmore needed the credits.

Davenmore cleared his throat, almost uncomfortably. For a man getting a payday, he didn't look pleased. "Fine, fine. Of course. So that's the little runt, huh? Hardly looks like a war hero, if you ask me."

"I didn't, and I'm not," Paul said, tone hardening. Wow, he'd switched from his 'favors to the senator' to his 'watch it' tone in record time. Was this what witnessing a triple solar eclipse felt like?

Was Paul Dealis actually capable of being something *other than* obsequious to someone with wealth and power? Heaven forbid.

She didn't think he'd ever had any qualms, corruption or otherwise. But right now, whether it was because of honor or war memories or some shred of something he still felt for her, he wasn't tolerating Davenmore's sneer.

"If you'd never seen Ms. Ryu," Paul asked, "how did you come to know her location?"

"By her ship." Davenmore laced his fingers together and grinned. "It really doesn't take a genius. Even if I am one. Details about its description have been available for weeks. I knew that the coordinate destination might interest her, and I watched the station two jumps before that one. Only so many ways to get to this horrible, desolate little corner of the outsystem, anyway."

"How did he know that coordinate would interest us?" she whispered. Both Paul and Kael twitched slightly, seeming to hear her.

"Clever. And so brave of you." Paul's voice was less than enthusiastic. Almost sarcastic. Was he... was he pissed off on her behalf?

"Thank you," Davenmore said, with too much pride in the words. A man used to being congratulated as a matter of course. "All right then. Just be done with it. I'd like to witness justice being served, if you don't mind."

Paul's brow ceased. "You have, sir. The deserter is in our custody. Thank you again, and your reward can be delivered by drone deployment now as you requested. Or if you prefer, credit will be instantaneous. We're awaiting your credential information."

Davenmore waved a hand in the air, still smiling. "That reward is pocket change to me. If that. Execute your duty, Captain Dealis. Or does your senator uncle need to know that you get squeamish about delivering justice when the criminal is fresh-faced and female?"

Paul's face flushed bright red. "I beg your pardon. I am following the orders of the admiralty."

"Orders you wouldn't be able to follow if it hadn't been for my information. And my ingenuity. You owe me."

"You have no right to request anything in this situation, Mr. Davenmore, aside from the reward owed to you. Which—if it's mere pocket change—I suggest you donate to a charity. I can recommend several. In fact, considering you haven't given us any payment information, I believe that shall be our starting point for the funds if you continue to refuse to cooperate."

"I can read the law as well as anyone can." Davenmore leaned closer to the screen, his black eyes sparking as his anger bled through. "The punishment for desertion in wartime is death. It is your law. It is clearly written."

"He doesn't have an ax to grind or anything, not at all, so definitely listen to him," Ellen muttered.

"Shut up," Paul snapped under his breath. Louder, he said, "The law also demands a court-martial in certain situations, Mr. Davenmore, and the location of her desertion is what determines the wartime status. That is not up to you to determine, but a military tribunal, which the admiralty has called."

"How hard is it to determine a location? She deserted. You've been at war for twenty years!"

"Harder than you would think," Paul said, straightening. "Cease fires occur all the time. Given her previous—and very young—

service to the Union, a court-martial has been called. While I appreciate your concern on behalf of justice, what you request is not within my purview at this time nor—"

"Not within your *purview*?" Davenmore sputtered, then burst into mocking laughter. "Not within your purview! What a weak-willed, limp—"

"That's enough, sir."

"This isn't justice. Execute her. You can't do this! You have to—"

"No, Mr. Davenmore, it is not within my power to—"

"Oh, yeah? It's within mine."

Ellen frowned. What the hell did that mean?

The feed cut, slamming the screen back into a multi-panel view of the space around the ship. Davenmore's yacht had vanished, though, its large green hull missing from any of the views, not even receding into space. What, had he invented teleportation?

"What the..." Paul frowned.

"The sensors—something's wrong." Yamamoto was near comms. His eyes weren't on the visuals but the readouts on the consoles, frantically scanning.

"Information systems breach, sir," said a younger officer beside him. "Moving to activate additional officers. Working to expel the threat."

"What does that mean?" Paul demanded.

"Sensor data unreliable, sir!" Yamamoto was running back to the command-center terminals.

A small silver glimmer on the viewscreen caught her eye. Was that a buoy? A satellite?

"How long till info sec expulsion?" Paul asked. Nobody answered him. "Other systems breached or only sensors?"

"I'm seeing anomalies in shields—" someone started.

Her breath caught in her throat. No, he hadn't discovered teleportation. He'd just used something far more basic, if complex in this context... A hologram, projected from something much smaller. The silver glimmer was no buoy.

"Canon turret, eleven o'clock!" she shouted, pointing. One arm jerked the other arm along like a marionette due to the cuffs.

A chorus of swearing erupted.

"Sensors, can you verify?" Paul snapped. "Shields, direct focus forward."

"We can't verify anything, sir. We can't see—"

A tiny red spot glimmered on the silver frame. "It's heating up," Kael said, under his breath.

"I can't see what it's doing over here!" someone shouted.

"Shield controls not responding, sir."

"Six operators online. At least six intruder programs running," yelled someone else.

Her eyes flicked from Kael to the turret, to the crew, to Paul, who'd rushed to Yamamoto's side. They were all focused on the hack. And if the ship hadn't been there, who knew if the turret was really there? The sensors were supposed to tell them that.

Except while they were waiting to get the sensors back online, they were going to get hammered.

"Evasive maneuvers!" she shouted. "Turrets mean evasive fragging maneuvers!" Who gave a monkey's ass if she had no authority to yell anything?

She was no one's CO, but that didn't seem to matter in this case. Heads snapping up, they listened, as best they could. Some systems weren't responding. The ship jerked hard, fighting to turn.

"Yes, evasive maneuvers. Get us some distance—" Paul put in. Engines flipped into reverse, throwing off his balance. He grabbed for a wall handhold.

They didn't flip fast enough, though. Nothing was truly instant on a ship this size.

The blast array fired—and hit.

The ship was already tilting erratically, trying to back pedal. The impact shook the deck underneath them, and they jerked to the side, but grav didn't let up—

She tried to keep her footing, but her arm hit the deck hard, then her head. Fragging cuffs. No great way to cushion her landing with them on.

The bridge tilted further, or maybe that was grav blinking out—hard to tell with her head spinning. She squeezed her eyes shut, trying to stabilize.

God, everything was red. Her stomach was in open revolt, and half her joints were screaming. And that red in her eyes—oh. An alarm blared. It wasn't just from the impact. Forcing her eyes open, she discovered a lovely mechanic's view of the weapons console. Warning lights were flashing—that was the incessant red.

"Hull breach, Sector Three," a computerized voice announced. "Fire, stage-two intensity. Three crew adrift."

Adrift. God.

She rolled and scrambled to her feet, clawing her way up the back of a seat.

She scanned the wreckage. A full meter away, Kael had pulled himself to a seat, shaking his head left and right and rubbing his temple. He glanced up when he felt her gaze and gave her a slight nod. There was a worry in his eyes, though, and some instinct told her the nod was hiding some injury or concern. He wasn't trying to stand up, which was probably the wiser strategy, considering the grav was stuttering in a way that could make the most seasoned sailor's stomach turn.

Paul had ended up closer to the hatch. He'd slid when he'd gone down and must have collided with the frame. Half his face was scraped, dripping red with blood from temple to jaw. And he was still sprawled flat on his back, eyes closed, the angle awkward.

"Medic!" She scrambled toward him. Better let them handle their own head injuries, especially where *he* was concerned, but she needed to check. "Officer down! Officer down on the bridge! We need a medic!"

"You—keep away from him," Yamamoto snapped as he gripped the commander's chair, getting to his feet. He must have gone down, too, but she hadn't seen it. "Medic *now*. Taking the bridge. Info sec status."

"Intruder repelled. Assessing damage," someone replied.

She stayed frozen where she'd been when Yamamoto had barked the order, crouched a meter away. Narrowing her eyes, she could see Paul's chest rise and fall slowly. Not dead, at least not yet. The blood pool was large, though, and growing. And the stuttering gravity wouldn't make the flow of blood loss as predictable as in normal grav, so it might be even worse than it looked. Damn, was the whole back of his head open?

Let it be just a scrape. He was an idiot, and maybe an asshole, but he didn't deserve to die. He'd just been doing his job like the rest of them. A job that had brought him after her, and she'd brought him here.

Into a trap. Nobody cared about the *Everest*. If they investigated, that wouldn't be a Puritan cannon. That cannon had been there for her.

"Shields status." Yamamoto had clasped his hands behind his back, looking calm and ready. Right. There was a battle to fight. She shifted her attention to the viewscreens; staring at the blood wasn't going to heal him.

"Raised," the computer replied. "Power ninety percent in most locations."

Yamamoto looked like he wanted to curse. Or kill someone. "What about at the breach?"

"Ten percent, but the error that caused them to lower has been corrected."

"Must've been multiple impacts," Yamamoto grumbled. "Gutier-rez, are the robots deployed for our dead?"

Ellen winced. Right. With a fire and a hull breach from that laser cannon, there was probably no saving those people. People that were dead now because of her.

"Robots deployed, sir," Gutierrez was saying. "Fire-suppression system activated. Damage isolated to Sector Three. Blast doors are down in Sectors Four, Five, and Seven."

The hatch slid open, and the medic team rushed in, so she backed off to make room. She scanned the bridge again—Yamamoto had vacated comms, but there was a second officer at the station. Targeting, sensors, the engineering liaison—everybody was fully staffed and then some. They didn't need her.

But maybe they needed Kael?

"Lieutenant Yamamoto," she said, "is that cannon still operational? Is there still a threat?"

"Sensors—status on the cannon," Yamamoto demanded.

"Unknown. Our forward sensor arrays are not responding, sir. Trying to get a read from aft, but there's interference. Teams wiping and reinstalling and—"

"Damn it, Janvier, get a visual instead." Yamamoto was shaking his head. "How many seconds since it fired? Those things have a reheat time."

"Reheat time is likely ninety seconds," she called as she crawled toward Kael. "Maybe seventy-five if it's fancy."

"It's still there." Kael kept his voice low, bending his head toward her as she slid to a seat on the deck beside him. "Pretty sure it's operational."

Yamamoto's eyes were on them, hard as little points of granite, but he said nothing.

"Can you reach it?" she murmured, turning her head away from the lieutenant.

Kael nodded once, sharply. "Should I?"

"Nobody else needs to die because of me." She glanced over her shoulder at the team tractoring Paul onto a levitating gurney.

"It wasn't your turret," he said. "Fuck Davenmore."

She propped her elbows on her knees, bringing her cuffed hands to her forehead, hiding. Hey, she *had* bumped her head in the fall. She had an excuse. "They might notice if you hit it. But good people might die if you don't. Up to you."

He closed his eyes, pain creasing his features.

"Aft sensors show an active probe, Lieutenant. I'd estimate thirteen seconds before—" Janvier faltered.

The viewscreen had been filled with the sight of the silver laser cannon as the sensors team worked for better and better visuals. And now, they all watched it abruptly spin, tip like it'd been knocked upside its head, and then shrink away into the distance.

"—before we solve our cannon problem?" Yamamoto finished Janvier's sentence as he turned to squint at her and Kael. "What a coincidence that the turret got blown away by that passing solar wind."

She kept her gaze flat, peeking out between her cuffed wrists.

Letting out a breath, Kael rubbed his temple. "I think I need a nap. Or maybe for them to just kill me already. My head…"

"You heard them, we get a court-martial."

"*You* get a court-martial. I don't think you can court-martial somebody who never served."

She waved a few fingers. "Details."

Yamamoto's eyes were still trained on them, but every other officer was focused on their battle stations. Meeting the lieutenant's gaze now, she lifted her chin, as his stare showed no sign of stopping. "Indeed. Lucky that solar wind came through."

"How fortunate for all of us." Yamamoto turned back toward the viewscreen, hands still clasped behind him. "That solar wind saved Union lives today, we should all be grateful to it."

Janvier was checking and rechecking every control at his station. "No other cannons detected in the area, sir. I don't detect any solar wind, sir, unless—"

"I believe that terminal is going to need an entire diagnostic overhaul. Please put in a requisition, Janvier."

"I've already requisitioned this three times, sir. They don't even make the parts for it anymore. They sent me a bolt, that was it."

Yamamoto sighed. "Then improvise. The *Everest* deserves our best."

"It sure does, sir. It'd be a lot easier to give her my best if I had one of those candies you're always chomping."

"Whatever it takes, Janvier. Here." Yamamoto produced a handful of bright candies from his pocket, and the comms specialist trotted up to get one like a happy dog earning a treat. "Everyone else, focus efforts on repair."

The medic stood up beside Paul. "Ready to transport, sir."

"Excellent. If no one else needs any candy, I'll be escorting Captain Dealis to the sickbay. Gutierrez, you have the bridge."

"I have the bridge, sir," Gutierrez replied.

She tensed as Yamamoto strode toward them, though, instead of the medic. "Lieutenant Rhee, are you injured?"

Kael had leaned forward and closed his eyes again but was still rubbing his temples. He could just barely reach both with the cuffs on. After a moment, he glanced up, seeming to notice Yamamoto for the first time. "Uh, a little. Maybe. Maybe I'm just a little tired, that's all. Can't tell the difference anymore, frankly."

"I think we all knocked our heads a bit in that fall," she said mildly.

"Thank you, Lieutenant Rhee." Yamamoto kept his voice quiet. "Your efforts today will not be forgotten."

Kael met the man's gaze for a long moment, then seemed to relax and shrugged. "Nothing special about keeping people from getting killed."

"I believe I already covered my opinion that gratitude is always worth expressing." Yamamoto's eyes twinkled with amusement for a moment. "But to be especially clear, I disagree. Many are unsuited to the task of protecting people. Some even work actively against it and try to kill them. Can you believe that?"

Kael let out a small laugh. "I can. But it's nothing."

"I don't know where you acquired those skills, but aside from a mention that I owe to Captain Dealis, I think I will quickly forget that they exist."

"That would be… appreciated. I'm nothing special. I'm sure you would have done the same, Lieutenant."

"Ah, but those were Union lives, and I am not a member of a people with a long-standing feud with the Union."

Kael straightened, his back pressing flatter against the wall as he frowned. "Neither am I. Not anymore. Nor did I ever choose to be."

"I see. Well, I hope you're both right that I'd have done the same. And I hope I never need to find out."

"I wish you the same," he replied.

"You've both done yourself a service today. You've demonstrated honor and competence. You're coming with me for the docs to look you over in sickbay. Then, I'm sorry to say, I'll have to escort you to the brig."

"Lucky us," Kael muttered.

"Three are dead," Yamamoto said, and he didn't smile now. "None of us are lucky today."

CHAPTER SIXTEEN

"IS SHE DEAD?"

That voice… no. It couldn't be who he thought it was.

Quentin Davenmore froze, his hand in midair, ice clinking in his glass that still hovered above the table.

He'd *asked* to be left alone. He *was* alone, at least he'd thought so. Getting revenge on his oldest rival required his complete concentration. He wouldn't grant Simmons the title of nemesis, because he had only escaped Quen's attempts once.

He wouldn't be doing so again. He was a rival, nothing more. The little prick had already lost the captain of his fancy ship, and Quen had been hard at work, inserting incriminating data into as many bank and law-enforcement databases as he could breach. As long as he could do it without leaving a trace. Soon the arrogant upstart would lose his freedom. And his fortune, too.

Yes, soon Douglas Oliver Simmons and his team of hired murderers would be ancient history, and Quen could move on from this whole disastrous affair.

But first, he had to deal with his uninvited guest. He cared nothing for hospitality. He had people for that. People he'd sent away so he could concentrate. In fact, one of those people would soon be paying the price for letting her in here to disturb him.

Right after she did.

"Cassandra! Fancy seeing you here." He forced himself to swivel and smile, raising the glass in his hand instead of sitting it down as he'd intended. The ice swirled in the amber concoction.

Her form was slender, draped in a pale dress that stood stark against the black expanse of space behind her. His quarters had a vast panoramic view on one side, and she stood beside the thin black rug, the silver throw pillows. He let himself leer a little. She was a pretty little morsel, blonde curls cascading over bare shoulders.

"Is she dead?" she asked again.

"Shouldn't you know that better than I would?" He grinned, mocking.

"Answer the question."

He sighed theatrically. "No. No, not yet. But the wheels of the machines are turning, and it'll be any time now. That's what matters, darling."

Her eyes narrowed—eyes that were as black as the vast night framing her form. "You're such a failure, Davenmore."

He struggled not to roll his eyes. "Me. A failure. Preposterous. Do you think I'd have all this if I was a failure?" He gestured at the casual opulence surrounding them.

"Yes, you would," she replied.

He made a noise of disgust. Some people had no vision. He hadn't even really failed yet. The Union could kill Ellen Ryu any minute now.

"If they were going to kill her, they would have done it already."

Had he said that out loud? He hadn't thought so. "Please. And if they don't, then her trial will. Her fate is sealed."

"How can you be so sure of your success when you've just failed me?"

"Failed you? You mean failed *us*. I'm the one who reached out to *you*, remember? We have a shared bounty in Ellen Ryu and the rest of those scum. This is the first step."

"They don't have to kill her."

"Prison guards are easily bought," he shot back. He'd have his way, one way or the other. "It's just a matter of time. And possibly money." Cassandra lacked his vision—and persistence. Yes, she was pretty, but so cold. So cold. Eyes like black holes, that's what they were. Nobody wanted cold. Oh, sure, he'd be happy to throw her down on the lounge over there for a roll, but cold was a turnoff in the long run. Not like Sahra.

"Time and money that didn't have to be wasted if you would have simply killed her as we discussed."

Instead of disagreeing with her, he just broadened his smile. "How did you get on my yacht?"

"I'm not on your yacht. I'm only in your mind."

"Sure, you are. I can see you, you know." He wiggled his eyebrows at her and took a sip of his bourbon. "I haven't had *that* much to drink."

"Telepathy is a powerful thing." It was a statement that could be delivered with a wry smile. But she didn't smile.

He scoffed. "Nobody has that kind of range."

"Who says I am far away?"

He kept his smile in place like a shield, even as his thoughts flew into a panic. He should have invested in telepathy-blocking opsepium shielding, like Sahra had said. It'd been on the list, but she'd always been leaps and bounds more paranoid than he was. Usually, he would dock in the middle of nowhere, the outsystem, anywhere physically inaccessible. Beyond that, his staff was thoroughly vetted. And truly volatile telepaths were so rare, and so quickly eliminated by their own kind. It had seemed like such an unlikely occurrence.

Apparently, they were not quite as rare as he'd estimated. It should perhaps have given him pause that Sahra—the more paranoid of the two of them—was already dead. It hadn't occurred to him, though, until just this moment.

Naive. Overconfident and naive. Sahra had told him so, but he'd just laughed. He'd thought she'd been joking. Nobody told him things like that and expected him to take them *seriously*.

How could he kill an illusion? A hallucination? A figment of his imagination? Because obviously she had to die.

Now a smile did touch the corners of her lips. "Illusion is the closest to accurate, Mr. Davenmore. As far as your brain is concerned, I'm really here."

He definitely hadn't said any of that out loud. "What do you want? Where is Dr. Arakovic?"

"Dr. Arakovic is a bit… busy at the moment. She, like you, thought getting creative might be a good idea. It was not."

"Getting creative? I'm not creative."

She snorted. "I will not dispute that. Perhaps you *thought* this little stunt was creative—"

"Little stunt?"

"We were supposed to be working together."

"We are!"

"I gave you her location. You were to eliminate her. And did you?"

He swallowed. "Yes, in a manner of— "

"You instead turned her in for a reward."

"It wasn't about the reward. Who has more ships to ensure her capture and death? You think this yacht goes around starting brawls with ex-military? No. I know my strengths. This is how I work. It is normally very effective. It just… can take time."

Her laughter was a chilling sound, echoing in his mind like glass tinkling, breaking, shattering.

No, wait—that was real. He'd dropped the glass. Liquid splashed amber and glossy across the glossy floor. He didn't move.

"Time," she said. "Time? What do you think they will do with that time? What if Ellen Ryu tells the Union everything she knows about my organization?"

"They won't believe a deserter."

"Is that how you would manage your own security intelligence, Mr. Davenmore? By allowing it to be told to whomever and hoping the poor credibility of the dishonored war hero would save you from anyone checking out what she has to say?"

"If you didn't want people to know, you shouldn't have let anyone find out. That's how *I* handle security intelligence." He wanted to *Ms. Something* her, too, but he realized abruptly he had never been able to locate her last name.

"Is that why your girlfriend is dead?"

He jerked back, like she'd physically hit him, and bit back a torrent of curses. What good would it do to curse at an illusion?

An illusion that was shaking her pretty blonde head. If she were here, he'd show her who really controlled this situation. He could just throw her down and—no, no. He cut off the thought.

The corner of her mouth quirked up. "Two Songbirds to kill or recapture, and you have delivered us zero. Do you know how we reward failure, Mr. Davenmore?"

"Call me Quentin," he replied. It was almost a reflex, trying to ingratiate her, more than a conscious effort. "And again, it's not failure. Give it time. I thought it best to overwhelm them with real, experienced military force."

"You thought it best not to get your hands dirty. Not to risk your own neck."

He winced. No. No, she was listening. That wasn't what he'd been thinking. Not that at all. His approach was simply reasonable risk management. "A public capture and execution will be widely reported and publicized. And wildly embarrassing and distressing to our mutual enemies." And that part *was* true. He wanted Simmons to suffer even more than this stupid minion Ryu. Ryu was only a pawn of Simmons.

"A deal was a deal, Mr. Davenmore."

"Quentin, please. Quentin. I will take care of it. I have a man onboard the *Denali*—"

"But they didn't put her on the *Denali*."

Fragging *Everest* had beaten the *Denali* to the chase. And somehow survived his turret. He'd had back-up plans for his back-up plans, and still that bitch was alive.

"It's that Captain Dealis." He was scrambling and he knew it. Maybe she was right. Failure. No—it wasn't his fault. He didn't fail. He just needed time to keep trying. "Dealis swooped in at the first mention of her and stole her away from us. From all of us. We go after Dealis, we get rid of him first, then we can convince one of the underlings to off her."

"All of those, in due time. Don't blame your failures on his enthusiasm. You shouldn't have trusted the Union. You should have just killed them. Like we ordered you to."

"Trust me, that bitch is dead eventually. You just have to be patient sometimes. Try and try again." He mustered a congenial smile. He'd never been exceptionally charming, but he'd had thousands of credits in appearance work done. Surely, he ought to be able to charm his way out of this, for all the money he'd paid.

"Patient. Really."

"Listen, I hear you. You want her dead pronto, but we're in this together. I mean, I dig the cold bitch thing, but how many allies do you really have? You need somebody like me at your side to—"

"Ms. Barakat would be disappointed in you, I think." Cassandra raised her chin. "I see why she was the mastermind."

"Excuse me!" He tried not to puff out his chest and bluster, but he found he'd already done it a bit. He scowled at her instead. "That's not at all true. We were equals. And you and I can be, too. Two of us against the world."

Her laugh was loud but tinged with bitterness. Almost a chuckle, if you could laugh without finding anything funny. "Equals? No such thing in this world, Mr. Davenmore. We roll the dice. We don't all come up with the same number. That's just how life works. *Equality* is for the weak. Men have always known that. Women, for once, have gotten the message."

He blinked. What the… What did that even mean?

"You don't want to get your hands dirty. You use other people to do the work, because you think that makes you respectable somehow. But you're just incompetent."

"Now, that's no way to talk to an ally. How many people with my financial and information resources do you really have that you can —" He faltered as pressure closed in around his throat, cutting off the air to his words. God, what was that feeling?

"We don't need allies, Mr. Davenmore. We are legion. And we will not make your same mistake. Getting your hands dirty can be… fun."

Was he having an allergic reaction? Was there a damned bar across his windpipe? He gasped for breath.

Not enough—it wasn't enough.

"What—are you—" He struggled to get the words out. What was she doing?

Cassandra's head was tilted, her form still in the same spot where it had appeared. Just the tilt of the head and her expression had changed.

Her eyes were alight, amused, inky wells as deep as the deepest vacuum of space. Like a cat playing with prey before the death blow.

We're getting our hands dirty. Your hands, actually. Like you should have in the first place.

He glanced down, but he couldn't lower his head all the way. His hands were in the way.

In the way, because his fingers were wrapped around his throat. Choking him.

He tried to break the grip with his chin, pull his arms away, lurch around. Anything—to break—

Yellow splotches clouded his eyes, then black ones.

His body writhed, collapsing from the chair and sliding to the ground. He struggled to regain control. Animal instinct took over, simply trying to survive, but his best tools—his hands—were not an option. How was this possible? How could they not be an option?

Struggling to breathe, he watched her stride toward him. She stepped over his body daintily, gracefully, and leaned over the tablet he'd set aside.

"Douglas Oliver Simmons," she said. "Now why, oh why, would you be so obsessed with him, of all people?"

Kill him. He killed Sahra. Make him pay. Kill him.

Cassandra raised her eyebrow. *That can be arranged.*

Let me live so I can help you. If he could just breathe one more time — The black splotches were growing larger in his vision.

She smiled. "Oh, I don't think so. You, Mr. Davenmore, have outlived your usefulness. But I can put one more name on my list in your honor. And more importantly, in Ms. Barakat's honor. A dying wish, if you will."

He writhed toward her, trying to catch her leg with his foot, but she neatly dodged and stepped away. Not that she was real, anyway. It was hopeless.

On his stomach, struggling to breathe, he watched her walk away, toward the endless starry expanse, as the darkness came in and engulfed him, too.

WANT MORE?

AFTERWORD

Thank you so much for reading! Hope you enjoyed. If you haven't discovered it already, check out the short prequel novella I wrote titled *Deserter* to learn more about Ellen's past.

If you'd like to be notified when new books come out, sign up for email updates here: www.rkthorne.com/get-updates/ I share upcoming book news and occasional free bonuses, like stories, maps, and character interviews, rarely more than once a month.

If you're feeling froggy, consider leaving a review. Reviews help readers discover their next favorite book—and avoid ones that aren't for them! Whether it's five stars or one, I truly love hearing from readers and appreciate your honest feedback.

ALSO BY R. K. THORNE

The Enslaved Chronicles

Mage Slave

Mage Strike

Star Mage

The Audacity Saga

The Empress Capsule

Capital Games

Child of Wrath

Songbird Rising

Oath of Duty (Forthcoming)

Deserter: An Audacity Prequel (Free)

The Legends of the Clanblades Series

Dagger of Bone

Blade of the Moon (Forthcoming)

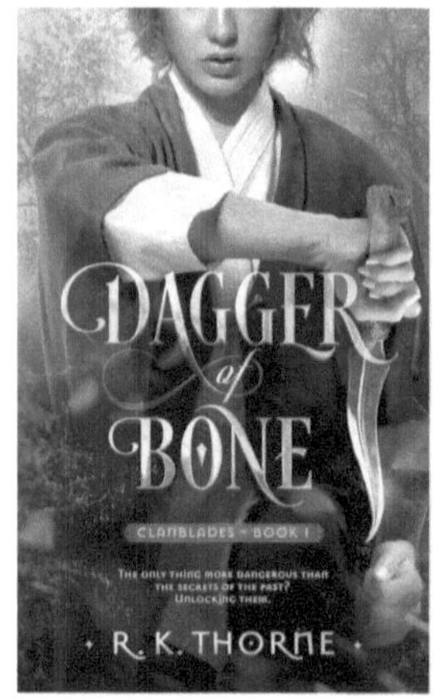

ABOUT THE AUTHOR

R. K. Thorne is an independent science fiction and fantasy author fueled by notebooks and imperial stouts. Coffee, role playing games, and her new puppy all keep her awake at night.

She has read speculative fiction since before she was probably much too young to be doing so and encourages you to do the same.

She lives in the green hills of Pennsylvania with her family, her pup, and two gray cats that may or may not pull her chariot in their spare time.

For more information:
rkthorne.com

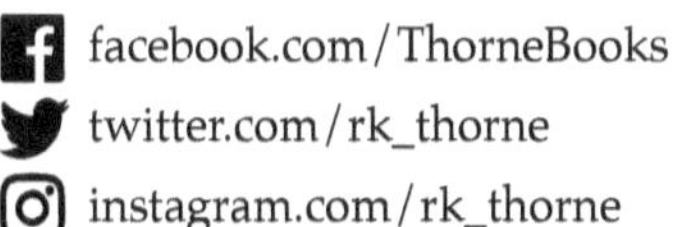

facebook.com/ThorneBooks
twitter.com/rk_thorne
instagram.com/rk_thorne